DANGEROUS SISTER

*To Denise Freeman
Thank you so much
God Bless*

*9-12-08
Joclyn Gipson*

BY:

JOCLYN GIPSON

© 2006 Joclyn Gipson
All Rights Reserved.

No part of this publication may be reproduced, stored in a retrieval system, or transmitted, in any form or by any means, electronic, mechanical, photocopying, recording, or otherwise, without the written permission of the author.

First published by Dog Ear Publishing
4010 W. 86th Street, Ste H
Indianapolis, IN 46268
www.dogearpublishing.net

ISBN: 1-59858-122-8
Library of Congress Control Number: 2006921968

This book is printed on acid-free paper.
This book is a work of Fiction. Places, events, and situations in this book are purely Fictional and any resemblance to actual persons, living or dead, is coincidental.

Printed in the United States of America

This book is dedicated to:
MY SISTER Amanda Gipson-Reynolds
My Mama Debra Gipson *"I love you"*

My biggest supporters...
Varry Surratt and Ruby Johnson
Ciara Fihiol
Vernita Lee
Raymond Joshua
SALON ENSTYL

A special thanks to all my readers

PLACE: NEW YORK CITY, NEW YORK
DATE: MAY 2000

CHAPTER ONE

*T*wo sisters with only a father in common.

Appearance, personality, and intellect, the two were the actual definition of opposites, night and day.

The oldest sister was ashamed of her younger sister, hating her with a red-hot passion. The younger sister's heart was filled with love, admiration, and the utmost respect for her older sister. If both young ladies didn't share the same last name and live in the same house, no one would suspect that they were even related.

No one would ever suspect Vanessa Thomas to be a troublemaker just by the sight of her, but she was, a real devil!

Gorgeous and sophisticated, she had the ability to enter a room and attract the attention of every man present. Just the right height with the sexiest legs, she had the figure most women desired. A round face with full, heart-shaped lips and a beauty mark just above her lip, she had the face of an angel. Her beautiful, smooth skin was a delicate golden brown, not a flaw to be detected. With chin length, sandy brown hair, she knew her beauty.

She walked and dressed with elegance, presenting herself as a princess, like royalty. She felt and flaunted her beauty. To uphold the *pretty-girl* image, she never missed a weekly hair appointment or a usual visit to the nail shop to keep herself well-groomed in all aspects. Her attire was only the best, as she wore nothing less than the most expensive brands of clothes and shoes.

Placid and at ease even in the stickiest situations, she would never be suspected of even being capable of mischief. To seek the attention of everyone around and to gain popularity was her main focus. She was used to having her way, being spoiled, and she was a real devil when she wasn't granted her every desire.

Jazzmine Thomas was the total opposite. Her beauty did not instantly attract the eye, as it had to be brought forth from beyond the surface. The exterior was crude and much unattractive, a real turn-off for the opposite sex. Her smooth dark brown skin was completely covered by acne, her dimpled cheeks chubby, her dark brown eyes puffy as if she were constantly losing sleep, and her nose appeared to be too small for her fat face. She was *definitely* not the model type!

Obesity was the most unattractive feature she possessed.

At two hundred and eighteen pounds, she was not the first choice to be featured on a magazine cover. She was short with short, thick, coarse black hair. Visiting the beauty salon was something she only did when her new growth was in dire need of relaxation. Her attire was usually whatever she could find that could comfortably fit. It was not of importance from where her clothes and shoes were purchased or what the cost.

Jazzmine was clearly not in Vanessa's league. Vanessa was the man winner, and Jazzmine was the admirer, as she was proud to even be her half-sister.

Vanessa was a twenty-year-old junior attending college in New York City and living with her father until she finished school and could afford to venture out on her own.

Jazzmine was a seventeen-year-old senior in high school who was contemplating attending the same college as her sister. As valedictorian of her class, Jazzmine had been offered several scholarships to excellent colleges. The difficult part was choosing the proper one to meet her academic needs.

James, their father who had practically raised them alone, was very proud of both of his daughters. No mothers, as he lost them both to death, he tried to instill in his daughters the importance of family. Vanessa's mother, his first wife, died in childbirth. Jazzmine's mother, his second wife, was killed in a tragic car accident when she was in elementary school. That alone was reason to cherish family, which he learned the hard way.

James treated both Vanessa and Jazzmine equally and looked upon them as his beautiful angels. He never favored Vanessa over Jazzmine because of her outer beauty nor did he favor Jazzmine over Vanessa because of her excellent brain. He had taught them that they were both equally smart and beautiful. It never dawned on him that his daughters felt so differently about each other.

Yes, James was quite aware that Jazzmine

looked up to Vanessa, but he had no idea Vanessa found her sister so repulsive. In his eyes, they were his angels, and neither could ever wrong the other. He had observed his daughters grow up together, and not once had it ever occurred to him that either of them could have hatred in her heart for the other.

It was true that Vanessa and Jazzmine appeared to be close in childhood. It clearly wasn't the case, however.

Vanessa was fully aware of Jazzmine's admiration for her, and the only reason she allowed her to hang around was because she had been able to manipulate her into doing whatever she desired.

Jazzmine had always been naïve and too blinded by love for her sister to say no to anything she requested of her.

Vanessa was cruel and vindictive, fooling everyone, as it wasn't common to have such hatred for one's sister. No one would be the wiser of her sinful ways.

Presently, Vanessa walked down the hall toward her bedroom, and she stopped at Jazzmine's bedroom door, hearing laughter coming from inside. A frown darkened her features, as she wondered who her half-sister was entertaining. Her eyes focused on the door, which was slightly ajar. *"One little peek won't hurt,"* she thought. Easing closer to the door, she peeped inside, eavesdrop to decipher about what the laughter was.

Jazzmine was sitting on the bed Indian style facing Maya, a friend of hers, who was sprawled all over the bed, laughing.

The laughter dying, Maya straightened to an

Indian style position as well and faced Jazzmine. "Girl! You are so crazy!" she giggled, remembering the funny comment Jazzmine made. Clearing her throat, she said, "So, you don't like him, huh? Well who **do** you like?" She leaned in enthusiastically with a smile on her face, anxiously awaiting Jazzmine's reply.

Jazzmine sighed heavily and slipped into a light daze. Her thoughts were of Keith Bedly, the young man she had been interested in for the past year. Blinking back to reality, she answered, "His name is Keith Bedly, and he is," she sighed and clasped her hands together with a big grin, "wonderful!"

Hearing the statement, Vanessa cringed, gasping with horror. She had no idea that Jazzmine was interested in Keith.

Keith Bedly, a friend of their cousin's, was a junior attending the same university as Vanessa. In fact, she had a business course with him.

She was familiar with the type of women he dated. Jazzmine was absolutely not his type. He preferred the thin, pretty, cheerleading type as opposed to dumpy and homely.

"Before we graduate, I'm going to confront him and tell him how I feel," Jazzmine, feeling confident, confessed.

Vanessa's eyes widened, and she backed away from the door, as if she had seen a ghost. It was unacceptable that Jazzmine was actually going to confront Keith about her feelings for him. It was unacceptable and embarrassing for Vanessa. Keith was sure to laugh in her face.

Of course, Jazzmine looked in the mirror on a daily basis. Did she not see how unattractive she was? Did she not realize that the only guys she attracted were fat and homely like herself or skinny, brainy little nerds? It was just plain ridiculous for her to even think she should waste her breath, and Keith's time, having that discussion with him.

Something had to be done to prevent Jazzmine from making such a horrible mistake and humiliating herself, not to mention her sister.

After a second of thought, the perfect strategy came to Vanessa, and she smiled mischievously to herself. There was something she could do.

Elated at how quickly the brilliant idea came to mind, Vanessa hurried to her room and immediately called her cousin.

"Hey, Tyrone," she smiled into the telephone. If all went accordingly, he was going to be a big assistance to her, and she really needed him.

"What's up, Vanessa?"

"Are you going to be busy Friday night?" she asked. There was no need to beat around the bush.

He shrugged his shoulders, as if she could see him through the telephone. "I don't know. I'll probably go out to the club or something. Why?" She never called and inquired about his plans for the weekend. "*Why is she asking now?*" he wondered. What did she want? It had to be a favor.

The club? To which club was he going? It couldn't be *any* club. In order for her plan to succeed, he had to cooperate. If he didn't offer the correct answer, she would just have to suggest it for him. "Which one are you going to?" She had to know.

"Probably *Club Ten*. Why? What's on your mind?"

Club Ten was perfect! It was a club that didn't emphasize women's identification on Friday nights. Friday nights were called *Ladies' Night*. Vanessa attended on *Ladies' Night* quite often. "Really? Well, I was just wondering because I was worried about Jazzmine. She's always stuck in the house, and she never gets to go out. Friday night is *Ladies' Night* at *Club Ten*. Why don't you take her with you? She adores you, and she'll be willing to go with you. I have a surprise for her, but she doesn't know it. It's a secret. Bring her for me."

Tyrone sighed deeply into the telephone. He usually didn't escort females to the club whether they were relatives or not. Jazzmine was his cousin, sure, but that was a typical thing for a male to say to another female. "Oh, she's just my cousin!" Women didn't accept that line anymore. Too many guys were players and jerks. He didn't want to be in the category with them.

Having Jazzmine on his arm would cramp his style. Females wouldn't talk to him if he was with her, and he loved to dance. They probably wouldn't even want to dance with him if he came with a date. Dancing alone was no fun. Jazzmine couldn't dance. It seemed as though Vanessa wanted him to have a boring night. "Vanessa," Tyrone sighed, again.

"Please?" she begged. He just had to do this for her. "You are the only person who can help me. Jazzmine is your cousin. Don't you want to see her go out and have fun for a change?"

Well, she did have a valid point. One night wouldn't hurt. It could be the best night of Jazzmine's life, and he did think she deserved to have fun just like everyone else. "Ok," he finally answered, pleasing Vanessa. "Hey, what's the big surprise? It's not her birthday or anything."

Vanessa smiled mischievously to herself, thinking of her surprise for her sister. It couldn't be revealed to Tyrone because he would surely renege on his discussion to help. He would have to find out when Jazzmine did. "You'll see. I have to go now. Bye." Before he could say another word, she hung up.

Thursday morning, Vanessa walked down the hall toward her business course with a huge smile.

Everything was set.

She just hoped Keith would uphold his duty, being the major asset in her plan. She needed him more than she needed Tyrone.

At the classroom door, she stopped and looked down at her light brown mini skirt, hoping it was short enough. Entering the room, she licked her lips when every guy in the room whistled at her, which she was used to by now. Ignoring the whistles, her eyes glanced toward the back of the room to Keith's usual seat.

He was there.

Walking with a switch, she passed all the guys who whistled at her and went right up to him. Sitting on his desktop, she forced him to look at her. Smiling at him, she crossed her legs.

His eyes studied her beautiful, silky legs, and he smiled, as well. Lifting his eyes back to her face, he almost frowned, wondering what she wanted.

"So, Keith," Vanessa lifted her eyes to the ceiling for a split second. Then she dropped them back to him, "what are you doing tomorrow night?

Do you have plans?" She was hoping he would say no.

Keith's eyes were drawn to the tight white top she was wearing, and he forced himself not to ogle her full-sized breasts. Redeeming focus, his eyes moved back to her face. "I might be free. Why? What do you have in mind?"

Vanessa's smile widened. There was a chance that her way would be rendered. "Well, I thought maybe you and I could go to *Club Ten*."

The expression on Keith's face did nothing to hide his surprise. Doing a mental reality check, his hand rose to his heart. "Are **you** asking **me** out, Vanessa?"

That was rather unusual and spontaneous of her. It was unpredicted to say the least, much out of character. Usually, she barely had a sufficient supply of air to breathe because so many men were swarming around, asking for a date. It intrigued him that she reversed the roles and asked *him* for a date. Pondering the situation, he wondered why her sudden change of heart. He asked her out *twice*, and she declined both offers.

Leaning back in his seat, he folded his arms across his chest with enthusiasm. Looking at her with a half-smile, he replied, "I recall asking you out a couple of times, and you turned me down." He placed his index finger on his chin and pretended to ponder the situation. "Hum. Where did this odd little change come from?"

Vanessa sighed and lifted her face to the ceiling, again. It was almost as if he was skeptical, questioning her motive. She didn't expect that at all. It was predicted that he would be all too willing to take advantage of any opportunity to be with her.

It took a moment to think of a feasible explanation as to why she would turn him down each time he extended an invitation for a date. Clearing her throat, she lowered her eyes back to him. "When you asked me out, I was involved with someone." It was an outright lie, but it would have to suffice. "It's over between us now. I'm available."

Keith dropped his eyes, as he was embarrassed for not giving her the benefit of the doubt. Then, he quickly lifted them, again. He wouldn't jeopardize any chance with her. "*Club Ten*, huh? Well, will you be picking me up or shall I come to you?"

Vanessa smiled with relief. That was more like it! Nothing could prevent her plan from succeeding now. Tomorrow night, she would stop Jazzmine from making the biggest mistake of her life.

Friday night, Vanessa ran down the stairs, wearing a sexy black dress suitable for a party or the club. She looked marvelous, as her hair was pinned up, and her makeup was flawless. She accessorized with gold jewelry. It was obvious that her agenda was to have a fun filled night.

James, sitting on the sofa with Jazzmine at his side, looked up when he heard her footsteps on the stairs. "Hey, baby!" he exclaimed with a smile. He examined her, as she came down the stairs. "Are you going out tonight?"

Vanessa stepped down the last step and turned to face her father. "Yes."

Jazzmine looked up and smiled, liking the dress her sister was wearing. Unfortunately, she would never be able to wear or look half as good in a dress like that. "I love that dress!" she told her sister, who was heading for the door.

Vanessa stopped and turned back with a huge smile. "Thank you!" she said for her father's sake. Personally, she was tired of constantly hearing how much her sister like an outfit or how pretty she thought she looked in it. Yes, she was fabulous, and her sister was not. Jazzmine needed to move beyond that point or she would be forever stuck on pause.

The doorbell rang, and Vanessa continued to the door.

It was Tyrone.

Vanessa invited him in with a greeting, and he entered. Going to the sofa, he plopped down on the other side of his uncle. "Hey, Uncle James!" He looked at his uncle, studying his face for a moment. It was often a wonder how he could produce two totally different children like Vanessa and Jazzmine.

James was his father's younger brother. The relation between the two of them was quite obvious, as the resemblance was immaculate.

James and his brother, Avery, were the same medium brown skin tone with the same dark brown eyes. Avery, of course, had a more mature face, as it was apparent that he was older. The noses and lips were normal, and the definition of both faces was strong, as their manhood was never dubious.

Avery, however, had facial hair, as he wore a nice trimmed beard to accentuate his manly features. James's face was bare, as he kept a clean shave. Both men were distinguished and quite handsome.

Even Avery's three children were similar in

resemblance. The oldest was a half-sister to the other two as was Vanessa to Jazzmine. It was difficult to comprehend, however, because one didn't have to ask the relationship between Tyrone and his older sister. There wasn't even a question between her and their younger sister. It was always a question between Vanessa and Jazzmine.

Looking at James, Vanessa, and Jazzmine, no one would instantly guess the nature of their relationship. Vanessa inherited his eyes, but nothing else. Jazzmine had no features from either of them. Of course, the two sisters were born of two entirely different women, but one would be skeptical of the blood connect to their father just by sight.

James looked at his nephew, who looked nice in the creased short sleeve shirt and slacks. He nodded his approval. "Hey, Ty! Are you going out, too?"

Tyrone nodded. "Yes, sir."

At the announcement, Jazzmine sighed, envying him and everyone else who would be painting the town tonight. Everyone she knew went out on the weekends except her. She always sat home with her father.

Tyrone looked at Vanessa, who was still at the door, holding it open, as if he hadn't made his entrance. Their eyes met, and she smiled at him, hoping he hadn't forgotten his responsibility. His job was very simple.

"Actually, Uncle James, I'm here to escort Jazzmine to the ball," he teased, leaning over to look at her.

Jazzmine looked back with a confused expression on her face. Tyrone was there to take *her* someplace? That was a first, but she didn't mind if he was offering. It would be better than sitting at home being lonely. "Where are we going?"

"*To Club Ten*," he answered. His eyes darted to Vanessa, who smiled and went out the open door, closing it behind her.

Jazzmine frowned and sat back, shaking her head. "I can't go to *Club Ten*. No one under eighteen is allowed! Newsflash, Ty, I'm only seventeen!"

"You can go," he assured her. "It's *Ladies' Night*. You'll be with me. They only check the guy's I.D. on *Ladies' Night*."

"Oh," Jazzmine wasn't aware of that. One wouldn't expect her to be since she had never been to *Club Ten* or any other club for that matter.

"What do you say? Would you like to go?"

"Well, can I wear this?" Jazzmine looked down at her tee shirt and jean shorts. Her feet were bare. All she needed to do was slip on some shoes, and she would be ready to go. However, she wasn't sure if it was appropriate, as she had no idea of the atmosphere. She definitely didn't want to feel out of place.

Tyrone shook his head with disapproval. "People usually dress up to go to *Club Ten*. You might want to change if you don't want to feel out of place."

Jazzmine looked at her father, whose eyes were on the television. "Go ahead, baby," he said, sensing her eyes on him. She leaned over, kissed his cheek, and stood up.

Heading for the stairs, she informed her cousin that she would be right back.

At nine o'clock, Tyrone made an entrance at

Club Ten with Jazzmine on his arm.

Upon their entrance, all eyes were on them. People stared with open mouths.

Tyrone came to the club quite often and never with a date even on *ladies' night*. Everyone knew that his sole purpose for coming was to meet women, which he couldn't do if he was with one. Since this was his first time bringing a date, people were shock to see that it was Jazzmine. No one ever expected to see him with her or anyone who looked like her.

As they moved farther into the room, people began to chatter among themselves, causing Jazzmine to feel very uncomfortable. It felt as if everyone was staring and whispering about her, which she couldn't understand. She changed her attire like Tyrone suggested. Her eyes went down to her white blouse and loose brown slacks. Nothing was wrinkled. She saw no dilemma. She even brushed her hair before leaving home. Mentally, she convinced herself that she was being silly. There was nothing wrong with her.

Tyrone escorted Jazzmine to a booth in the middle of the room, ignoring the whispers. He knew what it was all about, and he hoped that no one had hurt his cousin's feelings. He was not the least bit ashamed of her.

They sat down, facing each other.

Jazzmine surveyed the disco-lit room.

The beauty of the club was impressive.

The lighting was beautiful, as it was colorful from the disco ball. The room was huge. The booths and tables were neatly arranged in a section surrounding the dance floor, which was rather large within itself. There were mirrors in all four corners of the room, facing the dance floor.

The bar was in the very back.

It was rather crowded, and the music was at a comfortable volume.

Jazzmine was amazed to see so many familiar faces. Obviously, *everyone* did get out except her.

She looked at her cousin with a content smile. It was nice of him to invite her. The thought and gesture was flattering. She just didn't want to ruin his fun. It was a well-known fact that he didn't usually bring a date to a club. He was going to feel obligated to stay with her, and he didn't have to do that. She wanted him to enjoy himself as he usually would have if she hadn't been there. Surely, not many women were going to approach him if he was with someone. "Ty, why did you bring me here tonight?" she spoke her thoughts.

Tyrone almost frowned at the question. It wasn't an easy answer. Vanessa said she had a surprise for her. If he told her that, he could ruin it for her. Apparently, she didn't know about it. A quick thinker, he answered, "I figured you needed to get out of the house. I know you don't get out much, so I decided to rescue you from your room."

Jazzmine nodded, feeling grateful. That was true. He knew that the only places she went were to the movies and church, and she usually went to the movies alone. She did need to get out of the house and do something different for a change.

Tyrone searched the crowd for Vanessa. She was nowhere to be seen. He glanced at his watch, wondering where she could be. She left the house before they did, but she wasn't there, yet? Perhaps, she had to make a few stops. Deciding that she would be there soon, he dismissed the thought.

He stood up, telling Jazzmine that he was going to the bar to get a drink. He offered to buy her a soda or lemonade, but she politely said no.

As soon as he walked away, the door opened.

Jazzmine glanced over her shoulder with a smile, which quickly faded when she saw the couple making their entrance.

Vanessa was hanging on *Keith Bedly's* arm. The smile on her face was huge, probably from the excitement. She would be excited to be with him, too.

Jazzmine quickly surveyed Keith in the multicolored shirt and dark slacks. He looked great as usual. Seeing him, she wanted to melt. Remembering that he was with her sister, her heart sank, and she felt smaller than a dime. What was she going to do? She couldn't approach him now because she was definitely no competition for Vanessa. Tears threatened to surface. It was a waste of time to even think about him now, but with his handsome face, she couldn't help it.

Keith was definitely one to be admired with his gorgeous caramel skin and beautiful brown eyes. His eyebrows were thick and the facial hair was neatly trimmed, as he had a nice beard. The hair atop of his head was low, very fitting to his face. He was definitely nice on the eyes, as he attracted the attention of many women.

Jazzmine observed as Keith led Vanessa to a table near the entrance.

They sat down, facing each other. Vanessa crossed her legs and smiled at Keith with her usual dazzling smile.

Jazzmine swallowed hard, wishing she could be in her sister's shoes at that precise moment.

Sighing, she dropped her eyes when Keith reached across the table and took Vanessa's hand into his own. She wouldn't be able to take much more of his public display of affection. It was already sickening and heartbreaking.

It was purely coincidental that she was invited to *Club Ten* on the same night Keith invited her sister to join him there, but it was, also, painful. If only her sister had known her feelings for Keith, the outcome would have been different. It was too late to tell her now, though. She and Keith were probably going to start a life together.

It was possible.

Vanessa and Keith shared a common interest in the business field. Vanessa once told her that she and Keith had a business course together.

With a sigh, Jazzmine shook her head. Her desire was to go home and hide under the covers. She wished she could pretend this night never happened.

Vanessa sat with Keith listening to his boring conversation about his day. She didn't care. All she wanted was for Jazzmine to see them together.

When she left home, she met Keith at the gas station near the house because she didn't want him to pick her up. To stall time, she had him take her to a few miscellaneous places. Her goal was to give Jazzmine time to change and get to *Club Ten*. She wanted her to be there when she got there. If she got there first, there was a chance that she wouldn't have seen them the entire night. *Club Ten* was the hotspot. A crowd was sure to come.

Sighing to herself, she folded her arms across her chest and rolled her eyes. Whatever Keith was saying faded from her mind, as her eyes went around the room in search of her little sister. They had to be there by now. She thought she saw Tyrone's car outside.

Vanessa's eyes landed on Jazzmine, and she pretended not to see her. Satisfied that she had her sister's attention, she looked back to Keith with a real smile. "Do you want to dance?" she asked, cutting off whatever he was saying.

Vanessa slow danced with Keith, holding him as close as possible. Although she pretended not to, she watched her sister watching her, as her eyes were glued to them. Jazzmine was watching them with a frown of pain. The look on her sister's face was priceless and unforgettable!

Keith pulled back a little and looked down into her eyes.

Vanessa blinked and returned the stare, hoping he was going to kiss her. If he didn't, she would have to kiss him, but that wasn't part of her plan. She smiled and looped her arms around his neck.

Just as she had hoped, Keith lowered his head and closed his eyes, finding her lips with his.

The kiss was a long one.

When Keith lifted his head, Vanessa's eyes darted to Jazzmine, who shook her head with disbelief and looked away.

Vanessa smiled to herself, knowing that Jazzmine would be crushed. She definitely wasn't going to approach Keith now, *she hoped*. No, Jazzmine wouldn't be that stupid. She knew she was no competition for her. Keith would never look at Jazzmine now that he had been with her!

Sitting across from Jazzmine, Tyrone sipped from his alcoholic beverage and tried to make small talk with his cousin, who wasn't responding to him. "What's the matter with you?" he asked, seeing the hurt expression on her face when she looked away from Vanessa and Keith. "What have you been looking at all night?" He thought it to be rude that she hadn't paid him much attention all night.

Glancing over his shoulder to see what caught her attention, his eyes immediately connected with Vanessa and his friend. He frowned, catching on instantly to Vanessa's plan. He was quite aware of Jazzmine's mild crush on his friend, and he was, also, aware that her half-sister was ashamed of her. She didn't want her around any of her friends. This was a cruel way to tell her to stay away! It was coldhearted and vicious of Vanessa to do this to her own sister!

This was the surprise that Vanessa had for Jazzmine!

No wonder she didn't tell him! She knew he would be against something so devious. He wouldn't hurt his cousin that way. It was a shock to him that Vanessa could hurt her own sister so intentionally and not feel an ounce of remorse.

Tyrone looked back at Jazzmine, and he took both of her hands into his own, sympathizing with her. "I didn't know," he whispered apologetically. "Would you like to go home?" He was sure she felt bad and very uncomfortable now.

Going home wouldn't solve anything for Jazzmine. She would only hide out in her room and wish she was in her sister's body. Shaking her head, she faked a smile. "No. I'm fine. Vanessa didn't know how I feel about Keith. I probably should have told her."

Tyrone glanced back at Vanessa and Keith, who had gone from the dance floor to the bar. Jazzmine was so naïve! She just didn't realize that her sister didn't want her around!

Vanessa was ashamed of Jazzmine, and Tyrone was ashamed of her doing this to her. "*Want to bet she didn't know?*" he thought. Knowing Vanessa, she had to have found out somehow. She wouldn't have come here with Keith or asked him to bring Jazzmine there had she not found out secretly. Wanting to put a stop to Vanessa's evil plot to hurt her sister, he stood up. "Jazzmine, I'll be right back." He left her and crossed the room to the bar. Tapping Vanessa on the shoulder, he asked to speak to her in private.

Keith spoke to Tyrone and informed Vanessa that he was going to find a booth. She nodded at him.

He left them alone.

Tyrone sat beside Vanessa on the barstool Keith was sitting on and stared at her with disbelief. Her father would be ashamed of her if he could see her right now. He couldn't possibly know how heartless his oldest daughter was toward her sister.

Wondering what was on his mind, Vanessa sighed and shrugged her shoulders. "What?" she asked innocently.

"You knew that your sister is crazy about Keith. How could you do this to her?" Tyrone slightly tilted his head, waiting for her answer.

Vanessa sighed, again. So, he figured her out, and now he was going to try to convince her that she was wrong. She didn't have time for one of his little lectures. It was nice of him to try to protect Jazzmine's feelings, but she knew what was best for her. "Tyrone, I did this for Jazzmine's own good."

Tyrone shook his head, wondering why she was lying to herself that way. People don't hurt their own flesh and blood for their own good! "You did this to hurt her, and it will backfire, Vanessa!" he warned before standing up. Shaking his head in shame, he walked away.

Vanessa rolled her eyes. Nothing was going to happen to her. All she wanted was to get rid of Jazzmine, which she intended to do. In fact, Tyrone could tell Jazzmine the truth about her right now if he wanted. She wouldn't believe him anyway. In her eyes, she could do no wrong, which was why it was so easy to pull a fast one on her. She couldn't help it if she is young and stupid! It wasn't her fault.

Not knowing that Jazzmine was even in the club, Keith chose to sit in the booth directly behind her. His back was to her back, and her head was down, resting on her arm. She wasn't aware that he was behind her. She hadn't been able to stand the sight of him any longer after he kissed her sister. The sight of her sister in Keith's arms was too much for her, but when he kissed her, she wanted to die. She wished she could have been in his arms, holding him close, as they slow danced. For him to kiss her would have been a dream come true, but that was all it was, a dream. It would never happen for them. She wasn't that blessed, nor was she Vanessa.

Seeing him kiss Vanessa, she knew she

would never be able to have him or tell him how she felt. It would be humiliating to hear him say, "I'm sorry, Jazzmine, but I'm in love with your sister."

LaTerrio Tibs, a friend of Keith's, who was passing by, stopped at his booth. "What's up, Keith?"

Hearing his name, Jazzmine shook her head, feeling that she would never be able to lift it again.

"Hey, LaTerrio."

CHAPTER TWO

*J*azzmine sighed to herself, feeling uncomfortable and disturbed. Keith was closer to her than she anticipated by the closeness of his voice. Why did he have to sit behind her? The timing and everything was all wrong. It almost felt as if the incidents occurred to drive her over the edge, an adhesive situation.

"Why don't you sit down?" Keith invited.

Doing as requested, LaTerrio sat down across from Keith, making himself comfortable. "Hey, Keith, did you see the bow-wow Tyrone came in with?" He was curious to know because he had, and it was unbelievable. It was definitely going to be the talk of the town.

The question caught him completely by surprise. Keith was shocked. Was he referring to Tyrone Thomas? Surely, he couldn't be? "Tyrone who? Tyrone Thomas?" He asked to get clarity.

LaTerrio nodded with a gleam of laugher in his eyes. It was obvious that he couldn't wait to spread the news. "Yep!"

"What?" Keith was skeptical about the news, as he believed that LaTerrio had embellished. He hadn't seen the woman, as he and Vanessa had only recently made their arrival. It sounded nothing of Tyrone Thomas's character to make an entrance with a date on his arm. If she was a *bow-wow*, it definitely wasn't the Tyrone he knew. His taste in women was exquisite and unquestionable. He had never once seen him with an unattractive woman, especially in public. "Tyrone brought a date?" He shook his head, as he had to disagree. "No. I didn't see her." Curiously, his eyes scanned the room for Tyrone, as he had to see this *bow-wow*.

Tyrone was at the opposite end of the bar from Vanessa, speaking to a very attractive waitress. She wasn't his date. Why wasn't he with her? Where was she? He was still curious, as LaTerrio had intrigued him. "Well, what does she look like?" His eyes went back to him, as he directed the question to his friend.

LaTerrio shook his head quickly, disapproving of Tyrone's monstrous date. "Man! That girl is *fat* with a bumpy face! You would never believe how ugly she is!"

Fat? With a bumpy face? It was no longer a mystery of her identity. That description only fit one person to Keith's knowledge, Jazzmine Thomas. She was *no* woman nor was she fit to be called a date. She was Tyrone's cousin, and he agreed that she was *ugly*, very harsh to the eyes!

Tyrone stepped through the door with her as if he was sporting a trophy? What was he thinking?

"I already know who his date is. It's not actually a date. She's his cousin. I can't believe he would go out in public with Jazzmine." Jazzmine was definitely one to be kept under wraps. She should be a well-kept secret.

Wounded by the sharpness of his words, Jazzmine slowly lifted her head, listening quietly. She didn't see the dilemma with Tyrone bringing her to the club. To say he shouldn't take her out in public was elementary and vengeful! Who was he to monitor Tyrone's public affairs or who he took into the public's eye?

"You're right, she *is* ugly," Keith went on to say, shattering Jazzmine's self-confidence.

She was aware that she wasn't very attractive, but she didn't think **ugly** was an accurate description.

"I could never date her. Do you know how hard it would be to get air?" he continued, visualizing himself with Jazzmine. The thought was grueling.

LaTerrio laughed, amused by the statement.

"Think about what it would be like if I slept with her." He frowned, twisting his mouth with disgust. "I would always have to be on top because she would crush me if she got on top."

LaTerrio's laughter increased.

"No!" Keith shook his head with disapproval. "She is not the type of girl with whom I would ever be caught. Now, her sister," he looked at the bar, eyeing Vanessa with a nod of approval. Pointing her out to him, he whistled. "She is all that! I would love to get her in bed!"

Keith and LaTerrio exchanged fives over the table, as they were in sync.

After a moment of thought, LaTerrio frowned with confusion. His eyes moved from Vanessa back to Keith. "*She* is that girl's sister?" The relation was implausible.

"They're half-sisters," Keith explained.

LaTerrio nodded, comprehending more clearly. "They're totally different in every way. Vanessa is beautiful, the type of woman every man wants, and Jazzmine is a big fat blob. Nobody wants her! I know I don't! She'll never be anybody!"

Devastated, Jazzmine dropped her head in sheer shame. She thought she wouldn't be able to approach Keith because she was no competition for her sister. Now, she knew reality.

She couldn't approach Keith, nor did she want to, because he was a sex-crazed jerk! She had integrity, which made her highly above reproach. Keith would never be able to redeem himself from such a filthy mouth and a cold heart.

The atrocious comments he made about her caused her to feel like a complete fool. She had strong ambitions to be with him when he considered her to be some repulsive creature from outer space!

That was so horrendous!

Appearance wasn't everything, and neither was life all about sex! It was great to know Keith's true feelings for her, although the impact was traumatizing. At least now her heart would have time to heal, and she could recover. It would be a slow process, but now she could stop wasting her time constantly thinking about him. He wasn't worth her time nor was he worthy of a woman like her. He wouldn't know a good woman if she hit him in the face, which was exactly what she felt like doing.

Jazzmine swallowed hard, mustering up confidence from deep within. She may not look all that grand. According to Keith and his friend she was ugly, but she was going to be somebody someday. In fact, she was already somebody. She was Jazzmine Tankia Thomas, valedictorian of her class! So, Keith should stand corrected as he knew nothing about her. Besides, who was he?

Could Keith, his friend, or any of the other people who gossiped about her tonight actually say that they were somebody? Perhaps, everyone should look beyond the exterior and see that she was better inside than all of them for not passing judgment on them. She could judge them because they all had judged her falsely, by her looks. However, she had no intentions of stooping that low! If she said that everyone in that room was two-faced, she would be no better than they were.

Unable to repress her feelings or take anymore unscrupulous insults, Jazzmine slid out of the booth and stepped to Keith's side. Folding her arms across her chest, she tilted her head to the side and stared at him with a scowl on her face. "Oh, is that so?"

Hearing her voice, Keith snapped his head around to see her. He was taken aback, instantly feeling ashamed of himself. "Jazzmine!" he exclaimed.

"That's right," she hissed. "It's me! I heard every word you just said you bastard! You know, I used to like you until I found out that you're a low life. Looks really are deceiving!" She lifted her face to the ceiling and laughed.

Dropping her eyes back to him, she went on to say, "You know what else? You just said something that I just have to correct you on. I know that I'm not all that good looking, but so what?

Who cares? Looks aren't everything. And as far as me being somebody," she laughed, again, "I already **am**. You may not know this, but I'm valedictorian of my class. Were you?" She shook her head, answering her own question. "Oh," she laughed at him, "listen to me! I just made a joke! Of course you weren't because you're not that bright! So, maybe you're the one who'll never be anybody compared to me."

Without warning, she slapped him hard across the face and walked away.

Keith's hand rose to comfort his stinging cheek as he watched Jazzmine go. He felt terrible. It was never his intentions to hurt her feelings. She was Vanessa's sister. If she informed her of his harsh comments, he would be out in the cold. He was sure Vanessa would lose all respect for him for speaking so inadequately about her sister. He shouldn't have allowed the words to roll off of his tongue, and now he regretted it.

Keith watched Jazzmine go to Tyrone, skipping over Vanessa completely, and grab his arm. Practically dragging him away, they left.

Keith shook his head, wishing he hadn't been so uncouth. He could have had a little more couth in his decorum. He just didn't know she was listening. That was just a sign that he shouldn't have contributed to the conversation. He learned a valuable lesson at that moment. One never knew who was lurking nearby to catch him in the act of a sinful deed.

Jazzmine was probably a kind-hearted person, and he would never know it. He certainly didn't know she liked him. Her respect level for him had probably been demoted to near nonexistent. If it had, he could only blame himself.

One thing was for sure. He was going to attempt to salvage what little respect she might have for him and repent. If he could redeem himself and make up for the error of his ways, he most certainly would.

Attending her graduation was the first step to demonstrate remorse.

At two o'clock in the morning when Vanessa finally made it home, she went directly up the stairs. She was exhausted.

Keith had her going all night. He wanted to dance to nearly every song. Being that she loved to dance, she couldn't decline. She should have left when Tyrone and Jazzmine did. If she had, it would have ruined everything, however. Her mission was to push Jazzmine over the edge. Had she come home early, she wouldn't have succeeded. Jazzmine needed to think she had the time of her life. She wanted her to sit at home, pondering how much closer the two of them had become. Envy should eat away at her like a knife stabing her in the heart.

When she told her about her date tomorrow, she would embellish, tidy up the minor details, but that would be acceptable. Jazzmine wouldn't know the difference. It wasn't as if Keith was going to tell her.

Passing Jazzmine's bedroom door, she stopped, hearing sad sobs. Rolling her eyes with irritation, she thought, *"I know she's not crying over Keith!"* After a moment, a smile replaced her frown. If Jazzmine was crying over the episode at the club, her plan was working.

To drive the knife deeper into the wound, Vanessa pushed the door open, turning on the light.

Jazzmine was in bed under the covers, and tears were drenching her pillow. She actually was crying, and Vanessa couldn't help sympathizing with her. If she was crying because of the kiss Keith gave her, she didn't have to cry. He wasn't a good kisser. It was nothing she would want to experience.

When the light came on unexpectedly, burning Jazzmine's eyes, she was quick to pull the pillow over her head.

Vanessa moved farther into the room. "Jazzmine? What's wrong, honey?" she pretended to have no idea.

"Go away," Jazzmine hissed angrily.

Vanessa blinked, insulted. Jazzmine had never spoken to her so harshly. In fact, she never uttered less than a kind word to her. She must have really been hurt by what she saw, more hurt than Vanessa predicted.

Collecting herself, she moved to the bed and sat down, pulling the pillow away from her sister's face.

Jazzmine covered her face with her hands, sobbing harder.

"Come on, Jazzmine," Vanessa encouraged, "Talk to me. Tell me what's wrong."

Believing her sister to be genuinely concerned, Jazzmine sat up and looked at her. She didn't even know where to begin. What could she say? Trying to put her feelings into words, she swallowed hard. "Vanessa, Tyrone and I went to *Club Ten*." That was a beginning as she wasn't sure her sister was aware. She was so wrapped up into Keith that there was a possibility that she didn't know. She didn't acknowledge her presence, which meant that she probably didn't.

"Well, good! You needed to go out and have fun. I'm glad you decided to go," she was so convincing.

Jazzmine disagreed. "No, that wasn't good."

Vanessa cringed, pretending to be confused. Her forehead wrinkled into a frown. "It wasn't? I don't understand."

Jazzmine lowered her eyes with embarrassment. "Vanessa, I know you weren't aware of this, but I had a huge crush on Keith Bedly. When you came to the club on his arm, I was crushed. I felt like bailing then, but my pride wouldn't allow it. The sight of him holding you, while the two of you were dancing..." her sentence faded as more tears fell.

Vanessa looked at her sister with sad eyes. "Oh, Jazzmine! I'm sorry..."

Jazzmine stopped crying and sniffed, holding up a hand to silence her. She didn't know the whole story. "Wait! There's more."

Vanessa frowned, a real frown this time. To what more was Jazzmine referring? She wasn't aware of any incidents occurring under her nose, not on her watch. "What?"

Clearing her throat, Jazzmine swallowed hard, hating to relive the whole sorted episode. "I was sitting at a booth alone, feeling lower than dirt, and Keith came along and sat down behind me. I didn't know he was there because my head was down. I couldn't stand the sight of him at that point. Anyway, one of his friends, some idiot, joined him. Neither of them knew that I was sitting behind them. They joked and laughed at **my** expense. I heard them say that I was **ugly** and Tyrone should have been ashamed of himself for taking me out in public."

Jazzmine resorted to tears, again. After a moment, she stopped crying and continued, "I was so wounded and so confused that I didn't know what to do. I couldn't believe Keith was saying those things about **me**! I was so glad to find out his true feelings about me, though. I got up, told him a piece of my mind, and slapped him. Then, I had Tyrone to bring me home."

The first part Vanessa knew about, but what Keith said she didn't. Their feelings about being seen in public with Jazzmine were mutual, but he was stupid enough to say it aloud. Now, he had gone and hurt Jazzmine's feelings. How crazy could one person be? It was a good thing Jazzmine did slap him because he needed it. He was boring, a bad kisser, and stupid! No one knew her true feelings for her sister, and no one ever would because she was smart enough to keep them under wraps. Her father could possibly discovery her secret, and that would kill him! Her father was the one person she would never do anything to intentionally hurt.

Yes, Vanessa desired to get rid of Jazzmine, but she didn't want anyone to know about it. They were sisters!

"Oh, Jazzmine!" She reached over and locked her arms around her from the side, pulling her closer. Smoothing her hair down, she kissed her sister's hair. "Had I known you liked Keith, I would never have gone out with him. Had I known he was a jerk, I certainly wouldn't have! Why didn't you tell me?" she pretended to have no clue.

"I know. I know you would never do anything to hurt me. I should have told you. I just..." she shook her head, not wanting to talk about it anymore. "Never mind! It's not important anyway. I'm going to a university in California!" she announced, making the decision instantly.

Excitement rushed through Vanessa's entire body at the announcement, and she felt like kissing her sister, again. That was the best news of her life! If she went to California, thousands of miles away, she would be out of her hair at least for four years. Vanessa never wanted anything like she wanted to get her sister packed and on a plane to California! "What?" she pulled back and looked at her sister's face as if it hurt to hear the instant decision. "*California*! That's thousands of miles away! Everybody would miss you!" She tried to sound sincere.

Jazzmine didn't care. The more miles she was away from Keith, the better she would be, and it would be much easier to forget him. "I'm going to California," she repeated in a firm voice, letting her sister know it would be impossible to talk her out of it. She was aware that her family would miss her, and she would miss them, as well. It was just too painful to stay in the same city with someone for whom she felt so much compassion and love and who thought she looked like something that belonged in the zoo! Every time she saw him, the things he said about her would come crashing back, and she wouldn't be able to go on. She needed to get away and be free. If she was in California, and he was still in New York, there was no way they would ever have to see each other again.

"Well, if that's what you want to do," Vanessa said sadly, her insides bursting with happiness, "you should do it."

From that day forward until her Graduation day, Jazzmine locked herself in her room, refusing to see or talk to anyone. Vanessa never once complained. It was a joy to finally have her out of the way. No one could figure out why Keith called Jazzmine constantly every day, begging whoever answered the telephone to get her to answer his calls. He even dropped by the house four times, begging her to open her bedroom door to him.

She refused.

Trying every tactic that came to mind to get Jazzmine to talk to him, Keith even called Tyrone and asked him to talk to her for him. Tyrone tried, but she refused to hear anything about Keith Bedly.

Friday, the day of graduation, was a busy day for Jazzmine. She began by having breakfast with her father and sister at *The Pancake Sizzler*. After breakfast, she went to the Convention Hall for her graduation rehearsal. From there, she visited all of her relatives and friends to say good-bye. Her grandparents treated her to lunch to celebrate her decision to attend an excellent college.

By five thirty, she was home and preparing for her graduation. On her way to the Convention Hall, she looked over her notes for her speech. It wasn't very long. Her goal was to get straight to the point and to receive her diploma. The sooner she did, the sooner she could leave New York City. She was so ready to go.

The graduation ceremony began, and Jazzmine marched proudly to her seat. A huge smile was on her face.

She sat on the stage anticipating her moment to shine. Her eyes found her father as he was sitting close to the stage, and she smiled at him. She knew he was proud of her, and that was all that mattered. If her mother was still alive, she would be proud of her, too.

It was going to be hard to leave her father and her sister, but she was going to do it, and there was no way anyone could stop her. If the weather was bad, and she couldn't catch her flight, she would just have to catch a bus because she was getting out of there. If the bus broke down, she would catch a train. Somehow, she would get to California.

Jazzmine was introduced, and she smiled even broader as she stood up.

All was quiet as Jazzmine stepped to the podium in the purple cap and gown with the gold medal around her neck to make her speech. Her eyes panned around the crowded room. She wasn't as nervous as she expected to be.

Smiling broadly and feeling proud of herself for being valedictorian of her class, she said, "Good evening everyone. My name is Jazzmine Thomas. It is an honor to stand before you as a representative of my class. I would like to take a moment to tell you what I have learned during my thirteen years of schooling. I have learned that life is not about who you know. It is about what you know. One's knowledge is the key to success. I know that people can be cruel and insensitive to others when they do not look and dress a certain way. In my eyes, face value is not at all important. Neither are material things.

"It is not about the outside. No one can make themselves. A person's appearance is up to God. If you, the Class of 2000, have not learned to get along with people, no matter how they look, where they're from, what color they are, and what type of clothes they wear, you have not learned the most important lesson of all. I want you to learn this tonight. Every person in this class is going to be our future." She looked around. "You may be sitting next to your future boss."

"The future is what people make of it. If one wants his future to be the best, then he will strive for the best. Being the best cannot be done by prejudice judgments and unfair assumptions. Assuming that someone is not as good as someone else because of how he or she looks, or because of his or her color will get a person nowhere. As I close, I would like to tell you one more thing that I have learned. I have learned that in order to be treated a certain way, a person should treat others the way he wants to be treated. His reward will come in the end. I say to you, the Class of 2000, strive for the best and our future will be in excellent hands. We are in control. If we make the future the best it can possibly be, we will make all of our family and friends proud. I am proud to say congratulations to all of you. We have made it through thirteen long, hard years together. Hopefully we will continue to stay together and work together as friends. Thank you!"

Everyone applauded as she returned to her seat.

James smiled broadly, feeling proud of his

youngest daughter and loving her beautiful speech. It was a true message to everyone.

Vanessa was touched by the speech, feeling close to tears. She had to reevaluate herself and her own prospective. She had to wonder if she had judged her sister falsely all these years. It was wrong of her to treat her sister that way, and she wanted to go up on the stage and hug her. If it were at all possible, she would turn back the hands of time and erase every devious thing she had done to her sister, the only sister she had.

Keith sat behind Vanessa and her father. When Jazzmine took her seat, he found himself taking deep breaths. He was just as touched as Vanessa. Somehow it felt as if the speech was meant for him. Hurting Jazzmine happened unintentionally, and he wished she would let him apologize. Then, his conscience could be at ease, and they could restart their friendship.

After the ceremony, the crowd began to go down onto the floor to hug and congratulate the graduates.

Vanessa realized that no matter how pretty Jazzmine was on the inside, she was still ugly on the surface, and her feelings of guilt dissolved.

"Jazzmine!" Keith called to her in the crowded auditorium when he saw her, after she received her diploma.

Hearing her name called, Jazzmine turned with a huge smile on her face as she put her diploma under her arm. Seeing Keith, her expression immediately became serious, and she wished she hadn't turned around.

Keith hurried to her. He was glad she stopped.

He was afraid that she was going to run away. Approaching her, he took her free hand. "Congratulations! Your speech was wonderful!"

Slowly removing hand, she looked away. Her intentions were to direct the speech to him and all others who judged her falsely, but she hadn't been able to call names. If he gained nothing from her message, then that was too bad.

There was no need to reiterate the incident. They were both there, and neither of them needed to be reminded. Besides, he didn't have to see her again after tomorrow morning when she boarded the plane to California, anyway. What did he really want? Forcing herself to smile, Jazzmine nodded. "Thank you," she said in a weak, squeaky voice.

"Jazzmine, I want to apologize for what happened that night at *Club Ten*. I really didn't mean to hurt your feelings."

Jazzmine laughed and shook her head. "No. The truth is, you meant what you said, you just didn't mean for me to hear it. It's too late, Keith. I heard, and it hurt!" She felt the tears rising to the surface. Forcing herself not to cry, she blinked them back, repressing them. Keith wasn't worth her tears or ruining her makeup.

Keith dropped his eyes, wishing he could go back and erase what he had said that night and Jazzmine's pain. He just didn't know that she liked him. He later found out how deep her feelings were for him from Tyrone when they discussed the situation over the telephone.

"Hey, chin up," Jazzmine said, causing him to look up at her. "Don't worry! After tomorrow morning, you don't have to worry about seeing my *ugly face*, again. If I ever return to New York City, I won't bother you by trying to contact you!" Without another word, she walked away, leaving him behind.

Keith shook his head, watching her go. She had everything all wrong. He just wished there was some way he could make her understand before she left for California. He heard about her leaving for school in California the following morning from Tyrone and Vanessa, who confirmed Tyrone's story.

Jazzmine packed quickly, snatching clothes from her closest and tossing them into the open suitcase on her bed. She was angry with herself because she should have packed days ago. She knew she was leaving, and she wasn't even prepared. She was just so depressed over Keith that she couldn't function properly.

For days, she lay in bed too sick to move. She woke up with tears in her eyes and fell asleep with them. Graduation day was the first day she felt like getting out of bed, and that was only because she had to give her speech.

Not only was she angry with herself, she was more than upset with Keith. His comments about her at the club and his laughter replayed over and over in her mind. She couldn't shake it from her thoughts. He scarred her for life, and he just didn't know how bad it was.

"You idiot!" she scowled at him as if he were there as she began snatching things from her drawers. "I'll never forgive you for this. **NEVER!**"

Tears flooded her vision, and she fell to her knees at the foot of her bed. Crying her eyes out, she cursed Keith in her mind. She was so anxious for the following morning to arrive. The hands of time weren't ticking fast enough.

"Lord," she began, still sobbing, "if you let me get away from here, I won't come back unless it's an absolute emergency!"

This was her solemn vow, and she intended to honor it. New York City wasn't the place for her, and she was anxious to leave.

Vanessa, peeping through the crack in Jazzmine's door, smiled to herself. Jazzmine was serious about leaving and for a moment, she felt like volunteering to help her pack, but she couldn't. If she did, Jazzmine would feel that she was trying to rush her off, which she actually was, but she couldn't relinquish that information. She didn't want her plan to backfire and cause Jazzmine to want to stay. If she did anything, she would have to go in and act as if she was really going to miss her.

James's footsteps could be heard on the stairs.

Not wanting her father to catch her, she straightened up and dropped her head, wanting him to sympathize with her.

He reached the top of the stairs. When he approached her, he stopped. Looking at her, he frowned. "Vanessa, baby? What's wrong?"

Vanessa lifted her head with sad eyes. She looked at Jazzmine's bedroom door. "It's Jazzmine! She's really leaving, isn't she, Daddy?"

James, who did sympathize with her, nodded. "Yes, honey. She is."

Vanessa sighed. "I was going to go and talk to her, but I can't. I can't bear to see her now. I'm going to miss her, and it hurts too much."

James nodded, again. "Yes, honey, I know. I feel the same way, but we have to keep our heads up. This is for the best. We have to let her go. California could be the opportunity of a lifetime for her. Who are we to stop her?"

Vanessa didn't want to stop her nor was she going to try, not even for her father's sake. Jazzmine would be better off somewhere else. "Well, I guess it's just going to be you and me after tomorrow," she went on to say.

For that, she would be grateful. If Jazzmine was gone, she would be the only one there for her father to spoil, and she was going to love it.

The following morning at the airport, Jazzmine checked her luggage and prepared to board the plane. After hugging her father and sister, she stepped into the terminal and turned back to give New York City one last look. She was anxious to get away from this place.

All of her pain was due to her appearance. What did looks have to do with anything? Her looks didn't affect her heart, which was broken by the one person she thought respected her and looked beyond the skin surface to see the actual person. If only people would realize that looks weren't always what they appeared to be, they would be a lot happier. She learned this lesson long ago because she had a very deceptive face.

Her eyes lifted, hearing her name being called from a distance. She saw Keith running toward her as fast as he could. When he reached her father's side, he stopped, knowing he couldn't go any farther.

Not believing he actually came to the airport

to see *her*, Jazzmine's eyes locked with his and for a moment, she forgot all about that night at *Club Ten*. Her desire was to run to him as it was wonderful that he was there.

"Jazzmine, wait!" Keith called to her.

When he called her name, Vanessa snapped her head to him with narrowed eyes. What was he doing? If Jazzmine came back for him, she was going to kill him. What was he doing there anyway? No one invited him.

Memories of what he said about her came flooding back, and Jazzmine snapped out of her trance. Turning away, she walked down the terminal to the gate to board the plane. She would never be able to forget what he did to her, and there was no need to even try. She would just accept that he came to the airport to see her depart.

"Jazzmine, wait!" Keith called again at the top of his lungs. When she disappeared, and the door to the terminal closed, he dropped his head, realizing that she was gone, and that she probably hated him. His conscience was going to bother him forever now.

Satisfied that Jazzmine was finally gone, Vanessa looked at her father, who was holding up rather well. Knowing that he was sad, she placed a hand on his shoulder. "You still have me, Daddy."

James agreed. "I know."

Keith sighed with defeat and walked away.

PLACE: Beverly Hills, California
DATE: September 2006

CHAPTER THREE

*L*ife was fabulous!

Twenty-three-year-old Jazzmine Thomas had nearly everything for which anyone could ask. The only thing that she didn't have at this point was blood family living in the same city and state as she. Everything else was perfect, absolutely no complaints.

Upon arrival to Los Angeles six years earlier, she attended a university there, living on campus.

Life had been boring and lonely at that point as she had not a single friend.

Shortly, things began to progress, as her life was put into prospective. She became an active member of *Morning Glory Baptist Church.* In the church, she met some wonderful people. She was a faithful member, attending service every Sunday.

One Sunday, Erma Fistbourne, one of the mothers of the church introduced her to Levi Proctor, the pastor's son. She liked him, and to her surprise, he was compassionate, befriending her. Attracting each other's interest, they became fast friends. Actually, they became best friends.

Levi, although quite handsome, did not put emphasis on Jazzmine's outer appearance. He only saw her kind heart, which attracted him to her. Secretly, he begged Erma Fistbourne to introduce the two of them as he hadn't known how to approach her personally. Before their introduction, he observed Jazzmine every Sunday, and he loved her loving spirit. She was a beautiful person, very sweet and kind, but, also, sensitive and fragile. He pursued a friendship with her because of her compelling inner beauty.

During her freshmen year, Levi, a sophomore, escorted Jazzmine around campus and hung out with her, for which she was extremely grateful.

Initially, she felt uncomfortable hanging with him as it was a wonder if he actually wanted her in his presence. People always stared at them when they entered a room or a restaurant together.

After a while, things began to feel normal.

Levi introduced her to his family and friends, who became her family and friends. His home became her home away from home. She dropped by his parents' house at random, and she was invited to family dinners, which became a tradition. She spent birthdays and holidays with them as if they were actually her family, fitting in perfectly. It was not an act that they loved her, and she adopted them promptly.

By introducing her to his friends and hanging out with her on a regular basis, Levi displayed his feelings of respect for her. It showed that he liked being with her, and he wasn't ashamed to be seen in public with her. She felt comfortable with him, and she was positive that he could actually be labeled *"friend"*.

They shared practically everything from secrets to his car.

During Jazzmine's sophomore year, Levi, a theater art major, auditioned for and received a starring roll in a movie. It was produced in Beverly Hills. When the movie premiered, Levi became an instant success. Shortly, he was offered major roles in two other movies. Accepting both, he became a *Beverly Hills'* movie star.

Through his fame, he never neglected his responsibility to the university or Jazzmine. His priorities were in order.

Near the end of Jazzmine's sophomore year, Levi joined a health spa. He requested that she accompany him. Despite her lack of ambition or enthusiasm, she did.

At the spa, Jazzmine signed up for a personal trainer. Wanting to stay healthy, she received the best in the spa.

The first day with her trainer, Jazzmine was required to get a physical as a preliminary procedure. Doing so, the physician prescribed medication for her acne. It was to be taken daily until her face was cleared. It worked well, clearing her skin in as little as two months.

Jazzmine's trainer, Tina Worthy, was no amateur at her job, taking it very seriously. Every morning, she and Jazzmine were up at five, running five miles. Every other day they were in the gym exercising for at least an hour and a half.

Tina put Jazzmine on a strict diet, asking Levi to help her maintain it.

Compelled to comply, she maintained her diet.

As a result of Tina's ambitious drive, Jazzmine began to loose weight.

Effectively, she slimmed to a petite size six.

Jazzmine became a new woman! Her thick coarse black hair, in which she began to take great pride, grew long and lustrous. It was always well maintained. During the weight loss, her face actually shrank to the perfect size to fit her small nose. The circles and puffiness around her eyes and in her cheeks vanished. Her dimples were visible, an attractive feature.

Becoming the desired size and having an actual attractive face to stare at in the mirror, Jazzmine began to feel confident about her appearance. It was reflected as so as she began to dress trendy. Her new appearance did not change her attitude, however, as she still did not put emphasis on looks.

The new and improved Jazzmine Thomas was absolutely gorgeous, a new found wealth that she had never known. Feeling different about herself, she decided to shorten her name, requesting to be referred to as *Jazz* to fit her new look.

The summer before her junior year, Levi began to invite Jazzmine to his rehearsals at the studio more frequently as he wanted her by his side.

One day as they were leaving the studio, Beth Trenton, a renowned modeling agent, was making an entrance to pick up her daughter, Levi's co-star. Upon entering, she stepped directly into Jazzmine.

Captivated by Jazzmine's beauty, Beth offered her a contract with her modeling agency right there in the studio.

Her conversation was enticing as she said everything Jazzmine wanted to hear. She began by introduced herself. As a representative of her company, she baited Jazzmine in by telling her how beautiful she was, and her agency was looking for fabulous new faces like hers. Then, she offered her a lump sum of money that would take care of her for years to come if she agreed to train with her agency for the remainder of the summer.

A snap decision, Jazzmine accepted the offer, supported by Levi, who was proud of her. Training with *Beverly Hills' Beauties*, the modeling agency, she was still able to attend the university. As a model, she became a Beverly Hills' celebrity, a successful within itself. By her senior year, she was named among the top five models in Beverly Hills.

Jazzmine's face was plastered everywhere. She was on the front cover of *Hits Magazine*, and she was voted the *Sexiest Model of the Year* for the present year's issue of *Gorgeous Magazine*. Her face was on various posters, and she advertised for two commercials. In the first commercial she advertised for a popular nationwide shoe store. In the other, she advertised for her favorite department store in Los Angeles.

Missing her family back in New York City, Jazzmine wrote to her father and sister practically everyday, calling as often as possible.

During the first year, her father and sister returned her letters regularly. Then, Vanessa's letters began to come every-once-in-a-while. Soon her letters ceased altogether. Although her half-sister didn't return her letters, Jazzmine continued to write to her. Naturally, she assumed there was a logical explanation as to why Vanessa hadn't written back. Perhaps, one day, Vanessa would actually have time to sit down and write her a ten page letter, which she would enjoy reading.

Over the course of the past six years, James flew to California to visit with his youngest daughter several times, although not as often as he would have preferred. He was, however, able to see his daughter's transformation, of which he was proud.

Presently, Jazzmine was behind the wheel of her black Convertible, which was accented with gold rims and a license plate at the front saying *HOT BABE*, heading for her boyfriend's beach house. For the past five months, she had been dating Bartu Flexler, an interracial (black and white) Australian.

Bartu came to the states with his parents and three younger sisters as a teenager, growing up in Sacramento. When he was fresh out of high school, he and his family moved to Los Angeles. Upon moving, Bartu, who had always been interested in movie production, went into training for movie producing. Signing a contract with *Enlightening Productions*, one of the top television studios in Beverly Hills, he became a recognized producer. Eventually, he co-produced the last two movies in which Levi Proctor starred.

One Saturday in the middle of April, Bartu went home to visit his parents. His youngest sister, who was fourteen, was reading an issue of *Gorgeous Magazine*. She began to ramble on about her favorite Beverly Hills model, pointing out a picture of Jazzmine to her brother.

Seeing Jazzmine's picture, Bartu fell in love with her instantly. Taking the magazine from his sister, he read the entire article on her, discovering her relationship with Levi. Going back to the studio on Monday, he began to befriend Levi. Ultimately, he asked him to introduce him to Jazzmine.

Levi, with no desire, made the introduction.

Bartu and Jazzmine had been together ever since.

Upon meeting Bartu, who asked her out immediately, Jazzmine was dumbfounded by the fact that someone as handsome as he would be interested in her. He was an extremely attractive man! His black, naturally curly hair was always cut short. His medium brown, almost hazel, eyes were dreamy, and his skin was a beautiful caramel, almost almond, color. His torso was absolutely fabulous! His arms and legs rippled with muscles, and he was too sexy for his own good! His hands were strong and manly. His buttocks were shaped like basketballs, round and gorgeous.

Jazzmine was absolutely fascinated by the idea of dating a sexy movie producer, jumping at the opportunity.

Cruising with the top down, the radio on her favorite station, and dark shades shielding her eyes from the sun, Jazzmine allowed the wind to blow through her hair as it was down and flowing. Her right hand was on the steering wheel, and her left elbow rested on the door. Her hand dangled inside the car. The wind felt like a nice little air conditioner against her face, and she couldn't help smiling. It was a gorgeous day, and she felt great!

Pulling up to the beach house, she stopped the car and got out. Making sure she was presentable, she looked down at the deep yellow tank top and fitting jeans shorts. It looked all right she supposed. Lifting her eyes, she slipped her car keys into her front pocket. Lifting the shades into her hair, she went up the sidewalk to the door.

She rang the doorbell three times, and no one answered. Thinking he wasn't home, she turned from the door and started back to her car.

The door opened.

Batru saw her leaving. "Hey, babe," he called to her with his Australian accent.

Hearing his voice, Jazzmine whirled around to face him. Her eyes went over him. He was standing in the threshold wrapped in a towel. His torso was damp, and she could tell that he had just stepped out of the shower by his damp hair. Her eyes lingered on his sexy chest for a moment. Her heart was pounding rapidly as she stared at it. After a moment, she blinked to gain self-control.

Clearing her throat, she smiled. "Hey!" she exclaimed, glad to see him. Frowning slightly, she asked, "Did I come at a bad time?"

Ignoring the question, Bartu smiled and opened his arms to her. "Come here!"

With pleasure, Jazzmine ran to his warm embrace.

Glad to see her, as well, he kissed her passionately and swept her off her feet. Turning with her into the house, he kicked the door closed and carried her to his bedroom. Taking her to the king-sized bed, he sat her down on the edge. Stepping back, he kissed her forehead. "I'll be right back."

He hurriedly abandoned the room, not giving Jazzmine an opportunity to say a word.

Returning, he was wearing silk boxers and slippers. He moved to the bed and sat down beside his girlfriend. "I missed you, darling," he whispered, kissing her sweet lips.

Jazzmine returned the kiss, embracing him. Before she knew it, she was on her back, and Bartu was on top of her kissing her passionately. Her heart thumped in her chest with nervousness. Inhaling, she silently prayed that he didn't intend to pursue sexual intercourse. She wasn't ready for that stage with him. There was no guarantee that he was the one. "I missed you, too," she managed to say.

Jazzmine was tense, and Bartu could sense it as her body wasn't relaxed under his. She was practically shaking, which he didn't understand. They had been dating for months, and she knew he would never do anything to hurt her. "Jazz," he began in a soft voice. Desperate desire for her sensual sexy body threatened to erupt from deep within as he wanted to take her body to the heights of blissful passion. To stoke her body to a frenzied cry of pleasure would be like a ride on Cloud Nine.

Jazzmine wanted to melt inside as she felt like a crystal vase, delicate and easy to shatter. Her heart wouldn't easily mend if he was granted his desire, and he abandoned her the next day. Still, the sound of his sexy voice turned her on, sparking flames deep within. It was hard not to feel the throbbing sensation that was rising from her inner woman. Her body yearned to experience the passion that he could deliver, but her heart begged her to suppress those feelings. She just loved the way he said her name with that gorgeous accent of his.

With a clear head, she managed to tame her weak body. Sex could not transpire between them, not yet. "Bartu," she interrupted, gently pushing him off of her. "Please," she begged. She couldn't allow things go any farther as she felt that he wanted more from her than she was willing to offer at the moment.

Dropping his head with disappointment, Bartu groaned and rolled off of her onto his back. "Jazz, we've been together for quite a while now, and you've refused to sleep with me every time I asked or *tried* rather. What is it? What's the matter?"

Something was holding her back from him, and he wanted to resolve the issue quickly. He was a man with strong urges and needs. He prided himself on being a patient man, but Jazzmine was being unreasonable!

Jazzmine sat up and dropped her head. Her mind flashed back to the night she had gone to *Club Ten* with her cousin six years ago.

"Nobody wants her!" The words Keith Bedly had said about her rang in her head. *"Now her sister! She's all that! I would love to get her in bed."*

The scars he embedded in her that night resurfaced as she had done well to suppress them. A frown darkened her features.

Each time she and Bartu came close to being intimate, her mind would flash back to that night. She always wondered if he would have wanted her before her weight loss. Did he only want her because she was beautiful? The question never came forth for fear of the answer. If he said *"yes"*, it would break her heart, and she would only want to run away, again. She couldn't go through life running away because someone couldn't accept her for who she really was. Inwardly, she felt that

Bartu did only want to be with her because she was beautiful.

If he said *"no"*, she wouldn't believe him. He would probably say no because he thought it would sooth her ears. Then, she wouldn't be able to trust him because he would be a liar.

Bartu arched up on his elbows and glanced at her. The frightened expression on her face worried him. He sat up straight beside her and took her into his arms. Something *was* wrong! Someone had wounded her deeply. "What's the matter, babe?" His voice was filled with genuine concern as he wanted to support her through her tribulation.

"Bartu, I just don't think five months is a sufficient amount of time," Jazzmine explained.

Bartu felt neglected as he wondered how long she wanted him to wait. He had no intentions of waiting much longer. Five months was ample time as she was postponing his need for fulfillment. She was asking him to continue to neglect his own manhood, which was absolutely unacceptable!

In fact, he was ready to make love after the first month. Their main mission, before making love, was to better acquaint themselves. That didn't take long. He was well acquainted with her now. What more did she need?

"What do you want from me?" He had to know. "Are you looking for a wedding cake and a honeymoon? Come on, babe! You're acting like you've never done it before. It's not as if you're a virgin. How long did you make the others wait?"

There were no others!

Jazzmine closed her eyes tight. Bartu just didn't understand. She *was* a virgin. Of course, she couldn't tell him that now because he would probably laugh in her face. Levi didn't even know. It was the only secret she had ever kept from him. Besides him, Levi was the only other man who had been in her life for more than two minutes. She was too afraid to permit anyone to get close to her, fearing that her beauty was all anyone would see in her. She wanted her first sexual experience to be with her husband. Her prayer was that he would be someone who respected her and wanted her for who she was not just because her pictures were in magazines!

She was sure Bartu had seen pictures of her prior to their first encounter. He wouldn't understand how she felt, and she wasn't even sure how to explain it to him.

Hurt that he would even ask her if she intended to make him wait until marriage, Jazzmine stood up, forcing him to drop his arms. Walking away, she turned her back on him. It was insane to even argue about the subject, especially since the case had been argued several times before and neither of them won. It was useless. Neither would see the other's point.

Holding up a hand in surrender, the other hand went to her forehead. "Bartu, please, I don't want to argue with you about this. I came here to tell you about Levi. He..."

Insulted, Bartu's mouth dropped with disbelief. How dare she? *Levi?*

Levi Proctor was definitely not a topic of which he wanted to hear or discuss. He had absolutely no significance in his life. It was an ongoing process with her, however.

Levi seemed to be her favorite topic as she

always had to update him on the current events in his life. Frankly, he didn't care, and he wasn't going to receive the information anyway.

Now was not the time for her to be bringing up her *best* friend as he wasn't a fan like she. The only reason he even tolerated their relationship was because he had used him to get to her. Now, it was getting old. Levi needed to the boot!

"Levi?" Bartu shook his head with anger. "I want to make love to you, and you want to talk about Levi? What makes you think I would even care?" His voice displayed his anger.

Affronted by the question, Jazzmine dropped her hand from her forehead and blinked with disbelief. How could he even ask that? He should care! Levi was *supposed* to be his friend as well as hers. "What?"

Bartu laughed with amusement as she had no idea. Now was the moment of truth. "You don't get it, do you? I could care less what happens to *your friend* Levi. I only used him to get to you. I was hoping that after we got to know each other, you would lose interest in his friendship and become **my** best friend. I didn't want to say anything before, but things are starting to get out of hand now. You have to make a decision, Jazz. It's either going to be me or him."

Infuriated, Jazzmine lifted her head to the ceiling, not knowing what to say. How dare he give her an ultimatum! If it weren't for Levi, they would never have been together. Now, he was telling her to choose between the two of them? There was no question of which of them she was going to choose. Levi had been by her side for the past six years, and he made her feel beautiful even before her weight loss. She had only known Bartu for five months, and all he seemed to want to do was get her in bed. If he succeeded at his mission, how did she know he wouldn't leave her and go off to brag about sleeping with a model? He used Levi to get to her, and now, he wanted to use her for her body. It wasn't going to happen. Obviously, he didn't care about her or her feelings at all.

She couldn't believe he had used Levi to get to her, and now he was telling her that she couldn't see him anymore if she wanted to stay with him. From the look in his eyes, he was dead serious! It was fortunate that she discovered the true Bartu before she made the biggest mistake of her life. Like marriage, sexual intercourse was a major step, a commitment not to be taken lightly. It had to be something for which one was ready, and Jazzmine wasn't, especially now. Gratefully, she found out about him before it was too late!

"Well!" Bartu stood up and moved to stand before her. Collecting her in his arms, he hugged her tight. "Since you're still here, I assume I have my answer?" He was confident.

Amused that he thought she was actually going to stay with him now that she knew his true colors, Jazzmine laughed and pushed him away. "No one is going to choose my friends for me, or tell me who I can and cannot see! You are not my father, and you cannot control my life! If you think I'm going to remain with you, think again! Good-bye, Bartu! I choose Levi!" She pushed him backward to the bed and left, not giving him a second glance.

Devastated, Jazzmine sat on her living room

sofa in a trance. Her mind was on Bartu and what happened between them. Everything happened so quickly that she couldn't believe it was reality. Did she really break up with him? Surely, he was joking. He didn't mean anything he said. Perhaps, she should call him and give him a chance to apologize.

No! A little voice in her head demanded. She would not go crawling back to him. He was the one who made all the demands. He should call her if he wanted to apologize.

The front door opened.

Levi entered the house in an excited mood. His smile was huge as he had wonderful news for his best friend. He moved to the end of the sofa and stopped. "Hey, Jazz! It's over! We just finished the movie! And guess what! Mr. Bradley Stratford, you know the top producer in New York City, called me at the studio and asked me to guess star in that new sitcom *Doctor's Order* with Leila Brewer." He smiled as the beautiful actress crossed his mind. It had always been a fantasy of his to meet her. "I haven't decided whether I'm going to do it yet because I wanted to tell you the news, and..." His voice trailed off as he realized that Jazzmine hadn't blinked once, turned to look at him, or given him any words of encouragement.

Something was wrong. This was so unlike her. Her usual, when good news was rendered, was to display some form of excitement.

Jazzmine was sitting in a light daze as if something terrible had happened. She was rather fazed.

Concerned, he moved to sit on the sofa next to her, taking her into his arms. It was naturally his duty to be comforting. "Jazz, what's wrong?" His voice was a whisper.

Jazzmine, who was listening silently, suddenly realized that he wasn't across the room anymore by his embrace. It didn't really startle her, however. She was silent for a moment, wondering what to say? It was actually a blur to her. She went over to Bartu's to tell him *something*, and the next thing she knew, they were breaking up. She couldn't even recall the news she was supposed to tell him. "How could he do this to me?" she finally blurted in a tearful voice.

How could Bartu do this to her? He was her first actual boyfriend, and the first man she actually allowed to get close to her in that way. He had the nerve to hurt her this way! She even considered giving him what he wanted. She thanked the Lord she didn't sleep with him. If she had, then they broke up, it would have driven her crazy!

Levi, marveling the feel of Jazzmine in his arms, blinked at the sound of her sweet voice.

He had secretly been in love with her for the past six years, and it was eating him up inside. Never courageous enough to express his love for her, he hated every passing second away from her.

When she and Bartu became a serious couple, he gave up hope of ever being with her. He even tried dating other women to get over her, but it was an impossible quest. No other woman could make him feel as happy as Jazzmine had the potential to do. He knew she was the woman who could fulfill his every dream and love him as every man deserved.

His greatest fear was that she viewed him as an older brother and not in a romantic way. That was his sole reason for keeping quiet all these years.

The reality of Jazzmine's statement registered with Levi, and he frowned with confusion. "Who did what? What happened?"

Jazzmine stood up, freeing herself from his embrace. She walked away, turning her back on him. "I trusted him and he hurt me."

Following her with his eyes, Levi's frown deepened as he had no idea of what she was saying. Surely, she couldn't be referring to Bartu. The two of them were getting along so well. Who had her so upset? "Who?" He practically demanded.

Jazzmine turned back to Levi with sad eyes. Unable to stop them, tears streamed down her face. It was just so painful. She had often heard that breaking up was hard to do. Now she understood the meaning of the saying. "It's over, Levi. Bartu and I are through!"

The relationship had been terminated? What happened? Levi wasn't quite sure how to feel at this point. Was he supposed to be happy that their relationship was over as there was a chance for him now? Was he supposed to empathize with his best friend as she was hurting? Perhaps, he was supposed to remain neutral.

Feeling both empathic and joy at once, Levi abandoned his seat to embrace her, again. He was there for her. Mentally, he cursed Bartu for making her cry! "What happened?"

Not wanting to discuss it, Jazzmine pulled away and wiped her eyes. Sniffing she said, "Oh, hey, congratulations on finishing the movie!" They could change the subject. "So, are you going to New York?"

Levi was amazed at her mood swing. He couldn't believe she actually thought he would leave her in this state. She needed him. He would just have to call Bradley Stratford back and explain his situation. "I'm not leaving you like this!" he insisted.

"Levi, I'm fine."

No. She was not fine. One minute she was crying, and the next minute, she was talking as if nothing happened. That didn't sound like a person who was fine to him, and he refused to leave her side. "Jazz, I'm not leaving you," he told her in a firm voice, closing the subject.

Realizing that it was useless to argue, Jazzmine plopped back down on the sofa and stared up at him. With a half smile, she said, "You're a good friend, Levi." She really didn't want him to be so far away right now. She loved him for his devotion to their friendship.

Levi sat down beside her and took her hand. Regardless as to whether they ever got together or not, he would always be there for her. She had to know that. He would rather have her friendship than nothing at all. Her friendship meant the world to him, and he couldn't loose it by trying to become more deeply involved with her. He couldn't right now at least. If he pursued her romantically now, she would probably turn to him because she needed someone to fill the void Bartu left. He didn't want to tell her how he felt while she was in such a vulnerable state. "Are you all right?" He had to ask because he didn't think she was.

With a sigh, she squeezed his hand. "Yes, I'm fine. Thank you!"

He looked at her with an unconvinced expression. He knew she was just saying that to get him off her back. She couldn't be over Bartu that swiftly even though he didn't know what happened. They could have been having problems all along, but he doubted it. She would have told him by now. He wouldn't pressure her into telling him. She would tell him when she was ready.

Catching his eyes on her, Jazzmine shook her head. No one knew her better than he did, and he knew that she was hurting right now. He didn't have to say a word. The expression on his face said everything. Who did she think she was fooling? Needing his comfort, she practically threw herself into his arms.

He embraced her, wanting her to hold her anyway. She didn't have to say anything. He already knew.

PLACE: New York City, New York
DATE: September 2006

Twenty-six-year-old Vanessa Thomas entered her house feeling great. Her life was absolutely fabulous! She was the desired career woman, having a partnership in business. She was intending to take over as sole proprietor once her business partner decided whether or not she was moving to London. If she didn't go, Vanessa intended to buy her out anyway. She owned the house, which she designed and had built. She even had her ideal car. Her name was known from abroad as she was a renowned business woman.

A successful businesswoman, Vanessa could

walk into a restaurant, inform people of her identity, and everyone would fall at her feet. She loved the attention, especially from men.

She was especially glad to be close to her father, who, missing Jazzmine, began to bury himself in his work. In the beginning, things were fine, but then, he began to miss having both of his daughters at home with him, which he was too proud to admit. The problem got worse when Vanessa moved out a year ago. There was no one at home with him, and he got lonely with only the maid for company.

James began to travel a lot, going on all sorts of business trips for his company, which he owned with the intent to sign over to Vanessa when he retired.

Vanessa's greatest fear was that he was going to soon ask Jazzmine to come home. She prayed that it never happened. She was glad to be rid of her. No one even knew she had a sister besides the people who had known Jazzmine when they were growing up and the majority of them had gone to other states to college to pursue their careers. As far as her business partner and employees were concerned, she was James's only child.

Vanessa was proud to have Jazzmine behind her. She just wished there was a way to get her to stop writing her those constant letters. She had hoped that when her letters stopped, Jazzmine would get the picture and their line of communication would stop altogether.

Foolishly, Jazzmine continued to write her. Every letter she received, she put with the last in a box, never reading it. She never even opened the envelopes. Jazzmine's life and letters were boring.

She didn't have time to sit and read about how much her little sister admired her for becoming the woman she was and that she missed and loved her.

Vanessa was aware that Jazzmine wished she could be like her, and she didn't want to read about it anymore.

Vanessa went to the sofa and plopped down, dropping her brief case on the coffee table. Slipping out of the black pumps, she pulled her feet up on the sofa at her side. She was glad to finally be able to sit down and relax.

She reached over on the coffee table for the remote, and her eyes landed on an issue of *Gorgeous Magazine*, which must have come in the mail. She picked it up.

Flipping through the pages, she opened the centerfold to a beautiful woman in a bikini, who caught her attention, causing her to stop and look at her. She was lying on her stomach in the sand with one leg in the air and her chin resting in her palms. At the very top of the page was the title *Sexiest Model of the Year*. Vanessa examined her thoroughly. Yes, she was truly a beautiful woman. She had to admit.

Her eyes dropped to the very bottom of the page for the woman's description. She read that she was originally from New York City. "*Humph*," she thought. "*This woman is the only woman I've seen who is even as remotely beautiful as I am. As long as she stays in Beverly Hills, neither of us will have any problems.*" Tired of the magazine already, she closed it and tossed it back to the coffee table.

Yawning, she curled up on the sofa and fell into a light sleep.

New York City, New York
10:50 p.m.

CHAPTER FOUR

Driving for many hours from Boston, Massachusetts, James Thomas finally crossed the line into New York City.

Yawning, exhaustion overtook his body, and he felt weak and tired. His desire was to climb into his warm bed. He should have taken an airplane like Vanessa suggested. Then, he would have been able to sleep on the plane. Stubbornly, he chose to drive. At the time, he felt that he could handle it by himself.

The trip was exhausting, and he would be glad to get home.

Unconsciously, his mind wondered off to Jazzmine, whom he intended to call all weekend. He was just swamped with too many things to do, which shouldn't have been an excuse. He should have been able to take out five minutes of his busy schedule for his daughter.

They hadn't spoken lately, and he was missing her severely. He was so very proud of her, and he wished she were closer to home.

James was proud of Vanessa, also, and... He yawned, wiping his watery eyes.

He wanted so desperately to stretch out in his

own bed and fall asleep. *Sleep...* was all he thought about as his eyes closed, and he drifted off to dreamland.

Jeff Marshall, the highway patrol officer, slowed down. Up ahead it looked as if a car had been run off the road. He needed to get a better look.

He pulled the car over on the side of the road. Getting out, he grabbed his flashlight. Shining the light as he walked across the road, he saw a luxury car up on the curb. It looked as if the front end was wrapped around a tree. Walking up to the car, he shined his light inside.

The sight inside was horrendous!

The front end of the car was totally smashed. The windshield was shattered and pieces of glass were inside on the seat.

James was wearing his seatbelt. The airbag saved him from hitting the steering wheel. Blood was everywhere, dripping down the side of the door. The windowpane was shattered, and James's head was lying in the frame. If he were conscious, he probably wouldn't have been able to move.

Jeff backed away from the car, walking around to check the license plate. The door couldn't be opened without James hitting the ground. Instead of opening the door to check for identification, he would call in the license plate number.

Flashing the light on the numbers, he radioed help from his walkie-talkie. To be sure the call was received, he pulled out his cell phone and called the operator personally. His request was that an ambulance and the police be sent to his whereabouts.

The ambulance arrived first, just ahead of the police, who blocked off the road.

The paramedics had to nearly cut the door off to get James out of the car. The impact was so powerful that the door was jammed.

They stretched James out on the gurney and began medical treatment. His face was bleeding heavily, and the bandages weren't of much assistance as the blood continued to seep through. For precaution, a neck brace was around his neck.

"He probably never knew what hit him," Jeff was saying to one of the policemen as the paramedics were lifting James into the ambulance.

When he was finally out of the car, Jeff was able to recover James's wallet from his pants pocket. He handed it to Officer Donaldson, who looked inside for his driver's license. Finding it, he looked at it with a worried frown.

"What is it?" The expression on his partner's face frightened Jeff. He was deeply concerned.

"That's *the* James Thomas!" Officer Donaldson reported.

Jeff's heart ached for his family as he sympathized with whoever had to contact them. It was definitely a job in which he wanted no part. "Sad," he said. Flashing his light on the ground, he shook his head with pity. "Well, he didn't try to stop. That's for sure."

There were no skid marks whatsoever on the ground. It was an indication that no other vehicle was involved in the incident. No one ran him off of the road as he had assumed. It was still a tragedy, very awful.

"He must have fallen asleep," another officer offered a solution from the other side of the car, "because he couldn't have lost control of the car." She didn't see any way he could have. It didn't seem feasible for the looks of things.

"Must have!" Everyone agreed.

Beverly Hills, California
7:15 p.m.

Jazzmine, who was resting uneasily on Levi's sofa, sprang up to a sitting position. Her eyes shot open as an eerie feeling disturbed her, waking her from her dream. Something terrible had happened, and it was real. It was uncanny because she had no idea what was wrong.

Levi, sitting in the easy chair next to the sofa, looked up with concern when Jazzmine sprang up so abruptly. He lowered the paper he was reading. "Jazz? Are you all right? What's wrong?" She must have had a nightmare. It was probably about Bartu.

Jazzmine shook her head as she had no answer for him. She was actually petrified as the feeling couldn't be shaken. "I don't know. I just have this terrible feeling that something's wrong."

"You must have had a bad dream," Levi offered his explanation.

"No." She was convinced that it wasn't a dream. Her dream was about Bartu apologizing. She was about to slap him when she woke up. It wasn't a dream. A strong feeling attacked her, waking her. She sat up on the edge of the sofa. "I'm telling you, Levi, something is wrong. I can sense it."

Levi had nothing else to offer her. He didn't

know what she could be sensing. Nothing happened. He was right there when she fell asleep and when she woke up. Everything was just as calm as it had been when she closed her eyes. "What could be wrong?"

Her father crossed her mind, and butterflies fluttered in the pit of her stomach. *"Daddy!"* Jazzmine thought as it had to be something dealing with him. "I don't know, but I'm about to find out." She grabbed her cell phone from the coffee table. Nervously, she dialed her father's number.

"Who are you calling?"

"My dad," she answered, placing the phone to her ear. After three rings, the maid answered. "Hey! It's Jazzmine. Is my dad there?"

"No," she answered, "he hasn't made it in from Boston, yet."

"Boston?" Jazzmine frowned to herself. *"What is Daddy doing in Boston?"* She hadn't heard anything about him going to Boston. Her expression brightened as she went on to say, "Oh, all right. Well, thank you." She flipped the phone closed. Her eyes traveled to Levi, who was looking at her with curiosity. "He's not there. The maid said he hasn't made it back from Boston. I'll call Vanessa."

That was a terrible idea to Levi. She was going to the extreme. What was the point? If something was wrong, the injured party should have gotten word to her. It couldn't be that serious that no one knew to contact her. He met her father when he came to visit. James didn't seem to be the type to purposely withhold important information. His vote was that it had something to do with her dream, but she always had been a worrier. Sometimes, he thought she worried too much. This was definitely one of those times.

If something was wrong, someone should have contacted her by now.

He consulted at his watch. The time zones were different. New York City was four hours ahead of California. It was bedtime there. Vanessa could very well be in bed. Jazzmine shouldn't disturb her. Besides, if there wasn't anything wrong, she could frighten her. "Oh, Jazz," he sighed in a whispery voice, wishing she would listen to him.

Jazzmine tried to reach Vanessa at home. When she didn't get an answer there, she tried her cell phone. Still, she received no answer. Flipping her phone closed, she decided that, perhaps, Levi was right. She was just going to go home and lie down. She wasn't feeling her best. "Maybe she went with Dad to Boston." She considered the possibility.

"Maybe, she's asleep," Levi spoke his thoughts.

Jazzmine consulted her watch. She was inclined to agree with him as it was definitely a strong possibility, also. "Maybe." Jazzmine just could not shake the feeling that something was wrong as it seemed to stay with her. *Everything's going to be fine,"* she tried to convince herself as she silently prayed for her father.

New York City, New York
11:15 p.m.

As though water was poured in her face, Vanessa woke up from her dream in a panic. Petrified, she had the strangest feeling that something was wrong. Her eyes went around the room as she tried to figure out what it could be.

Everything appeared to be normal, nothing out of place.

She tried to shake the feeling, but it didn't go away. Her heart rate sped up as she wondered what could be wrong. *"The office,"* she thought. *"I have to call the office."* After a second, she glanced at her watch and realized that it couldn't be the answer. It was after eleven o'clock. It was too late to call the office now. Besides, if something had gone wrong at the office, Cassandra would have called her. She was so positive.

Inhaling a deep breath, she looked around again with a confused frown. If everything was all right at home and at the office, where else could there be a problem?

The telephone rang, startling her.

Inhaling another deep breath to calm herself, she reached back on the sofa table and picked up the receiver on the second ring. "Hello... Yes, this is Vanessa Thomas." She nodded to herself, listening. "Yes, James Thomas is my father."

Fear rose in her chest at the question of whether or not James was her father. Her mouth dropped, and her eyes widened as the highway patrol officer on the other line informed her that her father had run into a tree, totaling the car completely. Her heart rate sped up as he announced that James was on his way to the hospital, and he was in critical condition.

Dropping the telephone before he could finish his statement, Vanessa grabbed her purse from the coffee table, slipped into the pumps, and she was out the door.

Anxious and breathing deeply with fear, Vanessa rushed down the long hall to the emergency waiting room. At the nurse's station, she stopped, waiting for one of the nurses behind the desk to look up.

Neither of them did.

Tired of waiting and anxious to know her father's condition, she banged on the window, calling for the attention of all the nurses.

All three of them looked up at the disruption.

A red haired nurse with green eyes reached up to open the window. "Yes? May I help you?"

"Yes, I am Vanessa Thomas. I was informed that my father was brought here. Could you please tell me how James Thomas is doing?"

The nurse closed the window and referred to her computer. Opening the window again, she stated, "All I can tell you is that your father is in critical condition. He's had several tests run, and the doctor is waiting for the results. Have a seat. The doctor will be with you shortly."

Critical condition? How bad was that? Was it near death or seriously injured? Both thoughts were terrifying. Vanessa was too afraid to sit down and wait for the doctor. She wanted information about her father's condition now!

Realizing that waiting was the only thing she could do, and not wanting to make a scene, she slowly found a seat and sat down.

Impatiently checking her watch, Vanessa sat on the edge of her chair, tapping her foot. She had been there for an hour, and she hadn't heard a thing. What was taking so long? All she needed to know was that her father was going to be all right. He had to be. She would go insane if anything happened to him.

Her foot tapping stopped when a tall, bright, and handsome doctor came through the emergency doors. "Miss Thomas," he called in a strong masculine voice. His eyes went around the waiting room in search of the woman he called.

At her name, Vanessa sprang up from her chair. "Yes, Doctor?"

When she stood up, the doctor's eyes landed on her. He focused and moved closer to her. With a clipboard in one hand and an ink pen in the other, the doctor cleared his throat. "I'm Doctor Lawrence Larch." He placed the pen behind his ear to extend his hand to her.

She shook it anxiously. "Vanessa Thomas," she announced firmly, wanting him to tell her what he knew about her father's condition. Ordinarily, she would have examined him thoroughly and flirted a little, but now wasn't the time for that. Her father was the only person on her mind.

Dr. Larch stepped beside her and placed a comforting hand on her back. "Apparently, the driver's window caved in on your father and slashed the left side of his face. It did a great deal of damage. The cut went very deep. We had to operate immediately. Fortunately, we were able to stop the bleeding and remove all the glass. There are minor cuts and bruises on his shoulder, arm, and hand." He took a deep breath and continued, "Somehow, his spinal cord was injured. We ran a few tests on him, and when the results come back, we'll know for sure what's going on. We've done several x-rays, and we suspect that your father may be paralyzed."

"Paralyzed?" Vanessa's eyes widened with disbelief and fear. It just couldn't be! No. Panicking wouldn't help matters. She had to remain calm until the doctor could tell her for sure that her father was paralyzed, which she was afraid of hearing. If he was, what was she going to do? She couldn't take care of her father alone. If he was paralyzed, she was going to have to run his company for him until he was back on his feet *or out of the hospital* in that case. Who would be home with him until then?

At the frightened expression on Vanessa's face, Dr. Larch took another deep breath and went on to say, "If he is paralyzed, once the test results come back and the swelling goes down, we will be able to determine whether it is permanent or due to trauma."

"Oh, God!" Vanessa thought. *"More waiting!"* Now how long did she have to wait? At least now there was hope. If her father wasn't permanently paralyzed, he would be able to walk again. That would be a blessing within itself. She wouldn't throw in the towel, yet. Pulling herself together, she sighed softly. "How is he now? Is he ok? May I see him?"

"He isn't awake, yet. You may see him, but only for a few minutes. Why don't you go home and get some rest. We'll call you if any changes arise."

Go home? Get some rest? How could she rest when her father could be paralyzed? The doctor's suggestion was out of the question. She couldn't go home now. Her father needed her. She was going to be there for him when he woke up. "No," she was quick to shake her head. "I can't go home."

"Miss Thomas, it wouldn't do any good for you to be here, and..."

Vanessa shook her head, again. "No, it's ok. I'll be all right."

"There's no need to worry, Miss Thomas. I assure you, if any change arises, you will be contacted."

"Dr. Larch, I'm sorry, but there is nothing you can say to me to make me leave. My father is lying in a hospital bed possibly paralyzed. I need to be with him."

Seeing the serious look on her face and hearing the firmness in her voice, Dr. Larch surrendered. He held up his hand and the clipboard. "Ok. Fine! You can stay."

Satisfied at having her way, Vanessa nodded and followed the doctor beyond the emergency room doors.

Vanessa opened the door and stepped inside. Standing just inside the door holding it open, tears threatened to fall at the sight of her father.

James lay stiffly in the hospital bed, connected to various machines. The left side of his face was bandaged from his forehead all the way to his chin. His hands were crossed over the covers. There were bandages on his left arm and hand.

Hating to see her father in this condition, Vanessa forced herself not to cry as she moved to his bedside. Taking the chair next to the bed, she reached for her father's hand, which she held lightly to avoid squeezing his cuts.

Forcing herself to smile at him, she swallowed the lump in her throat. She began to talk to him in a soft voice as if he could hear her, and he was going to respond. "Daddy, it's me, Vanessa. I'm here. You're going to be just fine." She nodded with assurance. "How did this happen? Oh, I know. You tried to avoid something in the road and..."

At three in the morning, Vanessa's eyes began to feel heavy, and she closed them for a split second. She snapped them open them again when she felt her father's hand twitched in hers. Her eyes shot to his handsome face. His visible eye was open. Elated that he was finally awake, she smiled broadly and forgot her sleepiness. "Oh, Daddy!" she exclaimed. "How do you feel?"

James turned his head to see her clearly, hearing her voice. "Vanessa? Where am I? I can't see you..." Removing his hand from hers, he raised it to the bandage over his eye. "What happened to me?" he asked in a panicky voice. He must have blacked out because he couldn't remember a thing.

Vanessa explained everything to him, excluding the possibilities that he could possibly be permanently paralyzed. He didn't have to know until she heard the news herself. If he was, she would find a way to break the news to him. If he wasn't, there was no need to worry him. "Do you remember anything?" she asked.

James shook his head slowly, feeling sharp pains in his face. "No," he answered in a soft voice. He flinched as the pains worsened. Groaning, he placed a comforting hand to the bandage and closed his eye. "My face hurts," he complained.

Vanessa lowered her eyes. Did his back hurt, too? Did he even feel the pain in his back or his legs? She couldn't ask him, however. If he didn't mention it, neither would she. "I know, Daddy," she whispered. "Would you like for me to call the nurse for some painkillers?"

"No, I think I'll be ok."

"Are you sure?"

"Yes." James was positive. It was minor pain, nothing excruciating. A vision of his youngest daughter popped into his mind, and he recollected what happened. He was thinking of his baby. He meant to call her from the car, but he didn't recall doing so. Everything was a blur from that point. "Jazzmine," he whispered.

"Oh, no!" Vanessa thought. *"Here it comes!"* She secretly dreaded the day when her father would ask her to call her sister home. She didn't want her to come home. She didn't long for the day when she had to look at her ugly face. This was an emergency case, however, and she would have to make an exception if he did ask her to call her sister home.

"Vanessa, I want to see Jazzmine. Could you call her for me?" James looked at her with sadness in his good eye, causing Vanessa to weaken.

The more she thought about it, Vanessa decided that the idea was a good one.

Jazzmine could be very beneficial to her. She had always been an excellent homemaker, which she wasn't very good at herself. If she came home, she could take care of things at the house for her, and she could hold down the fort at the office.

"That's an excellent idea!" Vanessa thought with a half smile.

Jazzmine would be so busy going from the house to the hospital that no one would even know she was there. She always thought that Jazzmine was good for nothing! She glanced at her watch. "It's late. She's probably in bed. I'll call her first thing in the morning," she promised her father.

James smiled and closed his eye. "Thank you, baby!"

Jazzmine was finally going to come home, and both of his daughters would be reunited with him. That would be fabulous!

With happy thoughts of his youngest daughter on his mind, James drifted off to sleep.

The following morning...
Beverly Hills, California

Jazzmine was lying on the sofa in her robe and slippers. It was almost nine o'clock, and she had been too lazy to get dressed. She hadn't eaten since lunch yesterday due to lack of an appetite. Her head ached, and she didn't get much sleep. She tossed and turned practically all night.

When she woke up, the taunting feeling that something dreadful happened still remained.

Her eyes were transfixed on the wall. Her mind constantly replayed the incident between her and Bartu, sending her into a deep depression. Five months was a long time to just throw away.

Bartu had been everything to her. She couldn't believe he could hurt her this way and not feel the tiniest bit guilty.

Jazzmine just didn't realize how hard it

would be to let go. Part of her wanted to call him and mend things between them. The other part didn't. She wasn't sure she wanted him back. If she gave him a second chance, how did she know he wouldn't hurt her even worse the next time? Why would she even subject herself to such turmoil? It would be insane to give him a second chance to hurt her.

The telephone rang, and she didn't bother to answer it.

The answering machine picked up on the third ring.

"Hey, Babe!" Bartu's voice sprang into the room after the beep. Hearing his voice, tears streamed down her face. She didn't want to talk to him. What could he possibly have to say to her? "Jazz! I know you're there. Please, pick up the phone. I need to talk to you." He sighed heavily when she didn't pick up. "OK! I admit that I was wrong. I'm sorry. I really miss you!"

Not wanting to hear the rest of his message, Jazzmine reached back on the sofa table and clicked the phone twice, hanging up on Bartu.

The front door opened. Levi entered with his key.

Not wanting him to see her depressed mood, Jazzmine sat up and wiped away her tears.

Moving toward the sofa, Levi stopped and examined her from a distance. She wasn't dressed, which was unusual for her at this hour. He listened. Unconsciously, Jazzmine sniffed, and he could tell that she had been crying. He went to her side and sat down beside her, taking her into his arms. "You aren't slick. I know you've been crying," he whispered.

Jazzmine lowered her head, unable to deny the truth. Levi knew her better than anyone, and she couldn't lie to him.

"I know how you feel. This is normal, but you can't let it bring you down. I'll bet Bartu isn't moping around like this. He..."

The telephone rang, interrupting him.

Jazzmine stood up and screamed with aggravation. Walking away, she shook her head. "It's him! He keeps calling!"

The telephone rang, again.

"Would you like for me to answer it?" Levi offered. He would love to tell Bartu a thing or two.

Jazzmine shook her head. "No. Let the machine get it. He doesn't have to know I'm here."

On the third ring the answering machine picked up.

"Jazzmine? Are you there? It's me, Vanessa. Honey..." the feminine voice burst into the room.

Hearing Vanessa's voice, Jazzmine sprang to the telephone and picked up the receiver. "Hello? Hello? Vanessa? I'm here." She listened to Vanessa. The tragic news about her father hit her like a truck running over the curb. The impact was almost unbearable. Her heart leaped to her throat as the taunting feeling was released. That was the answer for which she waited so long.

Horrified, her eyes darted to Levi, and he went to her side at the worried expression on her face. "Well, is he ok?" her voice squeaked, giving her fear away. "Yes, yes," she nodded as if Vanessa could see her. "I'll be there as soon as I can. Bye." She hung up, turning her attention to her best friend. "Levi, I have to go to New York City right away."

"What happened?" Levi was anxious to know.

"I told you something was wrong. It's my father. He's been in an accident, and he wants to see me."

"Well, is he ok?" Levi didn't know what else to say. He felt guilty now. She did tell him that she had a bad feeling that something was wrong. He should have trusted her instincts. He was the one who convinced her that everything was all right, and the whole time her father was lying in the hospital.

Jazzmine nodded. "Vanessa says he is, but I have to see for myself."

"If you're going to New York City, I'm going with you. You just broke up with your boyfriend, and now your father is in the hospital. You really don't need to be alone right now."

He was so right. She didn't need to be alone nor did she want to be. This was not the time to argue about it anyway. Having Levi with her would make her feel better. She did need his company, and she would be glad to have him there. Jazzmine nodded again. "Great! Hey! If you go, you can take that job Mr. Stratford offered you."

Sitting in a First Class seat next to Jazzmine on the first flight to New York City, Levi watched her sleep while she rested her head on his shoulder. She was finally asleep, and she needed her rest. He knew she didn't get much rest because her mind was on Bartu. He could tell when he saw her this morning. There were bags under her eyes. He had no idea why she put herself through that. Going to New York City could be good for her. It would get her away from Bartu and possibly take her mind off of him. She didn't need to be bothered with him. She had enough worries without him adding to them. If they conversed, he would only try to make her feel guilty for breaking up with him. She didn't need that right now. Her father was in the hospital. That was more than enough for her to concentrate.

When the plane landed, Jazzmine and Levi stepped off the plane and into the airport.

Jazzmine's heart sank. It was a great disappointment that Vanessa wasn't there to meet her. She called her right back to tell her what time she was leaving California and what time she would be arriving in New York City.

Vanessa sounded happy to know that she was on her way, and she just assumed that she would be there to meet her at the airport.

As she and Levi went to collect their luggage, Jazzmine decided that Vanessa must have lost track of time. She could have been tied up in something for which she couldn't tear herself away.

She understood that her sister was a busy woman. There could have been several reasons for her absence. Realizing this, she brushed the thought aside. Her feelings of disappointment passed.

"I'll be back later," Levi told Jazzmine as he walked with her up the hospital steps. At the door, he stopped and turned to face her. "I'm going to the studio to talk to Mr. Stratford. That will give you some time alone with your father."

Jazzmine was appreciative. "OK."

Being a gentleman, Levi opened the door for her and watched her walk down the hall. When she was out of sight, he returned to the limousine he rented from the airport.

Going to the nurses' desk, Jazzmine was introduced herself to the first nurse who paid her any attention and inquired about her father's condition.

Dr. Larch, who was standing at the corner of the nurses' desk checking his charts, looked up when he heard a woman introduce herself as James Thomas's daughter. He already spoke to his daughter last night. He was under the impression that he only had one child. How many did he have? Were his sons coming along later? Why hadn't his other daughter taken the courtesy to inform her siblings of their father's condition? That was very rude and selfish of her.

His eyes went across to Jazzmine. For a moment, he was captivated. She was beautiful, equally as beautiful as her sister. Her face was so familiar as he had seen it somewhere.

Hearing her questions and wanting to answer all of them since James was his patient, he closed his chart book and moved around the desk to her. "Excuse me." Jazzmine looked up at the tall doctor. "Did I hear you inquire about James Thomas?"

Jazzmine nodded. "Yes."

"I am his doctor, Dr. Lawrence Larch. I will be happy to answer any questions that you have."

Relieved to be offered information, Jazzmine smiled. "I'm Jazzmine Thomas, his younger daughter. I'm sure you've met my sister."

Dr. Larch nodded with agreement. "Yes, I have."

Walking with Jazzmine down the hall toward James's room, the doctor explained his condition to her and allowed her to go to him in private.

At the door when the doctor left her, Jazzmine took a moment to compose herself. It was worse than she predicted. She thought her father had hit his head on the steering wheel and got a few bruises, but it turned out to be much more serious.

The doctor said that his face was going to need plastic surgery once the stitches were out and the wounds healed. He also said that her father could be *paralyzed*! That was the worst part. The thought of her father not being able to walk again frightened her. He wouldn't be the same person he had been six years ago when she left him. He, also, wouldn't be the same person who walked through her front door when he came to visit her.

Why didn't Vanessa tell her any of this earlier when they discussed the situation on the telephone. Why did she leave her to be surprised this way?

"Well," she sighed. *"I'll talk to Vanessa about that later."* Right now, she needed to see her father. Opening the door, she found him sleeping peacefully.

With a dozen roses in her hand, Vanessa opened the door to her father's room to find some young woman standing at his bedside holding his hand while he slept.

Who was she? How dare she come into her father's room? She definitely wasn't one of his employees because she was well acquainted with all of his staff members. Obviously, she read about his accident in the newspaper and decided to come in and make her move on him while he was down.

Did she plan to stick her claws into him when he was up again?

Vanessa did not need some young tramp chasing after her father for his money. She had to get her out of there before her father woke up and saw her.

When the door opened, Jazzmine glanced over her shoulder. The smile on her face was huge as she hadn't seen her sister in years. She was a mere child when they last saw each other. She stood before her now a full grown woman. She opened her mouth to speak, but Vanessa dropped the roses and leap forward, grabbing her arm.

Tugging her toward the door, Vanessa demanded in a loud and harsh tone, "You get out of here! My father doesn't need to see you. If you're trying to make a move on him, you can just go somewhere else!"

Insulted at her sister's behavior, Jazzmine jerked her arm away. Was this a joke? Was Vanessa teasing her? Surely, Vanessa knew who she was because she sent her dozens of pictures with long detailed letters, explaining each one. What was wrong with her? How dare she speak to her so gruffly and so loudly! She must have lost her mind!

Loosing Jazzmine's arm, Vanessa turned to face her with an angry expression. Obviously, she had no intentions of leaving. Who did she think she was? "I'm warning you! I will call security!" she yelled.

"Stop it! Just stop it, and keep your voice down!" Jazzmine said in a loud voice, as well. "What is the matter with you?" It was just too outrageous!

"*Me?*" Vanessa's hand rose to her heart as she was insulted. "You come into my father's room uninvited, and you dare to ask what's wrong with *me?*" Vanessa opened the door, yelling, "**GET OUT**! I don't know who you are, but I don't want you here!"

What did she mean she didn't know who she was? Of course, she did! Did she not receive any of her letters explaining her success? Did she not get any of the autographed photos that stated: *To my dearest sister with the deepest and sincerest love?*

Before Jazzmine could say a word, Dr. Larch stepped into the open door.

"What is going on in here? I could hear the two of you all the way down the hall." His eyes went to Jazzmine, who was standing in the center of the room with a horrified look on her face. "Is there a problem, Miss Thomas?"

Vanessa nodded, looking at the doctor. "Yes, I..." Realizing that he was speaking to the other woman, she snapped her head to her. She wasn't Miss Thomas. She was...

Suddenly, her mind snapped back, and she recognized her to be the centerfold model she had seen in *Gorgeous Magazine*. What *was* she doing in her father's room? She was supposed to be living the life in Beverly Hills, California. *California!* Could it be that she was...? No! Vanessa refused to believe such an implausible story. It was too exaggerated to be true.

"***Wait!*** *Who* are you?" She had to be

absolutely certain that she was wrong.

Jazzmine shook her head with a sigh. "Vanessa! It's me, Jazzmine!"

Jazzmine? Yes, that was it! The model's name was *Jazz*! *JAZZ*! This gorgeous woman was Jazzmine Thomas? This was her little sister?

In total awe, Vanessa turned fully to face her. How else would she know her name? Could it be? She checked the time.

Yes, Jazzmine's plane should have landed by now, but *this* woman was not Jazzmine Thomas. She was an impostor! Who was she really? What had she done with the real Jazzmine Thomas?

"Jazzmine?" She shook her head with disbelief. It couldn't be her sister. Her sister was fat and homely. "Why should I believe you're my sister?" She dared her to prove herself to be the authentic Jazzmine, as it was impossible.

Jazzmine was totally stunned and embarrassed by her sister's skepticism. It was utterly ridiculous! Why should she believe that she was her sister? She should believe it for the same reason she should be willing to prove it. Because it was the truth, that's why! Perhaps, the letters with the pictures she sent her somehow got lost in the mail, but **all** of them? That was just too farfetched!

With confidence, she lifted her head and answered, "Vanessa, it's really me. I'm Alexandria's daughter. Daddy used to take us horseback riding in the woods, and we used to go fishing at the lake. I was valedictorian of my high school class right here in New York City." Was that adequate proof or did she need more? She could go on.

At the mention of her father's second wife, Vanessa's expression softened. It really was Jazzmine. Her eyes widened.

Jazzmine was a model? Jazzmine, her little sister, was actually a model! Surely, this wasn't the same girl who was once dumpy and homely? "Jazzmine? It *is* you! Well, what happened? You look so," her eyes ran over her sister, not missing a thing, "*different!*"

Vanessa couldn't believe her eyes. Jazzmine didn't just *look* different. She had changed drastically, a full transformation. Her hair was longer and gorgeous as it flowed, hanging down her back and cascading over her shoulders. It looked so soft and beautiful. Her hairstylist deserved a metal! Her face was no longer fat, and her acne had completely vanished. There were dimples in her cheeks that she wasn't even aware existed.

She had no idea her sister was that beautiful underneath all that fat! Her fabulous body was definitely that of a model. There wasn't an ounce of fat anywhere to be detected.

Jazzmine dressed with so much taste and elegance, which was an indication that she cared about her appearance. She stood before her dressed in a lovely two-piece ivory suit. The jacket was very appealing with its fabric-covered buttons and lace trimmings. The skirt was just as appealing. To accessorize, she wore gold earrings in her pierced ears and a thick, gold herringbone necklace around her neck. Vanessa took note of the sparkling diamond bracelet on her right arm and her eyes lingered on it for a moment. It was beautiful! The diamonds had to be at least two carats.

Vanessa's eyes traveled down to Jazzmine's

hands. On her right hand, she wore only one ring. It was on her index finger. On her left hand, she wore three rings. They were on her index, ring, and pinkie fingers. Her nails were long and well-groomed.

Vanessa was impressed with this Jazzmine. The Jazzmine she had known dressed sloppy, had short hair, hated jewelry, and bit off her nails. This was a woman she could come to envy, although that would never happen!

For a second, she checked herself to be sure she was as well-dressed as Jazzmine.

She was.

She was wearing a cream top with a long burgundy, green and cream skirt. A silk scarf with splashes of burgundy and green was pinned over her shoulder, crossed her left breast, and was tucked into her green belt. Her hair was pulled back into a ball at the back of her head with a gold crown with tiny cream pearls was pinned over it. Her bangs were feathered. Satisfied that she looked just as good as Jazzmine, she smiled to herself.

Jazzmine did a full turn for her sister's approval. "Do you like it?"

The doctor sure did! He found himself ogling her sexy body with a huge smile of appreciation.

Vanessa nodded, unable to speak.

"Thank you! When I left New York City, I matured in more ways than one." Jazzmine was glad to have her sister's approval of her new look.

Realizing that the doctor was staring at her, and she had to look ridiculous to him, Vanessa laughed and turned her attention to him. "This is my little sister. We haven't seen each other in years. She was a little girl when we last saw each other. She has grown up so much. In fact, she looks like an entirely different person," she explained to put herself in a better light. It was pitiful when a person didn't recognize her own sister.

Looking at her as if she had lost her mind, Dr. Larch said nothing. His eyes moved to Jazzmine. "I will remind you two that you are in a hospital. If you can't keep your voices down, you'll have to leave. There are other patients in this hospital who need their rest."

Vanessa held up a hand in surrender. "Sorry, Doctor. It won't happen again."

The doctor left them alone.

CHAPTER FIVE

*V*anessa sat on one side of her father's bed, and Jazzmine sat on the other. They conversed for hours while their father slept. They reminisced about old times, going back to Jazzmine's not so beautiful days.

Vanessa updated Jazzmine on the current events in her life, most of which their father informed her during his few visits to California. Jazzmine was quiet, listening attentively as she took mental notes of the things her father didn't mention.

Jazzmine, too, updated her sister on the current events in her life, but Vanessa wasn't quiet. She asked questions and gave input on some things that she was told.

Vanessa consistently told her sister that she was proud of her. All the while, with every fabulous detail of her life, hatred formed in the very pit of her stomach. The more Jazzmine spoke, the more her sister wished she had stayed in California. Had she known Jazzmine was so successful, she would never have called her home. She could have just as easily remedied the problem by hiring someone to take care of her father. She probably should have!

"The letters!" Vanessa thought. If she had read those stupid letters, this wouldn't have come as such a shock. How could she have known? *"Dammit! Now what am I going to do? Nobody's going to believe she's my sister because no one is aware that I have one."* This was a fine fiasco into which she had gotten herself.

James squirmed a little and moaned.

All eyes went to him, as he slowly opened his eyes.

He looked from Vanessa to Jazzmine. Blinking, he cleared his vision as he stared into his baby's face. When his eye was focused, he recognized her with a smile. "Jazzmine," he whispered. "You made it."

He recognized Jazzmine! Vanessa was shocked. He recognized her, and she didn't. He must have taken the time to read her stupid letters. Why did this have to happen now? Her life was going so well without beautiful Jazzmine stepping into the picture. Somehow, she would find a tactic of dealing with it. Of course, it would have to be something inconspicuous, as she had to maintain her loving sister image.

"Yes, Daddy," Jazzmine patted his hand. "I'm here. How do you feel? I've missed you!"

"I've felt better," James was honest. "I've missed you too, baby." It wasn't that long ago that he was in California with her, but it felt as though it was. In fact, he had been there earlier this year. Still, he was delighted to have her home, close to her sister.

Selfishly panging for her father's attention, Vanessa patted his other hand. "Are you in any pain, Daddy?"

James turned his attention to her. "My face throbs, but I'm a tough guy. I can handle it. How did you sleep last night? The nurse said you didn't leave until early this morning. Honey, don't do that. You need your rest."

Vanessa was glad to have his concern. "Daddy, I'm fine. I got plenty of sleep right here by your bedside. I didn't need to go home. I needed to be with you. I went home and showered this morning. Then, I went to the office. I checked on things at your office for you, too."

"Thank you, dear. Handling business was always something at which you were good," he had to complement her as he was proud of her accomplishments.

Jazzmine smiled across at her sister with inspired admiration. It was wonderful that she was doing so well in her career. She was proud of her. Their father told her all about her partnership in business. She and her partner owned one to biggest multi-corporations in the city. She made quite a name for herself. It was always known Vanessa would success at her goal, as making money had always been her mission.

The two of them had so much catching up to do! Jazzmine had so much to tell her sister. There were so many buried stories to be uncovered. Although she missed Beverly Hills already, she was glad to be home in the presence of her *real* loving family.

Jazzmine and Vanessa walked down the hall toward the emergency waiting room together.

As they walked along, a nagging sensation

tugged at Jazzmine's brain. There were questions she needed to ask Vanessa. These were questions she had no desire to bring up in front of their father. It was rather personal.

She felt rather neglected and humiliated when Vanessa didn't come to the airport to collect her. It bothered her, remaining on her mind all day. It was, also, insensitive of Vanessa to leave her to discover their father's life-threatening condition on her own. There had to be a logical explanation.

Now, they were no longer in their father's room, as they were in private. The situation could be discussed openly. Vanessa was rather trapped as there was no way around it.

Jazzmine had to speak her peace for closure. Clearing her throat, she asked, "So, Vanessa, what happened to you earlier? You didn't meet me at the airport." She had to present the question in such a way to get a straight answer.

Actually, after much consideration, Jazzmine concluded that it was best Vanessa didn't come to the airport. She wouldn't have known for whom she was waiting. She didn't even recognize her after she was told who she was. She had to be convinced, and Jazzmine was embarrassed that the doctor had to witness the scene. She would have been more so embarrassed for all the people at the airport to witness it, especially Levi. She raved about Vanessa all the time to him from her father's letters and what he told her in person. It was a pity that her own sister didn't even know who she was.

Levi would have become skeptical as he speculated on their actual relationship. Two close sisters wouldn't have acted so *distant*.

Still, it would be nice if Vanessa's absence was explained. She owed Jazzmine that much.

The question caught her completely off guard. Vanessa didn't think Jazzmine actually expected her to meet her at the airport. She would have been expecting to see the old Jazzmine anyway. She had to think of something to say. She couldn't leave her hanging. "I'm sorry," she began as it came to her. "I was in a hurry when I called you. I wasn't expecting you to call back so soon. You arrived so abruptly! You didn't leave me much time to get things done. You know I wanted to be there."

As the answer was acceptable, Jazzmine offered mental forgiveness. She guessed as much. It was no big deal. She just wanted to hear Vanessa confirm her thoughts. There was another issue on her mind, however. "Why didn't you tell me the seriousness of Dad's condition? I know you knew. Dr. Larch told me he discussed it with you. Vanessa, Dad could be paralyzed. I had a right to know."

Why didn't she just let Vanessa handle everything her way? All she needed her to do was take care of their father. She had too many questions already. She did not need this pressure.

Trying to sound innocent, Vanessa's response was, "I didn't tell you because I didn't want you to worry. I know how much you worry about everything. I didn't want you to be upset when you got here. If you were upset, you could have upset Dad. I definitely didn't want him to be worried over what could be nothing. I think it's best he not be told until we know for sure."

Jazzmine corroborated that decision. Their father needed no added stress while he was in the hospital. The news could have traumatized him. It was a wise decision, but she still thought *she* should have been told. The news was just sprung on her, catching her completely by surprise. It hurt that Vanessa didn't clue her in even though she thought she was doing it with her best interest at heart.

Letting it all go, Jazzmine sighed to herself. She was the same caring Vanessa.

Vanessa pushed the door to the emergency waiting room open.

Levi, who was sitting in a chair next to the door, was the only person in the waiting room. Seeing the door open, he stood up when Jazzmine came out. He went to her. "Hey! How's your father?" He was concerned, and he really wanted to see him. He didn't intrude, however, because now was Jazzmine's time with her father. She should see him first. He would see him later.

"He's ok. How did everything go with you?"

"I didn't stay long. We start the first shooting next week. I took the liberty of reserving two rooms at the *Maza Hotel*. Your luggage is waiting for you in your room, and the limo should be here any minute. I've made reservations for us at the hotel restaurant so you can go straight to bed after dinner if you like."

Vanessa was mesmerized as her eyes landed on the handsome Levi. She surveyed him, examining him thoroughly. Who was this marvelous looking man? *"Yum!"* she thought as her eyes moved from his head to his feet.

Levi was tall, an estimated five foot nine. He

was possibly six foot, but he was definitely nothing taller. With his young face, Vanessa guessed him to be her age, which could pose a problem if she were to pursue him. Her ideal man was someone older, a mature well-established man. Someone as young as Levi couldn't have much to offer her. She desired someone as equally established as she.

His hair was low, a brush and go length. His smooth golden brown skin was sexy and so were his dark brown eyes. His shaped beard was attractive, a nice touch. His full lips were perfect as they appeared to be soft, very kissable.

His body was nice, that of a sexy male model or a professional body builder body. It was like being up close and personal with a well tuned wrestler. He was well dressed in a deep yellow crew neck shirt, as it wasn't actually a turtleneck, with the matching blazer. His black slacks were of obvious expense as were his shoes. His outfit must have come straight from the designer himself, as it seemed that the clothes were tailored just for him.

Vanessa smiled as her eyes moved back to his face, which was so familiar. *"I don't know him, but I've definitely seen his face somewhere!"* After a moment, her eyes moved form Levi to Jazzmine.

Was he a male model as he very well could be, especially sine he seemed so well acquainted with her sister. He couldn't possibly be Jazzmine's husband or fiancée because she wasn't wearing a wedding or engagement ring. He wasn't wearing a wedding band. Was he her boyfriend? It was possible as he checked them both into the most expensive and elegant hotel in the city. He had to be if he came all this way just to be with her. He was handsome, and he liked to travel in style... a *limo*! Vanessa liked that quality in a man. If he was her sister's boyfriend, so what? That was only a minor setback, not much of a dilemma.

"We don't have..." Levi tried to continue.

Tired of Jazzmine getting all of his attention and wanting him to be aware of who she was, Vanessa casually pushed her sister aside and stepped in her place. Smiling flirtatiously, she said, "Hi! I'm Vanessa, Jazzmine's older sister."

The smile on Levi's face disappeared when Vanessa pushed Jazzmine, brushing her aside like she was a mere unimportant being. From that alone, he formed a much demoted opinion of her. She was rude and somewhat arrogant. At that moment, he could care less who she was as he was speaking to her sister. Her opinion of herself was much too high as she was actually a diminished minded idiot! Obviously, she believed she had to be noticed as soon as she entered a room.

The expression on Levi's face was unimpressed as he said, "Yeah, hi." There was no enthusiasm whatsoever in his flat voice.

"What a nasty attitude!" Vanessa thought as she was clearly offended by his lack of interest. *"He could have at least smiled! Jazzmine can't be all **that** spectacular!"*

Jazzmine stepped between them, feeling obligated to make the introduction. Clearing her throat, she smiled at her sister, disregarding the fact that she pushed her. "Vanessa, this is my best friend, Levi Proctor."

It surprised her that he even needed an introduction as everyone knew him. He was *THE Levi Proctor*! Apparently, there were a few who were clueless. Perhaps, Vanessa was too busy with her work to get around to a movie.

Jazzmine turned her eyes back to Levi. "Levi, I guess you know this is my sister."

"Yeah," he answered flatly and glanced at his watch. "The limo should be here by now." He had more indispensable things on his mind.

Even more so offended, Vanessa narrowed her eyes at him as he was a dreadful person. She had no idea who he thought he was, but she was important! She deserved to be treated with the utmost respect.

The door to the emergency room opened.

Three teen-aged girls entered.

They spotted Levi and Jazzmine. Their loud screams caught the attention of everyone in the room. They surrounded them, requesting autographs and asking dozens of questions.

Standing on the sideling feeling like an outcast, Vanessa folded her arms across her chest and narrowed her eyes at them with pure anger.

Levi Proctor! The name suddenly registered in her mind. He was the famous movie star, a celebrity! Jazzmine's best friend was a handsome movie star! It was so unbelievable and unrealistic that she could cry!

When the girls finally walked away, Jazzmine returned to her sister. Levi was at her side. There would be plenty of time to check into hotel. Right now, they needed to settle a few issues on their father's behalf. Several unanswered questions remained. Vanessa couldn't possibly have the answers to all of them. They would resolve the issues together. "Vanessa, have you been to the police station yet?"

Now that she mentioned it, Vanessa meant to

stop by the police station on her way to the hospital to pick up their father's wallet. It completely slipped her mind. "Oh, no! I was intending to do that. I forgot."

"Let's go now!" Jazzmine was prepared.

Vanessa was appalled. It was nice of Jazzmine to render her assistance, but it was much unneeded. It didn't take both of them to go to the precinct to recover the wallet. If Jazzmine had to go, she could go by herself. For Levi's sake, she pulled herself together. "Let's go!"

Jazzmine turned to Levi. "Levi, I'm sorry. I'm going to ride to the police station with Vanessa. I'll have her drop me off at the hotel when we're finished."

Levi understood completely. She and her sister had essential business to handle. "That's fine. Go ahead! Handle your business! I'll see you at the hotel."

Jazzmine entered the police station. Vanessa was right behind her. They approached the desk together.

The policewoman, Officer Henderson, sat behind the desk. She looked up. She was a pretty woman with short, bouncy red hair and crystal clear green eyes. "May I help you?" Her voice was soft as she was polite.

"Yes, I'm Jazzmine Thomas, and I would like to know what happened to my father's car. He was in an accident the other night, and we haven't been told anything. I..."

Vanessa cleared her throat over whatever Jazzmine was saying. She stepped forward. That wasn't all they wanted to know. The fact that

Jazzmine didn't introduce her was unacceptable. They came together. Taking over, she said, "**We** are James Thomas's daughters, and we're here to pick up his wallet and anything else that belonged to him that you may have recovered from of his car."

Officer Henderson's eyes switched from Jazzmine to Vanessa, when she spoke, and back to Jazzmine. She would deal with them one at a time. Jazzmine came first simply because she didn't particularly care for the way Vanessa overthrew her sister, taking charge. It was so uncouth. She spoke to Jazzmine, ignoring Vanessa. "Miss Thomas, I'll look his accident up in the computer. I can tell you who was working on that case. You can get a police report if you like."

Jazzmine was grateful for her assistance. "Thank you!"

"What was his name again?"

"James Thomas," Jazzmine and Vanessa sang in unison.

Officer Henderson turned to her computer and typed in the necessary information, reading the screen as she scrolled down. Looking at Jazzmine again after a moment, she said, "It says here that the detective who investigated the grounds reported that your father must have fallen asleep behind the wheel because there was no sign of a struggle with the car. Therefore, he couldn't have lost control of the car. There were, also, no skid marks. That means he didn't attempt to stop."

At the announcement that their father could have possibly fallen asleep behind the wheel, the Thomas sisters exchanged glances with open mouths.

Vanessa's eyes were full of pain as she looked

away. The accident happened the night their father drove in from Boston. She recalled begging him to fly or to take one of his employees with him. He was just too stubborn. Tears welled up in her eyes. If she had insisted that he not go alone, he wouldn't have been in the accident. The fault was within her. **She** could have gone with him. A teardrop trickled down her cheek as she was rattled with guilt.

Jazzmine, wanting to comfort her sister, placed her hand on her back. Rubbing it gently, she said, "Oh, Vanessa, it's all right. Dad is going to be fine."

Vanessa wiped away the tear as more fell. Sniffing, she said, "No, Jazzmine, that's not it. Daddy's accident was all my fault."

Jazzmine cringed with utter disbelief. Her heart was pounding. Vanessa wouldn't do anything like this to their father intentionally. It simply wasn't true. "What? What do you mean?"

"Dad was coming back from a business trip the night of the accident. He was coming from *Boston*. Do you know how far that is? *I* allowed him go alone."

Jazzmine exhaled with relief. She thought Vanessa was serious. She was just being ridiculous. "Oh, Vanessa, that wasn't your fault. You couldn't have known."

Unintentionally, Vanessa spilled over in uncontrolled tears. "I should have gone with him," she whispered, kicking herself mentally.

Jazzmine pulled her closer, wrapping her arms around her. "It's ok. Dad's going to be all right." Her voice was full of confidence as she had to be the strong one.

After a moment, Vanessa pulled herself together and backed out of Jazzmine's embrace. Holding up a hand, she sniffed. "I'm fine." With a satisfied nod, she turned back to Officer Henderson, who was at the end of the desk at the printer waiting for her paper to come out. "About that wallet," she said with another sniff. She wiped her eyes.

Officer Henderson nodded. Her eyes were on the paper coming out of the printer. "I'll be with you in a minute."

Jazzmine rubbed Vanessa's back, again. Her eyes were sympathetic. "Are you sure you're all right?"

Vanessa needed no one's sympathy. She was no child. She especially didn't need Jazzmine's sympathy. "Yes, I'm fine."

When the police report was out of the printer, Officer Henderson handed it to Jazzmine, who paid for it. Then, she directed her attention to Vanessa. "I'll get your father's wallet for you, but you'll have to pick up the other things if there are any for yourself." To Jazzmine she finished, "If you'll follow me, I'll take you to Detective Horn's office. He'll be able to take you to the grounds where your father's car was found. He'll, also, be able to take you to the wrecking yard to see the car."

"Thank you."

While Detective Horn showed Vanessa and Jazzmine the grounds where their father's accident was discovered, neither of them said a word. He discussed his theory as to how the accident happened.

At the wrecking yard, Vanessa felt close to tears when she saw the car.

It was completely totaled.

Jazzmine glanced at the car. She hadn't been able to stand the sight of it. It had been too much for her to bear, and she had to walk away. It was amazing that her father survived an accident as horrible as that.

Levi sat on the edge of Jazzmine's bed as she sat up against the propped pillows, telling him about her entire day, her father's condition, and her sister's successful career. He listened quietly. His eyes ogled her full breasts as the silk fabric of her nightgown molded them. The thin spaghetti-straps did nothing to hide her smooth skin. His desire was to caress her body and take her to the journey of the passion triangle. It was a place of love where he longed to take her for the longest of time. If only he could taste her erect nipples and kiss her beautiful mouth. He could give her...

He blinked when she placed her hand against his chest, sending sparks to his spine. Her touch was so gentle and soothing, and... She couldn't possibly know what type of affect she was having on him. If she did, it was wrong of her to tease him.

"I just don't know," she was saying. "Things don't feel the same. I don't know why, but I'm not sure Vanessa..."

"Shhhh," Levi silenced her, pressing his index finger to her sweet lips. "Don't worry. Everything will be fine. You'll see."

She smiled and kissed his whole palm. "Thanks, Levi."

He didn't want to tell her that he had no good feelings about her sister, and he didn't want to hear anymore about her. Vanessa and her father were all she raved about back in California, and he didn't want to cause any friction between them. Perhaps, he misjudged Vanessa, and she really was the woman Jazzmine described her to be. Somehow, he doubted it. He had his suspicions about her. She came off as devious and too controlling, and he only met her today. It was just the vibes she unleashed.

"Get some sleep. I'll see you in the morning," Levi promised.

Jazzmine opened her arms to him for a hug as that was sweet of him to say. When he hugged her, she felt the strangest tingle inside. Momentarily, she didn't want him to let her go. Releasing him and trying to shake the feeling she knew she imagined, she stretched out in bed, and he pulled up the covers.

"Good-night," he whispered as he leaned down to brush her lips with his without thinking.

"Good-night," she whispered back as she watched him go to the door. Turning off the light, he left her alone in the dark hotel suite.

When she was alone, her hand rose to her lips. Although Levi gave her a friendly goodnight peck, a strong sensation lingered behind. Touching her lips, she could still feel his mouth there. She had to wonder if she imagined the peck and the sensation it caused.

When Levi was on the other side of the closed door, he leaned against it for a moment for composure. *"I shouldn't have done that,"* he told himself. He felt so much from the kiss even though it was just a peck.

Jazzmine aroused so many urges deep within him that it would take every fiber of his being to contain himself. The kiss was probably out of line as he should have been content with the hug she offered.

If Jazzmine didn't approve, she would have said so or slapped him, anything to let him know. She didn't, but still he didn't want to jeopardize their relationship if she didn't return his feelings of love. He would have to be more careful and control his urges next time. It was just too hard to resist. She was right there, too close, and he wasn't thinking. It happened before he knew it.

With a sigh, he left her suite to go to his own, which was next door.

At midnight, Vanessa sat by the fireplace in her pink pajamas with the box of letters Jazzmine wrote to her at her side.

On the floor in front of her was a pile of letters she had already read. With each line she read of the letter in her hand, she shook her head as teardrops fell. She had once been ashamed of her little sister, and now she hated her with a white-hot passion. How could this be? All of Jazzmine's letters were very detailed on her life and her fabulous career.

Vanessa couldn't believe it!

Jazzmine made more money in six months than she accumulated in one year! Even her boyfriend was someone important. Vanessa didn't even have a boyfriend! That was so unfair. She was better than Jazzmine. So why did Jazzmine have the life she deserved?

Jazzmine owned two vehicles, a convertible and a sport utility vehicle. She even lived in a Beverly Hills mansion with a hot tub in the upstairs bathroom and an outdoor pool! Why did she have all the luck?

What did Vanessa have compared to her? She had a luxury car, a mansion with no hot tub or swimming pool, a great job for half the money and no boyfriend. She was seeing several people, but none of them were steady dates, and none of them were fit to be called her boyfriend.

"Oh God!" she thought, tossing the letter to the floor and snatching up a big yellow envelope. "This is so unfair! I wish she were never born to my father!" More tears fell as she opened the package and pulled out a page of pictures of Jazzmine and Bartu. They even autographed it! Tossing the envelope and the pictures to the floor, she stood up and yelled, "I hate her! I hate her! I just hate her!"

Something had to be done about *Miss Beautiful* before things got out of hand. It was going to take her a few days, but she was going to come up with something.

During Sunday morning service, Jazzmine sat next to her sister with a real smile. She was so glad to be back in her home church. It was the church in which her father raised her and her sister. It felt good to be surrounded by a lot of her old church family members, even though they probably didn't recognize her. There were a lot of new faces.

Levi sat next to her listening attentively. The choir was marvelous. He couldn't help clapping and standing in the spirit. Even though he was a visitor in the church, he felt extremely welcome.

Vanessa sat up straight, not too pleased to have her model sister and her celebrity friend sitting beside her. If she could have sat on an entirely different pew, she would have, but Jazzmine insisted on sitting with her. They were in church, so she couldn't refuse.

In the pulpit, Pastor Jackson stepped to the podium calling for everyone's attention after the choir's selection.

All eyes were on him.

"Good-morning, brothers and sisters!"

There was a song of good-mornings from the congregation.

"First off I would like to make an announcement." He spread his hands out on the podium. "I regret to announce that our own Brother James Thomas is in the hospital. He was in a tragic accident the other night, and he's in critical condition."

There were moans of sadness from the congregation. A few members, who sat behind Vanessa, leaned forward to pat her on the shoulder and tell her how sorry they were to hear about her father's accident.

The pastor's eyes landed on Jazzmine, who dropped by his house last night to tell him about her father's condition and to ask for his prayers. "Sister Jazzmine Thomas, Brother Thomas's younger daughter, is home. If Brother Thomas were here, I'm sure he would be proud to announce that Sister Jazzmine has been doing well over the past six years. She left New York City six years ago to pursue a higher education in California. She has done so," he nodded approvingly. "Along the six year journey, the Lord opened many doors and gave her many blessings. Sister Jazzmine is now a very successful model. I remember when she was a young girl growing up in this church. I always knew she was going to make something of herself. In California, she made the acquaintance of some good people, Brother Levi Proctor, the actor, for one."

He nodded again. "She and Brother Proctor," he indicated them with a sweep of his hand, "have come all this way to commune with us and to be by Brother Thomas's side. Sister Jazzmine, would you like to have a word?"

Jazzmine stood up and walked to the front.

Whatever Jazzmine was saying, Vanessa turned a death ear to it. She was more than upset. Pastor Jackson only announced Jazzmine and Levi. He was acting as if James wasn't even her father, and Levi was her long lost brother. Levi was no relation to them. He had no right to be announced. James was her father! He was her father way before Jazzmine was even born. The pastor said that if James were there, he would have been proud to let everyone know how successful Jazzmine had become.

Vanessa pouted. If her father were there, Jazzmine wouldn't have been. Why did this have to happen?

Pastor Jackson had to go and let everyone know she had a little sister. No one, except for the ones who remembered her as she was years ago, needed to know. Now everyone knew about *Jazz*, the fabulous model. Oh, Vanessa could have screamed.

Jazzmine was destroying everything already, and she had only been there for three days.

As the day progressed, Vanessa's hatred for her sister increased by the minute. Everywhere they went together, Jazzmine got all of the attention, and she had to be introduced as **her** sister. The situation should have been reversed. Vanessa should have been the one getting all the attention, and Jazzmine should have been introduced as the little sister, but she was in the shadow. Vanessa Thomas was only a well-known name in New York City. *Jazz* Thomas was a well-known face and name nationwide. Things were getting out of hand, and Vanessa was going to have to come up with something fast.

Monday morning, Vanessa was glad to escape Jazzmine's presence and to be behind the desk of her own office. That was the one place where she could be herself and get all the attention. At the office, people fell at **her** feet, not Jazzmine's.

She sat behind her desk wearing a lovely gold suit with black outlines. Her shoulder length hair hung about her shoulders in a bouncy body wrap. Around her neck, she wore a nice choker with the matching earrings.

Being away from Jazzmine, she felt better and more at ease.

Switching from her paperwork to her computer, she smiled to herself.

At least her father was doing better. If he continued to progress in this way, perhaps he wouldn't ask Jazzmine to stay. If he told her she was free to go, she wouldn't have to do it herself.

There was a soft knock at the door.

"Come in," Vanessa commanded cheerfully. When the door opened, she looked up, and the smile on her face almost disappeared.

Jazzmine entered the office looking more beautiful than ever. She was wearing a charming white blouse underneath a navy jumper dress. Her hair was curled all over with bouncy spirals that hung to her chin. If she weren't actually a model, one could easily mistake her for one. The smile on her pretty lips made Vanessa want to slap her silly.

"Hey! There was no one at your secretary's desk, so I decided to knock. I hope that's ok."

Vanessa wished her secretary had been at her desk to warn her that she was here. She could have told her to tell her she was busy or to come back tomorrow. Too bad she didn't get the warning. "Of course," she answered, beckoning for her to come closer into the room. Jazzmine stepped closer to the desk. Pulling open the top drawer of her desk, Vanessa took out her office remote control and pressed the red button at the very top to close the door. "What's on your mind?" She really didn't want to know, but she did want her to hurry up and get out of her office.

Hearing the door close behind her, Jazzmine's eyes went back to the door. *"Mmm!"* she was impressed. Her eyes went around the beautifully decorated office, her hair bouncing when her head moved. "I came to see your office," she announced when she turned her attention back to her sister. "This is so nice!"

"Of course it is!" Vanessa told her mentally. *"I have excellent taste!"* Aloud, she said, "Thank you."

"Oh! Look!" Jazzmine's eyes went over Vanessa's head to the window and all the tall buildings that were visible through it. "You have a view of the city." She moved pass the desk to the window and stared out at the beautiful scenery below. "I forgot how beautiful New York City is." She smiled down at the pretty green lawn and the busy streets.

Was that all Jazzmine wanted? She just came to see her office and to enjoy her office view? She could have come later for that! With her back to her sister's back, Vanessa rolled her eyes and shook her head with pity.

The door opened unexpectedly, and Vanessa quickly pulled a straight face.

Hearing the door open, Jazzmine turned around as if she expected to know the person coming in.

Cassandra DuMars, Vanessa's business partner, entered the office with her head down and a stack of folders in her arms. "Vanessa, you have to help me," she was saying when she entered the office. Moving closer into the room, she lifted her head. "I don't know how..." her eyes met with Jazzmine, and she froze in mid-sentence.

Recognizing her, she dropped the stack of folders in front of Vanessa and to extend her hand to Jazzmine anxiously. "Hi! I... You're..." She laughed at herself when Jazzmine accepted her hand with a firm shake.

Vanessa, who was watching her partner fall all over her sister with disgust, shook her head and cleared her throat. "Before you get all tongue tied, I think I should tell you that this is my sister, Jazzmine. Jazz, this is my business partner, Cassandra DuMars."

Jazzmine smiled. "Nice to meet you."

Cassandra turned her eyes on Vanessa with disbelief. "Jazz... *The* Jazz Thomas is your sister. **This**," she pointed to Jazzmine, "is your sister?" She was shocked. "I didn't even know you had a sister."

"That's because I did well at hiding the fact up until this point," Vanessa wanted to say aloud, but she didn't. Cassandra should have stayed in her own office. If she had, she still wouldn't know she had a sister.

Jazzmine turned her eyes on Vanessa with a questioning glance. *"What does she mean she didn't know you had a sister?"* she wanted to ask.

Apparently, Vanessa didn't talk about her much if at all because not many people were aware that she had a sister who lived in Beverly Hills. Several people came up to her at church, telling her that they were pleased to meet her, but they didn't know that Vanessa wasn't an only child. It was painful to hear such a statement. Back in Beverly Hills, she talked about Vanessa all the time.

Not giving Vanessa an opportunity to respond, Cassandra turned her attention back to Jazzmine with a cheerful expression. Her hand rose to her heart, and she blushed. "Oh, Miss Thomas, it is such an honor to meet you."

Jazzmine half smiled. "Please, call me Jazz." Miss Thomas was a bit much. She was an ordinary person just like everyone else. Just because she was a model, she didn't need special attention or to be put on a pedestal. She had no desire to fly too high and above everyone else.

Giggling with excitement, Cassandra was overjoyed. "OK! So, you're Vanessa's little sister?" She still found it hard to believe. "Oh," her mouth dropped. That reminded her. She read about their father's accident in the newspaper, and she was meaning to ask Vanessa about it. "How's your father?"

"He's better. Thank you." Answering her first question, she replied, "Yes, Vanessa and I really are sisters. Well, when I left New York City years ago I was her little sister in a sense, but now, I'm just her younger sister. We can't say little anymore, can we?"

"Yes we can," Vanessa thought, comparing her present appearance to how she looked before she left. If only Cassandra knew the truth, her reaction to her would be different. Even then, she probably wouldn't believe it. Vanessa barely believed it herself.

"Jazz, I just have to ask you, how do you keep that figure?" Cassandra's eyes went over her body admiringly. The jumper dress fit her so snugly in all the right places. If only she had a figure like that. Yes, her figure was nice, too, but Jazzmine was much more petite. "Aren't you afraid of getting fat? I would be. In fact, I am, and I'm not even close to being a model. I'm sure it's hectic."

Actually, Jazzmine wasn't afraid of gaining weight. Being that she was fat before, she already knew what that was like. She dealt with it before, and if she ever gained the weight back, she would deal with it again. "It's not hard. The diet is a little strict, but once you get use to it, it becomes natural. I'm not afraid to gain weight simply because I know that it's just as easy to lose weight as it is to gain weight. As far as my career goes, I know that as long as I have faith in God, everything will be ok. He'll never let me fall." She shook her curls.

Cassandra was impressed by her answer. Her smile was evident. "So, where did your motivation to go for it come from? I've read that you and Levi Proctor are close friends. Was it he who encouraged you?" She smiled to herself, thinking of the handsome actor. Now, he was a man she truly wanted to meet! Her husband wasn't too fond of the idea, but someday, she did hope to meet him.

"Well, actually," Jazzmine stepped behind Vanessa's chair and folded her arms around her neck, hugging her, "my sister encouraged me a lot when we were little. She used to say I was beautiful and I could be whatever I wanted to be."

Glad to finally get some praise, Vanessa smiled broadly and placed her hands on her sister's arms. Silly Jazzmine! She used to say those things out of obligation. It was her duty as the older sister. Jazzmine looked up to her back then. She didn't know she would actually believe her and blossom this way!

"Of course, Levi did encourage me a lot, too," Jazzmine laughed with a smile, thinking of her best friend. "He is a very good friend of mine." A sudden desire to be with him washed over her, and she straightened up, dropping her arms to her side. "Well, I'm sure you two are very busy. So, I'll let you get back to work." Stepping closer to Cassandra, she shook her hand again. "Again, it was a pleasure to meet you."

"Oh, same here!" Cassandra was flattered. "I'll have to tell my husband that I met you. He's a big fan of yours."

Jazzmine went to the door with an appreciative smile. At the door, she waved. "See you later, Vanessa," she said with her hand on the doorknob.

Glad she was leaving, Vanessa nodded. "Ok, sweetie!"

Jazzmine left, closing the door behind her.

Cassandra, who turned to watch the model leave, sighed. She was impressed. Turning back to Vanessa, she said, "She is so sweet! I wonder if they miss her back at the agency?"

"The agency! That's it!" Cassandra gave Vanessa a brilliant idea. She knew exactly how to get Jazzmine to go home!

Alone in her office again, Vanessa used her remote to close and lock the door. Picking up the telephone, she called information and asked for the number to *Beverly Hills Beauties'* in Beverly Hills, California. Jotting down the number, she hung up and dialed the number as fast as her finger would allow. "Ah, yes, I would like to speak with Beth Trenton, please," she remembered the name of Jazzmine's agent from her letters. Holding, she tapped her long fingernails on the desktop anxiously.

"Beth Trenton, may I help you?" the woman's voice was soft and sweet.

"Yes, this is Charlene Barks from *Above Beautiful Modeling Agency* in New York City, and I understand that you are Jazz Thomas's agent. Is that correct?"

"Yes," Beth answered nervously, wondering why an agent from an agency in New York City could possibly be calling her.

"Well, Mrs. Trenton, my agency would like to offer you double what you're getting for Jazzmine's publicity if you sign her contract over to our agency. She would be perfect for our next issue. I understand that she's here in New York City for a short while. Great! Great! We, also, understand that she's originally from New York City. That's even better. Next month's issue will be dedicated to her as a homecoming gift and to your agency for signing her to us. I thought it would be best to let you know we have our eye on her. I do intend to contact her first thing tomorrow morning."

Vanessa was quite aware that because of Jazzmine, *Beverly Hills Beauties*' was getting excellent ratings, and she was a great asset to their agency. They weren't going to be willing to part with her. If they lost her, they could lose other equally successful models. Their job was to hire models, not give them away. Vanessa refused to believe that Mrs. Trenton was stupid. She couldn't let money walk out the door. Vanessa was depending on her to get Jazzmine to come home.

"Um, thank you for calling, Ms. Barks. I'll keep in touch!" Beth Trenton hung up before Vanessa could protest her calling back.

Hanging up, Vanessa felt complacent. Beth Trenton was not going to let Jazzmine get away, and it was obvious in her voice. Besides, she didn't say she would confer with her colleagues and call her back. She didn't say she would consider the offer either. Now, all she had to do was sit back and let Beth Trenton do her job.

Leaning back in the big leather chair, she laughed with cheer. She couldn't wait to get Jazzmine on a plane back to California.

CHAPTER SIX

*V*anessa and Jazzmine sat side-by-side at the foot of their father's bed. Levi sat in the chair next to the bed with his legs crossed masculine style. James was sitting up in bed with his attention focused on Levi as he was bragging about both of his daughters.

"Did you know that Jazzmine and Vanessa..." he began to say when Jazzmine's cell phone buzzed.

All eyes went to her.

Hoping it wasn't Bartu, she anxiously dug the cell phone out of the small handbag she carried on her shoulder. Pulling the antenna up, she flipped it open, "Hello? ... Oh, hello, Mrs. Trenton."

At the agent's name, Vanessa had to hide her smirk. She knew Mrs. Trenton would call her today to be sure to get to her before *Charlene Barks* did. She dropped her head listening quietly.

Levi, who caught Vanessa's smirk, frowned as he felt an uncertain vibe from her. *"What is that about?"* he wondered. Vanessa was the oddest person.

"Well, yes, I did," Jazzmine continued. "What?

More shoots? Now? But," her eyes went to her father. Then, they darted to Levi with a sad expression. "I took some time off to be with my father. I thought I explained my situation to you..." She sighed and swallowed hard. "Yes, I realize that." Her eyes widened, and she arched her eyebrows. "*Double* my pay?"

At the mention of doubling her pay, Vanessa was secretly jealous. She didn't think Mrs. Trenton would go that far. She just thought she wouldn't take no for an answer. She had to go and offer her more money. That meant that Jazzmine would be making Vanessa's yearly salary doubled in less than a month. Oh, Jazzmine got all the luck! Even when Vanessa got her way, she still didn't get her way.

"Mrs. Trenton, how long do you suppose this will take... That long? Well, why does it have to be right now? ... I see... Ok... Well, can I get back to you... Yes, I will call you back today." She hung up.

James frowned at his daughter's sad expression when she stood up to face him. "Honey, is something wrong?"

Jazzmine dropped her eyes. "Yes, Daddy. That was my agent on the phone. She has a job lined up for me back in California. They want me to come home tomorrow morning. I don't know," she shrugged her shoulders, "why it's so urgent, but my job is at stake here. She says it will probably take anywhere from two to three weeks to finish. Oh, Daddy, I can't leave you now!" Not knowing what to do, she sped from the room.

Levi went after her.

Two to three weeks? That was music to Vanessa's ears. That would give her just enough time to come up with something to keep her in California permanently.

Having her father all to herself, Vanessa stood up and moved closer to his side. Taking his hand, she said, "Now, Daddy, you do realize how important Jazzmine's career is to her, don't you? If she stays, it could destroy her entire career. You're fine, aren't you? Three weeks will fly by before we know it, and she'll be back." The thought was horrifying! "You don't really want to destroy your daughter's life, do you?"

No. He didn't, but he didn't want her to go either. She had only recently arrived. James missed his baby, and he deserved time with her, too, didn't he? Seeing her again did him a world of good. Vanessa was right, however, Jazzmine's career did mean a lot to her, and he had no desire to jeopardize her promising future. He was going to be fine. He could hold up until she returned.

"Hey!" Levi gently caught Jazzmine's arm and turned her to face him. "Slow down. Where are you going?"

"I don't know." Jazzmine really didn't know. She would rather be anywhere else at the moment. She couldn't face her father right now. He needed her. If she chose to go back to California, she would be abandoning him. The decision was so hard to make.

The fact that she had no idea where she was going was obvious. She was moving so fast, Levi thought he would have to take a bus to catch up with her. He hated it when she ran away from her problems, which she normally did when she didn't think she could face them. The main reason she ended up in California was because she had been running from a problem. There were solutions to problems. She just needed to find them.

"Hey, hey," Levi said in a soft voice. "It isn't so bad, is it? Two or three weeks? I'm sure your father will understand. He's a reasonable man. Besides, you've finally returned home after six long years. Three weeks is nothing compared to that."

Jazzmine lifted her eyes to the ceiling with a sigh. He was right as usual. Her father was an understanding person. "He is. I know, but..."

"What are you so afraid of? He isn't going anywhere before you get back." Levi had to help her keep her priorities in line. She could have both a loving relationship with her father and magnificent career.

That was true. Her father wasn't the only person on her mind, however. "I know. If I go back now..."

Thinking he knew her dilemma, Levi held up a hand to silence her. "Ah! If you go back now, you may have to face Bartu."

She lifted her eyes, wondering how he knew what was on her mind. Her expression was her answer.

"Listen, baby, you're going to have to face him when you do go back anyway. Go, Jazz. Do the shoot. Hurry back because I'll miss you."

He was right again. Perhaps, she was worried over nothing. Maybe Bartu had stopped trying to reach her by now. If he still wanted to talk to her, he could have called her on her cell phone like Mrs. Trenton did. That was the smart thing to do. He had the number, and he hadn't used it. Her conclusion was that he had given up on her by now. Had there really been a chance for them to reconcile? Did she actually want to be with him anymore? She hadn't been available that long, and she felt better already. "Oh, but, what about Dad? I came to be with him. I took time off to be with him. Levi..."

"I'm sure the two of you can compromise. Just go back in there and talk to him," Levi encouraged, caressing her cheek.

His touch was so gentle. His voice was so sweet. Jazzmine thought she would whither away. Placing her hand to his, she held his hand to her face. "Thank you, Levi. I'm going to miss you, too." She gave him a hug.

Returning the hug, Levi wondered if Jazzmine could hear the fast pace of his heart as it pounded against his chest. Her nearness always had that affect on him. When he held her in his arms, a million emotions attacked him at once. It never ceased as he knew his arms was where she belonged.

Exhaling, he closed his eyes, savoring the moment.

Before entering her father's room, Jazzmine slightly pushed the door open and peeked inside.

When the door opened, James looked up at her. Seeing her, he smiled and waved her in. "Come on in. It's safe."

Jazzmine pushed the door all the way open. She stepped inside at the welcoming invitation.

Levi followed her into the room.

Jazzmine went to her father's bedside and took his hand. "Daddy, I know I came to be with you, and..."

James glanced at Vanessa, who was on the opposite side of the bed waiting patiently for him to tell her to go, and back to his youngest daughter. "You have a job to do. I understand, honey. Go!" He gave his permission without her asking. "I'll be here when you get back."

Loving her father, Jazzmine hugged him. "Oh, Daddy! Thank you! I'll try to get back as soon as I can."

"Oh, don't hurry back on our accounts," Vanessa told her mentally. She was pleased that her father told her to go! Now, she could get some fresh air, and things could resume to normal. It was awful being in Jazzmine's shadow. She should be in front because she was one number, and she was better than Jazzmine by far!

Tuesday morning, Levi found it very odd that he was the only person who could arise early to see Jazzmine off safely. Her own sister didn't even come to the airport. He thought something to be strange about Vanessa from the very beginning, however. He, too, had a sister. He was positive that if he were in Jazzmine's shoes, she would act much differently than Vanessa. Actually, she did. He had only been out-of-the-state for a few days, and his sister had called him a total of four times already, inquiring about Jazzmine and her father's condition. She showed concern for other people as she was a loving, sensitive person. Vanessa was the opposite. The only person she seemed to have genuine concern for was herself.

Jazzmine lived thousands of miles away from New York City. Levi had never known Vanessa to call her. Had she called, Jazzmine would have told him. James called her quite often, and he visited when possible. Vanessa did neither. Her call about their father's accident was the first ever to Jazzmine in six years! Even then, it wasn't a courtesy call. It was a straight to the point call that **had** to be made. Had James not asked her to, she probably wouldn't have called then.

Something wasn't right about Vanessa as everything couldn't possibly be right in the upper level of her brain. No one was that busy or wrapped up in his own life to take time for *family*!

Levi refused to believe Vanessa was the *great woman* her sister proclaimed her to be. Vanessa Thomas was a fraud! He deemed this from their very first encounter.

PLACE: BEVERLY HILLS, CALIFORNIA
EIGHT DAYS LATER...

Wednesday morning, Jazzmine was at the studio for her photo shoot bright and early. Her goal was to get her work done and get back to New York City as soon as possible. For the past seven days, she did her best to avoid any contact with Bartu Flexler. When she returned home and checked her answering machine, there were dozens of messages from him asking her to contact him as soon as possible. He even came to the studio and left messages for her there.

When she returned to the studio after her arrival Tuesday, she discovered that he left her two-dozen roses and a jumbo box of candy along with the messages. She sent them back with a note telling him not to send her anything else and to stop calling. Not giving up, he sent Devin Ringer, a renowned singer, to her house to serenade her with a sad love song, apologizing for his mistake. It was a romantic gesture, but it didn't achieve his mission. She got to know Devin, and she still refused to speak to Bartu. She saw no future between the two of them. Devin was a nice man, however.

Entering the building wearing a lovely turquoise pantsuit, Jazzmine jumped in surprise when Bartu stepped in front of her from nowhere. He startled her. She almost screamed. Her hand rose to her heart as she took a moment to calm herself.

"Oh, I'm sorry, babe. Did I frighten you?" he asked with that sexy Australian accent that made her quiver as usual.

"Yes!" she snapped. What did he think? Of course, he frightened her, stepping out in front of her like that. He could have given her a heart attack! The way he stepped out, he would have frightened anyone. Not wanting to talk to him, she stepped pass him.

Bartu grabbed her arm and pull her into his warm embrace. He missed her dearly, and he wanted her in his arms. It felt wonderful to have her back in them. He savored the moment for a second before he spoke. "Jazz, why are you doing this to me? Do you know what I've been going through for the past few weeks? Without you, I've been going crazy!"

He sounded sincere, but was he truly?

"Oh!" Jazzmine almost lost herself in his

arms. His embrace felt so warm and familiar. It was as if they hadn't been separated. Had her feelings for him actually changed or had she been trying to convince herself that they had? She wasn't sure anymore. All she knew was that for the past seven days, she had been anxious to get back to New York City to see her father and *Levi*.

She missed Levi tremendously! Hearing his voice over the phone, as they kept in constant touch, only made matters worse. The two of them had never been separated by distance in an entire six years. They were always together. Now, the distance was an awkward adjustment.

For seven days, Jazzmine went home to an empty house expecting Levi to rush in with some fabulous news about with whom he made acquaintance at the studio, or in what type of movie he was offered a role. For seven days, nothing happened. She spent seven nights alone in her dark room thinking of her best friend's handsome face and all their memorable times. For seven days, Bartu never once entered her mind, which was why the present situation was so confusing. She wasn't sure how to feel or what to do. She couldn't deal with Bartu asking her to give up her relationship with her best friend again. She never asked anything so drastic of him.

"I've missed you!" Hugging her tighter, Bartu snuggled up to her. "Ah!" he moaned with pleasure. "Doesn't this feel good?"

Jazzmine had to admit that it did feel good to be in his arms again. She sighed, saying nothing. Her response was resting the back of her head against his hard chest. Her eyes closed for a moment as she slipped into the land of nowhere.

She forgot all of her problems and even where she was. Her eyes snapped open again when thoughts of the sensation she felt in Levi's arms that night in her hotel room invaded her mind. It was a secret that couldn't be revealed as it was unexplainable even to herself.

"Jazz, I've thought of nothing but holding you for the past few weeks. I've been dying to do this!" Bartu whispered in her ear. "Oh, baby, I am so sorry. I would love to make it up to you. Will you let me?"

She didn't know if she should. "How? How will you make it up to me?" Jazzmine wanted to know.

Bartu smiled to himself, knowing exactly how. "I was thinking of inviting you up to the beach house for a glass of champagne and some cozy music. We could cuddle up on the beach after it's deserted, and perhaps, you'll let me show you how much I've missed you in my own little way."

Everything sounded so blissful right up until that last part. He was talking about *sex*, again. Nothing had changed. He was the same old Bartu, who let his hormones get in the way of a good time. No! Jazzmine just couldn't deal with this. Pulling away, she turned to face him. "There you go again! I thought you said you were sorry."

Bartu frowned innocently. "I am. What' wrong now?" He held his arms out at his side, not having the faintest idea what was so upsetting.

"You may have missed me, but you haven't changed. You still want to get me in bed. I have to go, Bartu. Good-bye!" She walked away.

Bartu shook his head. Jazzmine just didn't understand. He never said how he wanted to show her. He said he wanted to show her in his own little way. Naturally, she assumed he meant sexually. Actually, he had something else in mind. He had intentions of salvaging what was left of their broken relationship, but she didn't offer him an opportunity to elaborate. "Jazz Thomas, I'm not going to give up on you!" he yelled after her.

Hearing his statement, Jazzmine treaded faster. She didn't think he would.

Beth Trenton stood to a distance watching as Jazzmine did the photo shoot she had arranged. Even though Jazzmine smiled on the set, she knew she wasn't actually happy.

The only reason she arranged the photo shoot was to ensure that Charlene Barks didn't get to her first. They could not afford to lose her. Now that Jazzmine was home, and she received no call from Charlene Barks, she was beginning to feel guilty. Naturally, Jazzmine wanted and *needed* to be with her father. Every single break she received, she was on the phone calling New York City to check on him.

Beth folded her arms across her chest. She had to let Jazzmine go back now. Her conscience wouldn't be at ease as long as she knew she tricked her into the emergency flight home.

"That was an excellent job!" Shane, the photographer, told Jazzmine when he ran out of film. "The camera loves you! Let's take a break, and I'll see you back here in an hour. I need to reload."

Jazzmine blushed, taking off the white hat she was posing in. The idea of taking a break was marvelous. She was overdue for an intermission. She wanted to call and check on her father anyway. "Thanks, Shane."

Beth unfolded her arms. Tossing her long blonde hair off her shoulder with the back of her hand, she swallowed hard and moved closer to the set.

When she stepped onto the black carpet, Jazzmine's smile faded, causing her to drop her head in shame. Jazzmine was expecting her to bring more bad news. Lifting her head, her blue eyes found Jazzmine's brown ones. "Jazz," she began with a sigh, "I'm so sorry I had to call you away from your father like I did. I was wrong, and..."

Jazzmine shook her head as she understood completely. "No, Mrs. Trenton, that's all right. I was happy to do the..."

Beth Trenton held up a hand to silence her. "Jazz, dear, you don't understand. Just listen."

Jazzmine nodded, listening anxiously. She had no idea what to expect Mrs. Trenton to say. She explained everything to her over the phone when she called her back to California. She told her she was needed for the winter issue of *Essential Magazine* as she was the icon. What now? Was there more work for her to do? She did not want to hear that right now.

"Jazz, I feel guilty about this now, but the only reason I had you come back here was because Charlene Barks from *Above Beautiful Modeling Agency* in New York City called me earlier that day. She informed me that they had an eye on you. They were intending to offer you a contract with them. They offered us double what we are getting for your publicity now. Ms. Barks said she was going to dedicate next month's issue to you and us if you accepted their offer. I had to get you back here before she could call you. If you were otherwise engaged here, you couldn't go." Beth placed a hand on Jazzmine's arm.

"Jazz, you know I can't let you go. You *are* my VIP model! I didn't mean to trick you. I know I should have been honest with you from the beginning, but I..." She shook her head. There was no excuse for what she did. She was just afraid at the time, and now, she had to rectify the situation. Never finishing the sentence, she went on to say, "I had a contract drawn up for you for ten more years with us. If you sign it and promise not to break it, you will be free to go back as soon as you finish the shooting today."

Everything Mrs. Trenton said was flattering. Jazzmine was speechless. It was nice to know that she was so well valued at *Beverly Hills' Beauties,* and other agencies were interested in her, as well. When she told her that she would be free to go, Jazzmine's face lit up with surprise and burst with happiness. "Really? I can go back to New York City, or do you mean I can go home for the day?"

Beth laughed with amusement. "You can go back to New York City if you like, and I promise you, I won't line up anymore jobs for you until you get back. Just don't move or stay too long. I'll keep your father in my prayers. Say hello to Levi for me."

"I will," Jazzmine promised, "and thank you!"

Mrs. Trenton patted Jazzmine on the arm, and walked away.

PLACE: NEW YORK CITY, NEW YORK
IN VANESSA'S OFFICE

Vanessa stood in the center of the room, holding up a picture of Jazzmine and herself when they were younger, which she had blown up. She had the perfect plan that would run Jazzmine back to California for good when she returned. She was just preparing early. Looking at homely Jazzmine, she pitied the vision. "You were a sight to see, Jazz," she told the girl in the picture. Smiling at herself, she said, "And I am still as stunning as I ever was!"

There was a soft knock at the door. She glanced back at the door as she commanded, "Come in."

Levi entered the office.

Levi? What did he want? Seeing him instead of one of her employees, Vanessa lowered the picture and turned to face him. "Well, what is it?" she demanded in a harsh tone. He was not one of her favorite people. She wasn't a *Levi Proctor fan* as he was so very disrespectful to her. There was no reason she should offer him better treatment than he offered her.

Levi ignored her rudeness, as he was positive that their feelings for each other were mutual. The only reason he communicated with her was because she was Jazzmine's sister. Were she not, he would have nothing to do with her. "I came to pick up a package for your father," he announced his reason for gracing her with his presence as it was probably unwanted.

He promised Jazzmine that he would tend to her father in his spare time while Vanessa tended to her business. He was appreciative of the fact that it worked out so well. While Vanessa was at work, he had time alone with James as he enjoyed his company. As long as he and Vanessa weren't in the same room together for too long, he was fine. He just wished James hadn't asked him to come here and collect the package for him.

"Oh! Oh, yes," Vanessa remembered. She had completely forgotten that her father was going to send him over for his things. Going to her desk, she laid the picture on top and reached inside the top drawer for her remote control. "It's down the hall in the storage. Excuse me. I'll be right back." She left him.

Looking around the well-decorated office, Levi moved closer to the desk. His eyes landed on the picture. He had to smile, recognizing young Jazzmine. A frown overtook the smile when he realized that Vanessa had been admiring this particular picture when he entered the office. Why? Would Vanessa cherish this picture of her and her sister, whom she seemed to have no interest in whatsoever? It wasn't likely that she missed the old Jazzmine, as she didn't continue the line of communication with her. She undoubtedly didn't care for the new Jazzmine. It was obvious from the way she perked up when Mrs. Trenton called Jazzmine insisting that she return to California. Something was abnormal about the whole scenario.

Levi turned around just as Vanessa was entering with a giant shopping bag and a small box.

"Here you are," she handed them to him politely, shocking him. He didn't think she was capable of being polite.

Accepting the things, he was just as polite. "Thanks."

Vanessa watched him leave. If his attitude were different toward her, there could be something between them. He was a *famed actor* for goodness sakes! His money was right! She once thought he could offer her nothing, but that had been dead wrong. He had so much to offer her. He could take her to elegant restaurants and buy her expensive things. That was just for starters! As things began to progress between them, naturally he would fall in love with her. If they were to get married, she imagined the diamond ring would be so enormous that she would have to keep her hand a great distance from her face to keep from hitting herself in the eye. She would have the bragging rights of being a celebrity's wife. Her face would be all over the television because every time he was nominated for an Academy Award, she would be right by his side.

Yes, Vanessa identified a lot of potential in Levi. He was just too stubborn to realize how privileged he was just to know her!

Levi stopped the rental car at a red light. Sensing that something was seriously wrong with Vanessa, he glanced over at the items he collected from her, which was in the passenger's seat. He was curious of the contents of the bag and the box. He couldn't invade James's privacy, however. It was none of his business. If James wanted him to know what it was, he would have told him.

Shaking his head, he turned his attention back to the light only to snap it around again when his cell phone rang.

Reaching for his cell phone, which was lying in the seat next to the box, he opened the small flap and pulled up the antenna. "Hello?"

"How is my father?"

Jazzmine's voice warmed Levi's heart. They seemed to talk nearly every hour, but he wasn't complaining. "I'm on my way back to the hospital now," he answered as the light changed, and he pulled out into traffic. "But, he's fine. He was eating when I left him."

That was good. "I saw Bartu today," Jazzmine reported.

Levi inhaled, wondering if he really wanted to hear what she was about to say. She didn't sound angry. Perhaps, they reconciled, which was what he didn't want to hear. "Well, what happened?"

Jazzmine shook her head as if he could see her. "Nothing. He is driving me crazy, Levi. I can't deal with him. He's incorrigible!"

Exhaling, Levi gave a faint sigh of relief. That was good to know. They hadn't reconciled, which restored his hope. She was talking in riddles, however. She never told him what happened between them. The reason for their break up was unknown. In what way did she want Bartu to change? What did he do to her? If it was something unspeakable, he would deal with him personally when he returned to Beverly Hills. He didn't want him harassing her. "Well, are you ok?"

It was sweet of him to be concerned as a friend should be. "Yes, I'm fine. Did you know that the only reason I'm even back here in Beverly Hills is because Mrs. Trenton got a phone call from *Above Beautiful Modeling Agency* there in New York City? They wanted her to sign my contract over to them, offering to double the amount of money they were receiving for my publicity."

Levi blinked several times at the announcement. That was shocking news! Why would a modeling agency in New York City contact the agency in Beverly Hills without consulting Jazzmine first? "Really?"

"Yes. Mrs. Trenton called me home before they could call me. She wanted to keep me busy so that I couldn't accept their offer. Somehow, they found out that I was in New York City."

There was logic in Mrs. Trenton's actions. There was none in the actions of the other agency, however. It was incomprehensible. Why had they called now all of the sudden? It was normal that the agency would go to the person and offer them the job, letting them decide whether or not they wanted to take it. It was not usual, however, for them to go to the agency first. In fact, they didn't even have to deal with the agency. It was up to the clients to handle that business for themselves. There was something wrong, and Levi wanted to know what it was. "What did you say the name of the agency was?"

"*Above Beautiful.*"

Levi nodded, repeating the name in his head. He was definitely going to investigate because something wasn't right. "Did she say who she spoke with on the phone?"

"Um, I think she said her name was Charlene Barks," Jazzmine answered with a shrug of her shoulders. She guessed that was the woman's name. She didn't really remember and she didn't know why it was important to Levi anyway. "Why? Have you heard of the agency? Do they have a bad reputation?"

"No, I haven't heard of them. I was just wondering."

"Oh," Jazzmine said. "Well, I guess I'll talk to you later." She deliberately forgot to tell him that she was finish with the photo shoot, and she was coming back to New York City. She couldn't wait to see the expression on his face when she showed up unexpectedly.

"Ok. I miss you."

"I miss you, too. Bye."

They hung up.

Levi parked the car on the hospital emergency room parking lot and turned off the engine. He started to get out, but then he stopped. He could not rest until he knew what was going on. He closed the door back and picked up the cell phone again.

He dialed the operator. "Yes, I would like the number to *Above Beautiful Modeling Agency* in New York City please."

He was put on hold for no more than a second. The operator came back to the line to inform him that *Above Beautiful* was a nonexistent company.

He frowned with confusion, feeling positive that *Above Beautiful* was the name that Jazzmine gave him. "Are you sure?"

"Yes, sir."

"Oh, well, thank you." He hung up the phone. Twisting his mouth with confusion, he narrowed his eyes. The wheels of thought were in motion. If

Above Beautiful didn't exist, who called Mrs. Trenton from New York City? *New York City!* After a second, he nodded to himself. He had a good idea who called. To confirm his suspicions, he called the operator again, requesting that she check the records to see who called *Beverly Hills' Beauties* on the day in question and from where. He didn't even need to hear the conversation.

Just as he suspected, she told him that the phone call was made from Vanessa's company. Naturally, he assumed that she made the call personally.

"No wonder she looked so happy when Mrs. Trenton called," he thought, remembering the smirk on Vanessa's face when Jazzmine's cell phone rang while they were in James's room that day. *"She called her to get her to lure Jazzmine back home, but why would she do that? What does this woman have against her sister?"*

Sighing, Levi shook his head, feeling ashamed of Vanessa. He climbed out of the car.

Thursday morning, Levi opened his eyes to the sound of knocking at his hotel suite door. Glancing at the alarm clock, he rubbed his eyes to rid himself of sleep. Whoever it was had to be at the wrong suite. It was five o'clock in the morning. Who could it be? It couldn't be room service because it was too early. He stepped into his slippers and reached for his robe, slipping into it.

Abandoning his warm bed, he went to the living room. Turning on the light, he went to the door. Opening it, he found Jazzmine wearing a huge overcoat and a big smile. Surprised to see her, he blinked to be sure he was actually awake.

"Jazz!" he exclaimed. They spoke over the phone several times yesterday, and she never once mentioned coming back early.

She opened her arms for him. "I'm back!"

Accepting the invitation, Levi hugged her and gently pulled her into the room. "So, what happened? I wasn't expecting you back for another week or two."

"I know! Isn't it great? Mrs. Trenton released me!"

It sure was! Levi missed her terribly while she was away. He was tempted to go home to be with her several times. Helping her off with her coat, he hung it up for her. Taking her hand, he led her to the sofa. They sat down together. "Well, come on. Talk to me. Tell me what happened. Did she cancel your shoot, or are you just here for a few days?" he sounded anxious to know. He hoped she wasn't going to say she was only there for a few days.

Jazzmine's eyes fell upon his robe and she remembered that it was only five o'clock in the morning. She sighed, knowing that she must have disturbed him from his sleep. He usually didn't get up this early. "Oh! Did I wake you? I'm sorry. We can talk later if you want to go back to bed."

"Come on now, Jazz! I haven't seen you in eight... nine days," he reminded her. "I would much rather talk to you."

She smiled. That was sweet of him to say. She answered his question, telling him that she said nothing to him about coming back early yesterday because she wanted to surprise him.

At five o'clock, Vanessa waltzed into her

father's room with a broad smile and a gift basket in her hand. Walking through the door, her eyes landed on Levi and *Jazzmine*! Her smile disappeared, and she almost dropped the basket.

"Jazzmine!" she thought with horror. What was she doing in town? She was supposed to be in California for at least another week. How did she manage to return so swiftly? Fortunately, she was prepared for such an occasion. Forcing a smile, she clinched the basket tighter. "Jazzmine!" she exclaimed, pretending to be happy to see her.

The horrified expression on Vanessa's face at the sight of her sister was enough to tell Levi that she didn't miss her at all. It definitely wasn't a look of happy surprise. When she faked a smile, he thought, *"Too late!"* and looked away with disgust. She couldn't fool him.

James smiled at Vanessa. "I told her you were going to be surprised to see her," he told her.

Sincerely happy to see her sister, Jazzmine hurried across the room to give her a hug.

"I sure am," she said truthfully. Not wanting to, Vanessa returned the hug with her free arm. She had to. Her father was watching. "Hey, honey! When did you get back?" she asked with concern in her voice.

"This morning."

"Why didn't you call me? I would have come to pick you up from the airport."

Levi pitied Vanessa for lying. If Jazzmine had called her, she probably would have made up some lame excuse as to why she couldn't come. She never came to the airport whether Jazzmine was coming or going. She probably would have said she was too sleepy to drive. If she checked her caller ID, she might not have answered the phone. Two seconds was much too long for her to devote to Jazzmine, her own sister. If she could work all day, she should be able to take time out for her sister. That was just too much to ask of Vanessa, however.

Dropping her arm to Jazzmine's waist, Vanessa and Jazzmine went to their father's bedside together. Handing the gift basket to their father, who accepted it with pleasure, Vanessa turned her attention to her sister. "So, how was your trip? Did you get to see Bartu?"

"Why do you care?" Levi asked her mentally, looking from Vanessa to Jazzmine, who dropped her eyes. He would have asked her aloud, but he didn't for James's sake. Surely, he wasn't aware of his oldest daughter feelings about her sister.

Jazzmine's heart sank as she could hear the cheerfulness in her sister's voice at the question. She wrote her sister so many letters telling her about her fabulous relationship with Bartu. She failed to mention their separation, which was saddening. Naturally, Vanessa would wonder how things were progressing between them. "Yes, I saw him, but..." She shook her head, not wanting to discuss the situation. This was actually not the time or place. Levi didn't even know the whole story, yet.

Jazzmine's reaction to the question puzzled Vanessa. She frowned with curiosity. What was going on? Surely, there wasn't trouble in paradise. If there was, she wanted to know all about it! She was anxious to hear every sad, painful detail. Anything that inflicted pain or sorrow in her sister's life was worth hearing. It could brighten her day.

"Jazz?" She placed her hand on her shoulder. "Are you ok?"

"No," Jazzmine whispered.

"Come on. Let's go get us a snack. You can tell me all about it," Vanessa encouraged, anxious to know what happened. She turned her eyes on her father. "Daddy, we'll be back."

James nodded, and Vanessa led Jazzmine away by the hand.

Levi watched them go. He couldn't believe Jazzmine was too blind to see her sister's true colors. He didn't know why Jazzmine thought Vanessa cared what happened between her and Bartu. She couldn't possibly. If she did, she would have called her while she was away. Vanessa didn't even have the decency to call her own sister!

Vanessa sat across from Jazzmine at a table for two in the snack room with her legs crossed. She was listening to Jazzmine tell her about her break up with Bartu, enjoying every second of her pain. The pain in Jazzmine's eyes as she spoke was priceless. She felt better, knowing that her sister's life wasn't so perfect after all. Horrific things happened to her, too! If she had anything to do with it, more horrific things would occur! As she listened, she ate white doughnuts to hide her smile.

Sipping from her bottled cola, Jazzmine concluded, "And he said that he had no intentions of giving up on me. I don't know what to do. I don't want to be with him as much as I used to. I don't even know if my feelings for him are the same. They aren't as strong anymore. I do know that."

Vanessa reached across the table, taking her

sister's hand. "Oh, honey, don't worry. Everything will be fine. I'm sure he's gotten the message by now. If he tried to reach you, he's probably figured out that you're long gone. Let me tell you a secret that I figured out a long time ago. If you let a man into your heart before he makes a commitment to you, a serious commitment, he'll take your heart and run with it! Don't let Bartu do that to you. If he wants you, let him prove it. You'll see the difference. He'll act differently and do things he's never done before. Then if you still want him," she nodded, "pull him in. If not," she shook her head and waved her hand, "say bye-bye."

Jazzmine considered the concept. It made a lot of sense. She was going to take her advice and let Bartu prove that he truly wanted to be with her and not just for her body. She smiled across the table at her sister. "I never thought about that. Thanks!"

Vanessa entwined her fingers and leaned forward, resting her chin on her knuckles. "So, how would you feel if he came here to...?"

Jazzmine held up a hand to stop her sister's question. She had an idea of what she was going to ask. "No," she shook her head. "Bartu knows nothing of my whereabouts. If he showed up here, I wouldn't be able to handle it. I already have a lot on my plate right now. He'll have to wait until I get home."

"Hum!" Vanessa thought. *"Their breakup must have been really horrible for her. Oh well!"* She sighed to herself. *"Things happen!*

Friday morning when Jazzmine and Levi got off the elevator on their way to the restaurant for breakfast, they saw a crowd of people gathered around the entrance window. Some of them were laughing, and others were pointing. They exchanged glances, wondering what was going on.

"Let's go see what's going on," Levi said, anxious to know. He and Jazzmine walked toward the crowd together.

Over a little girl's head, Jazzmine saw a jumbo picture of her and Vanessa when they were younger hanging in the window. Their names were written over their heads in bright red ink. Seeing herself, memories of why she departed New York City came flooding back. She felt so embarrassed. She thought she had abandoned that life six years ago.

The laughter increased, and someone pointed to Jazzmine on the photo, asking, "Who is that? She's fat and ugly! Wonder if anybody wants her?"

"No!" someone else responded, and the entire crowd laughed, minus Levi and Jazzmine.

Levi's eyes darted to Jazzmine. He knew what was happening, and obviously, Jazzmine didn't. She probably didn't have a clue as to what her sister was doing to her. She was just too blind when it came to Vanessa. In her eyes, Vanessa could do no wrong.

Vanessa was definitely behind the little scandal. This was the exact same picture he saw on her desk in her office the other day. No wonder she was looking at it. She was plotting to use it against her sister in her twisted mind. It hadn't been admiration at all!

It was quiet clear now. Vanessa was venting because she was jealous of her sister. Her desire was to get rid of her. That was the reason she had

Mrs. Trenton to lure her back to California. With Jazzmine around, Vanessa wasn't the center of attention, and it was eating her up inside. He suspected her to be spoiled from the beginning, but he had no idea it had escalated to the point where no one else could have the spotlight. She should be proud of her sister. Instead, she was jealous, too envious for her own good.

"Why is this happening to me?" Jazzmine wondered, feeling close to tears. Who could be this cruel? No. She didn't even want to know how the picture got there. She didn't even care. The comments restored her feelings of being the ugly duckling. Jazzmine wanted to die! No matter how she looked now, she was still the same person she had been then. Only her outer appearance had changed. Inside, she would always be the same sensitive person. "That's me," she whispered an answer to the person who asked the question. She turned and walked away.

Levi turned and watched her go. He knew that more than likely she was going into hiding now, which was exactly what Vanessa wanted. He cursed Vanessa under his breath for being so vindictive.

On the way to the hospital, Levi and Jazzmine discovered that the picture was plastered everywhere for the world to view. Each building they passed had the picture in the window, which was deeply upsetting to Levi. It took him an hour to calm Jazzmine down. He suggested that Vanessa was behind the crime, but she refused to hear him. She deemed that the picture had gotten into the wrong hands somehow, and whoever held it wanted to destroy her. Her father could have given the picture away years ago. He was proud enough to have given everyone pictures of his daughters. Suggesting that Vanessa would do this to her was absurd! Her sister loved her too much to hurt her so viciously. She was convinced.

As they drove along Jazzmine held her head down with shame and embarrassment.

Trying to solve Jazzmine's problem and come up with a way to retaliate against Vanessa, Levi thought of the perfect solution. It would resolve the whole ordeal. Apparently, Vanessa wanted everyone to see Jazzmine in a bad light. He had an idea how to stop everything before a huge disaster derived. Vanessa had a surprise for Jazzmine, and he had one for Vanessa.

When he parked the rental in front of the hospital entrance, Levi took Jazzmine's hand before she could open the door. She looked at him. "I have a little errand to run. I'll be back shortly. Tell your father I said good-morning."

She agreed, getting out of the car.

If everything went accordingly, Levi would be back at the hospital before Vanessa arrived. He didn't want her suspecting anything. To be sure everything would work out as smoothly as he hoped, he reached into his back pocket and pulled out his wallet. Flipping through the pictures in it, he found the most recent picture of his best friend before her transformation and the most recent photo of her afterwards. Taking them out, he drove off into traffic.

CHAPTER SEVEN

All day long, Vanessa observed Jazzmine, who moped around with embarrassment. Her reaction was much expected and exactly what Vanessa wanted. Soon Jazzmine would be on the first flight back to California. When something insufferable occurred in her sister's life, her usual was to bail, going as far away as possible. Not being accepted was the most insufferable thing in her life right now.

It was over for *Jazzmine the Beauty Queen!* She was finally going to be seen as the homely little girl she truly was, and Vanessa was anticipating the end result.

Vanessa would sympathize with her father, however. He was going to be hurt that Jazzmine was leaving again. She would be there to console him as always, however.

Jazzmine stayed in her hotel suite for the remainder of the weekend, wanting to keep her face hidden. The spotlight was relinquished to Vanessa, who felt victorious! She was very satisfied with herself for getting her sister to hide herself for at least the weekend. It wasn't enough, but it would do for the time being. Something more permanent would arise in the near future.

Monday morning, Vanessa sat behind her desk working on some files for her father. She was transferring new information from forms onto a disc for him. Working with her eyes on the forms, her fingers moving rapidly on the keyboard, she didn't hear the knock at the door. She looked up when the door opened unexpectedly.

Cassandra burst in with an excited expression on her face. A magazine was in her hand. It was obvious that she was anxious to spread whatever news, and it was detected by the vibes that she perspired. "Vanessa, why didn't you tell me?" It sounded as if she were accusing her of purposely withholding information. Vanessa looked at her with curiosity. She had no idea of what she was speaking.

"I didn't know about this!" Cassandra went on to explain herself. "I know several people who would love to go through this. They would probably come out feeling better about themselves! Confidence is a great thing!"

Vanessa was really confused now. Cassandra was making no sense whatsoever. Turning away from her computer, she shook her head trying to grasp the concept of what was being said. "Why didn't I tell you what? What are you babbling about, Sandra?"

Cassandra inhaled a deep breath to collect herself. Turning the magazine cover around, she exposed the cover. "About this!"

The magazine cover was horrifying! Vanessa was confused, petrified, and utterly disgusted all at once. Furious, Vanessa leaned forward and snatched the book from her business partner's hands. "Let me see that!" Her eyes ran over the headline, which read **Behind the Scenes, What You Didn't Know**. Below the headline were two pictures of Jazzmine, a before and an after. The before was nothing to brag about, of course, but the after made her look like a living angel!

Angry that her plan reversed to go in Jazzmine's favor, Vanessa flipped through the tabloid and quickly read the article of how Jazzmine blossomed into the beautiful model she was today. Closing the magazine and tossing it aside, she leaned back in the chair and sighed with irritation.

How did something good derive from the picture she spread around? This was supposed to be Vanessa's time to gloat.

The girl in her photo and the girl in the magazine were entirely different. The one from her photo was young, much younger than the one in the tabloid. From where did this picture of young Jazzmine come? Who did this for her? Why was it that every time she proceeded with the perfect plan to get rid of Jazzmine, everything seemed to backfire, and she stayed longer?

Vanessa had to do something. If she and her sister stayed in the same city much longer, she would go insane! There was no limit as to what she would do to get rid of her sister! What could she do, however? Nothing seemed to be successful thus far. The only thing that would really work was for their father to have a miraculous recovery and be released from the hospital. That was something for which she had no control. If she did, none of this would have happened. Her father wouldn't have been in the accident in the first place, and she would never have called Jazzmine home.

New York City wasn't large enough for the both of them. One of them had to go, and it wasn't going to be Vanessa! Jazzmine was the one who needed to go. She had a fabulous life in Beverly Hills. Vanessa had a fabulous life until Jazzmine flew into town and destroyed everything for her. Did she steal the spotlight everywhere she went? If she did, she needed to go somewhere else!

That evening, Vanessa came to the hospital barely saying a word to anyone. Her anger was too obvious. She refused to share with anyone, however. She sat on the window ledge staring out at the rest of the hospital with a wondrous expression on her face. She spent the entire evening trying to strategize a new approach of getting Jazzmine out of her hair.

Jazzmine wasn't even missed back in California, which was apparent because she was shipped back to New York City too swiftly. The fact that she was a former alien's twin was of no interest to anyone. The only interest anyone had was in her present life as a glamorous model.

It was driving Vanessa up the wall! Hopefully, Jazzmine would get bored of living a normal lifestyle and want to return to her own lifestyle. Surely, she wanted to make more money. What would it take to get her to leave? Vanessa was almost desperate!

Tuesday evening, Vanessa sat in her living room watching television.

Jazzmine was in the kitchen keeping the maid company while she prepared dinner, which Vanessa didn't mind at all. Not being in the same room with her was a relief. She preferred they not be in the same house, but Jazzmine just dropped by unexpectedly. To be nice, she let her in. She should have told her she didn't feel well, and to never come back!

Vanessa sat on the sofa with one leg drawn under her and the other foot on the floor. The television remote was in her lap.

Slippers were on her feet as she was lounging. As soon as she got home, she went upstairs to her room to slip out of the brown and gold silk pantsuit and brown heels. To relax, she showered and changed into a simple blouse and casual pants.

As she was leaving her bedroom, the doorbell rang. Too lazy to find suitable flats to put on, she slipped into the black fuzzy slippers and ran downstairs to answer the door. When she got there, she wished she had searched for the shoes. Perhaps, Jazzmine would have gotten tired of waiting and left. With her luck, the maid would have gotten tired of the doorbell ringing and answered it.

Now Vanessa sat on the sofa watching a TV show about two sisters who loved each other. It was so fake to her that she felt sick to her stomach. How could two sisters love each other so much that they would decide to go into business together? She could never see that happening between her and Jazzmine. She could never see herself loving Jazzmine enough to do anything with her! She certainly didn't want to go into business with her. That would mean seeing her on a daily basis, and that was definitely not an enticing thought. She would prefer to be sole proprietor before she let that happen! It was enough that they had to see each other everyday at the hospital.

The office was a whole different ball game. It was Vanessa's territory. Jazzmine wasn't going to take over that, too!

The doorbell rang, bringing her out of her trance.

Vanessa placed the remote on the coffee table, and went to the door. "I'll get it, Della," she called to the maid. At the door, she stopped and looked down at her outfit. *"Oh no,"* she thought. She wasn't expecting guests. Her appearance wasn't presentable. If she had known someone was coming by, she would have kept her pantsuit on. The way things were going lately, it was probably just Levi coming to see Jazzmine.

Assuming it was he who rang the doorbell, she opened the door. Embarrassment burned her face. She almost turned red. Támeo Dudley, one of her many associates whom she had gone out with on several occasions, stood on her doorstep with a lovely bouquet of roses in one hand and a bottle of the finest champagne in the other. He was wearing a charming navy suit, and he smelled excellent as usual.

"Támeo!" Vanessa exclaimed, surprised to see him. "What are you doing here?"

"Well, hello, to you too, Gorgeous!"

Vanessa smiled broadly. It was wonderful that someone still thought she was gorgeous.

Támeo returned the smile, extending the

roses to her. He lightly shook the bottle of champagne in front of her. "I brought champagne."

"Ah! Támeo, that's so sweet!" She blushed, feeling flattered that he thought about her at all. She hadn't gotten much attention lately, and she needed it. "Oh! Where are my manners?" She realized that he was still standing outside. "Come in! Come in!"

"Thank you." Támeo stepped inside and turned to face her. His eyes went over her attire, and he laughed with amusement. It was so unlike her to be dressed so plainly. He was used to her dressing up just to go to the bathroom, and the slippers were something he never would have expected to see in a million years. "What's the matter, Vanessa? Are you feeling ok?" he teased.

"Oh!" Her eyes went down to her outfit, as well, and her embarrassment returned. "Do I look that bad?" She imagined she probably looked like a spectacle of some sort. He had never seen her look so pathetic.

"Actually, I like it! It's a change, but I like it!"

Vanessa opened her mouth to speak, but Jazzmine's voice drowned hers out as she burst into the room from the kitchen. "Oh, Vanessa, Della..." she quickly silenced herself when she realized that her sister was entertaining company. "Oh! I'm sorry. I didn't know you had company!"

At Jazzmine's voice, Támeo glanced over his shoulder. Seeing her, his mouth dropped, and he turned fully to face her. At her breathtaking beauty he couldn't help staring.

Jazzmine stood in the kitchen door wearing a sleeveless cream top with a cream and burgundy skirt. Her hair looked fabulous as it was pinned up into an elegant updu. Burgundy earrings dangled from her ears.

Seeing Támeo, Jazzmine had to smile. He was very handsome, whoever he was. Vanessa's height with a clean baldhead, he had smooth golden brown skin. His mustache was thin, the only facial hair he possessed. He possessed features of an older man, possibly in his late thirties or early forties. He was nice looking for his age. He looked absolutely charming in the handsome gray business suit.

Before Vanessa knew anything, Támeo shoved the champagne bottle into her free hand, and he went to Jazzmine. She observed him silently.

He smiled at Jazzmine, taking her hand. "Well, hello, there!" he said in a flirtatious voice. "I don't believe we've met. I am Támeo Dudley, and you..." he lifted her hand to his mouth, lightly brushing it with his lips, "are beautiful!" He didn't release her hand.

Flattered, Jazzmine laughed softly. "Thank you! I'm Jazzmine, Vanessa's younger sister."

"Well! Come over here," he turned, switching her hand from his right hand to the left when she was behind him. He led her to the sofa, and they sat down together. "I want to know all about Vanessa's younger sister."

For ten minutes, Vanessa stood in the same spot holding the roses and champagne, listening to Támeo flirt with Jazzmine. He constantly told her how beautiful she was, and that he loved her eyes, into which he gazed. She couldn't believe he had completely ignored her to flirt with Jazzmine! Now, she could relate to how Jazzmine felt when she used to get all of the attention when they were younger. It was as if she were giving her a taste of her own medicine.

Vanessa hated it! Stealing the spotlight from her was one thing, but when it came to stealing her men, Vanessa was not having it! Now, she was desperate to get Jazzmine out of her life *forever*!

Enraged, she left the two of them in the living room and went to the kitchen to put the roses in water and the champagne on ice. Moving about the room in an angry manner, she disturbed the maid, who looked up at her in surprise. She had never seen her so upset. The maid inquired if she was all right.

She answered in a harsh tone, which led the maid to believe she wanted to be left alone. She held her hands up in surrender.

Vanessa went back to the living room to find Támeo leaning over Jazzmine as if he wanted to kiss her, which he probably did. Jazzmine seemed to be enjoying the attention. Loathing her sister to a point of strangling her, Vanessa ran up the stairs to her room and slammed her bedroom door.

The door slammed loudly enough to be heard downstairs.

Started by the door slam, Jazzmine jumped a little and looked back at the stairs as if she could see the door from where she was sitting. Having no idea what was wrong with her sister, she shook her head. She would be all right.

Wednesday morning, Vanessa tapped her nails on her desktop as she sat behind her desk, plotting. Her anger with Jazzmine had gone beyond a point of return. If she didn't get rid of her soon, her father would loose both of his *beautiful* daughters! He would loose Jazzmine to *death* as she would kill her! Of course, then, Vanessa would be confined to imprisonment.

The situation was out of control! She stayed in her room for the remainder of the night last night. After what happened with Támeo and Jazzmine, she didn't even bother to see Jazzmine out. It was just too hard to cope with the idea of *anyone* stealing men from her.

"What can I do?" she asked herself. Contemplating, she frowned with narrowed eyes. There had to be something she could do.

Suddenly, an idea popped into her head, and she arched her eyebrows, wondering if it would work. Biting her bottom lip with happiness, she picked up the telephone. *"There are a few people who owe me a favor,"* she thought, hoping at least one of them was available. "Yes, is Sam in? ... Hi, Sam, it's Vanessa. Look, I need you to do me a favor." She nodded when the person on the other end agreed to do whatever she asked. "Listen, all I want you to do is go to that place you went to the other night... Yes," she nodded, again. "Meet me there this evening. I'll tell you exactly what I want you to do for me. This is major! I really need your help. I'll be there as soon as I leave the office... Thank you! You're a lifesaver!"

With a mischievous smile on her face, she glanced at her computer and then away. After a split second, her eyes darted back to the computer as another idea popped into her head. The smile widened as she thought of the internet and her E-mail account. It could be very useful to her right now. She was going to use it to her advantage. *"Hum,"* she thought with a nod of approval. *"Maybe there is something I can do, and if all else fails, this one just might work!"*

She was going to get rid of Jazzmine one way or another. She was determined!

Turning to her computer, she nodded and typed in the code for her E-mail account.

As they walked down the hall together toward their father's hospital room, Vanessa wrapped her arm around Jazzmine's shoulder. "Hey, Jazz, we haven't had any fun since you've been here. Why don't we go out this weekend? It'll be just the two of us. I know just the place to go. They just opened a new club on Dell Boulevard, and it's definitely the hotspot! You'll love it!"

Jazzmine was all in favor of having a good time. It would be nice to finally get to hang out with her sister even though she wasn't a club person. She and Levi seldom went to the club together back home. It wouldn't hurt to go out with her sister just this once. "Ok. I'm game."

Vanessa smiled. She had a big surprise for Jazzmine. As long as Levi stayed home, nothing could possibly go wrong. She just didn't need his interference. Once Jazzmine was out of the hotel, it would be all over for her. There would be no stopping Vanessa. "I'll be by the hotel to pick you up around eight o'clock."

Jazzmine nodded with agreement. "I'll be ready."

Friday night, Levi sat on the edge of Jazzmine's bed, watching her apply her makeup. He didn't want her to go out with Vanessa, but it wasn't his place to say anything. She was a free woman.

Vanessa *was* her sister, but he still had reservations about the whole ordeal. Why did she suddenly want to spend time with Jazzmine? Vanessa had something up her sleeve. He could sense it.

Jazzmine, sitting at the vanity applying her lipstick, looked at Levi through the mirror. The expression on his face was that of worry, and he had no reason to be worried. Glancing over her shoulder at him, she said, "Levi, relax! I'm just going to have a little fun. I would invite you to come along, but you know how it is. Tonight it's going to be just the two of us."

Levi lifted his eyes to her with arched eyebrows. Did she actually believe he wanted to go? He didn't want to go anywhere with Vanessa because he wouldn't enjoy himself. He would feel obligated to keep an eye on her all night. There was no telling what she was capable of doing. She didn't seem to have any morals about herself. Shaking his head, he said nothing. He would keep his comments about her sister repressed. She wouldn't listen anyway. "Go, Jazz," he said in a low voice. "Have a good time."

She stood up. "I will."

He looked up at her. She did look gorgeous in the black halter dress. Her hair was in a nice updu. His heart almost skipped a beat, and for a moment, he wished he were going with her. He didn't want other men falling over her. But then, that was something he had been dealing with since she became a model. She was a beautiful woman, and he was quite aware. She wasn't his woman, however, which was, also, something in which he had been dealing even longer.

Inhaling a deep breath to calm himself, he

closed his eyes. Opening them again, he had to ask, "Where is this club anyway?" He needed to know just in case he decided to drop by, which he wouldn't. He just didn't want to not know where she was in case something happened. He could call her cell phone, but that didn't mean she would answer. They were going to a club! She may not even take it with her.

"Oh, it's just down the street on Dell Boulevard. I can't recall the name off hand."

"Oh great!" he thought. Jazzmine was from New York City. Getting to her destination was not a problem for her as she knew her way around the city. He knew no more than the little he learned since he had been there. He could get to the hospital, the hotel, the studio, Vanessa's company and a few other miscellaneous places without asking directions. He knew nothing about Dell Boulevard. The fact that she didn't know the name of the club was even worse. He didn't know where to find her if anything happened.

There was a soft knock at the door.

Jazzmine turned toward the bedroom door as if it were the front door. "Well," she turned back to Levi, "I'll see you later." She gave him a hug. Then, she was out the door.

Yes, Levi would definitely be waiting for her when she returned. He wouldn't be able to rest until she was safe back at the hotel with him. Closing his eyes when he heard the front door close, he silently asked the Lord to protect her while she was gone.

Jazzmine and Vanessa entered the club together.

The smile on Vanessa's face was huge. Tonight, she was equally beautiful as her sister. No one could say differently. The short navy dress was sleeveless with spaghetti straps that crisscrossed several times in the back. Her whole back was exposed. Her hair and makeup was flawless. Her hair was straight with layered flips. The flips were bouncy and soft. The navy earrings were pretty and dangly. One was exposed clearly as one side of her hair was behind her ear.

She held her head high as she was confident in her appearance. No one would push her over for Jazzmine tonight.

Walking through the entrance, the smile on Jazzmine's face faded. Her mind flashed back to the last time she made an entrance in a club in New York City. For a moment, she felt like that person again. Her eyes darted around the room as it felt that everyone was staring at them. *"This is not Club Ten, and you are not the same person you were that night!"* she had to remind herself. She looked at Vanessa, who was smiling from ear to ear. Apparently, she was expecting to enjoy herself tonight. For her sake, she would try to enjoy herself. *"Pull yourself together,"* she willed herself.

As Vanessa and Jazzmine moved farther into the room, Vanessa's eyes darted around the room in search of Sam.

He was there at the bar. He was watching the door over his shoulder. When he saw her, he threw up two fingers in greeting. Then, he turned back to his alcoholic beverage.

Satisfied, Vanessa led Jazzmine to a booth, and they sat across from each other.

They conversed, Vanessa making idle chitchat. Her eyes consistently found the bar as they were talking. She couldn't wait to get the balls rolling, but it was too soon. Her eyes went back to Jazzmine, who was saying something to her. She pretended to be listening. All the while her mind was elsewhere.

Jazzmine was having a ball! She danced and laughed with Vanessa and her many male associates. She couldn't wait to tell Levi about her evening when she returned to the hotel. He crossed her mind, and she decided to take a break from dancing. She abandoned the dance floor to return to the booth.

Vanessa followed her, but she didn't sit down. "I'm going to the bar. Do you want anything to drink?"

Jazzmine wasn't a drinker. She didn't particularly acquire the taste of alcohol. "No thanks."

Vanessa walked up to Sam and sat on the stool beside him. Crossing her legs, she rested one elbow on the countertop and the other on the back of the chair. "Well, Sam, you do remember what to do, don't you?"

Sam looked at her, his eyes going over her in the dress. With a half smile, he lifted his eyes to her face. "Yeah, I got it. You know I'll come through for you. It is the babe who came in with you, right?" His voice was deep and raspy, almost scary.

"Yes!"

Sam shook his head, glancing at Jazzmine over his shoulder. "I don't know why you want me to do this. She's sexy!"

Vanessa held up a hand. There was no time

for questions. She didn't particularly care to hear his summary of Jazzmine's appearance. He agreed to help her, and that was all she wanted from him. "Just do it," she whispered.

He wasn't there for an argument, and he did agree to help. Sam just didn't understand why Vanessa wanted to hurt someone as beautiful as the woman with whom she made her entrance. *"Oh well,"* he thought. It wasn't his business anyway. He nodded with agreement and stood up.

Vanessa watched him go with anticipation.

Sam walked up to Jazzmine, casting a shadow.

Jazzmine looked up.

Sam was a nice looking man. With his build, he could pass for a bodybuilder. His torso was very nice and firm as he was wearing a tank top, exposing his tattooed biceps. His hands and feet were big, larger than the average men she knew. His hair was in dreads as he, obviously, wasn't into getting a haircut on the regular.

Although he was nice looking, the way he towered over Jazzmine was frightening. She swallowed hard forcing herself to smile. Who was he, and what did he want? Perhaps, he had mistaken her for someone else. It was rather dark in the room as the lights were dimmed.

His voice was deep as he said, "Hey! You're Vanessa Thomas's sister, aren't you?"

She nodded nervously, wondering why he wanted to know. Her voice was lost somewhere as she couldn't even speak. She didn't dare ask the question on her mind as she was afraid of how he would respond.

"She was called away, and she asked me to

take you to her whereabouts," he explained, excluding to give his own name and his relationship with her sister.

Jazzmine was simple stunned. He was making no sense whatsoever because his statement was utterly ridiculous! She didn't even know him, and he expected her to just get up and leave with him because he gave her some line about Vanessa telling him to take her someplace? He was dumber than he looked if he believed that. Her eyes darted to the bar in search of Vanessa. She wasn't there.

She was even more nervous now. What was going on? Where was Vanessa really? With hope that he would leave her alone, she said, "No thanks. I think I'll just wait for her right here. I'm sure it won't be long before..."

"She's not coming back!" Sam objected to her staying. "She told me to be sure I didn't leave you here alone."

Jazzmine was curious as to why Vanessa left without saying anything to her. They came together, and they were supposed to leave together. If she was so concerned that she was left alone, why did she leave her? It was absolutely absurd! Perhaps, she should call Levi to come and get her because she had no desire to leave with this stranger.

Vanessa, standing off to a distance watching Sam and Jazzmine, frowned with dismay. She glanced at her watch, wondering what was taking so long. They were supposed to be gone by now. "Get up, Jazzmine," she hissed in a low voice. In order for her plan to work, Jazzmine had to cooperate. Her refusal to leave wasn't calculated into the plan. What could she do...? A mischievous smile tugged at her lips as the perfect idea popped into her head. She would get Jazzmine out of there.

She dashed off to the ladies' room.

"Please," Jazzmine was saying when she heard a vibrating ringing sound. It sounded like her cell phone, but she wasn't sure. When she heard it again, she glanced down at her purse, deciding that it probably was. Opening the purse, the phone rang, again. Pulling up the antenna, she flipped the phone open, clamping her hand over her other ear to hear. The music was too loud. "Hello?"

"Jazz, it's Vanessa. I'm sorry I had to rush off like that, but I got an urgent call, and I had to leave immediately. I sent a good friend of my, Andrew Pondexter, for you. He's going to bring you to me," Vanessa hurried to explain, not bothering to say hello.

Jazzmine's heart sank as she was expecting Levi to be on the other end. Hearing Vanessa's voice, she felt a weak feeling in the pit of her stomach. She really did expect her to leave with this stranger, which she didn't think was such a good idea.

The phone was echoing in Jazzmine's ear. Vanessa sounded distant. "Vanessa? Where are you?"

Why did everyone have to ask questions about everything? Vanessa was becoming frustrated as it was as simple as pie. All that was required was for Jazzmine to do as she requested. It wasn't hard. There was no time for questions. "Please, Jazz," she pleaded. "Honey, I really do have to go now. I'll see you in a little bit." She hung up in Jazzmine's ear.

Walking beside her, Sam led Jazzmine behind the building into a dark alley. She kept up with his pace, fear rising in her chest, as the alley grew darker. She had no idea they were going to walk to Vanessa's whereabouts. They left the club a little ways back, and now she had no idea where she was. She was extremely uncomfortable, and she should have followed her first mind, which instructed her to call Levi. Vanessa's phone call just threw her for a loop, the unpredicted. Had she known she was so busy, she wouldn't have agreed to come.

When they were in what seemed to be the middle of nowhere, he grabbed Jazzmine's arm, clutching it tight.

Shocked at his abrupt abusiveness, Jazzmine snapped her head around to see that Sam was gone. His replacement was a big husky man with a mask. He was even bigger than Sam, and his ski mask was black with yellow outlining. His short sleeved shirt was black with a skull on the front, which was scary within itself.

Just the sight of him was enough to make her knees quiver. She was scared. Her desire was to scream, but it seemed to get tangled in her throat. Trying to snatch her arm away, she found her voice and managed to say, "Ow! You're hurting me!"

He clutched her arm tighter, jerking her forward, at her words.

"Please, let me go," she pleaded, fear rising by the second. Her arm was throbbing, and she was sure it would be bruised tomorrow.

"You want me to let you go? OK!" His voice was much deeper than Sam's. It almost sounded as if his throat should hurt when he spoke. Releasing her arm, he slung her to the cold hard ground.

Landing on her back, she hurt her buttocks. Before she could move, he dropped to his knees, which he used to pin her arms to her side, paralyzing her. His hand clamped around her jaw, squeezing tight. "If you scream, you'll only make matters worse," he warned.

Jazzmine was petrified as she had no idea of his agenda. Obviously, he wasn't trying to make a new friend! She inhaled a deep breath, careful not to scream. She looked up at the masked man with fear in her eyes. *"Why? Why me?"* she wanted to ask. She was innocent as she wouldn't hurt a flee. Still, he must have her mistaken for someone else as she had no need for such cruel punishment.

He mocked the fear in her eyes with laughter as he was enjoying it. Using his free hand, he produced a roll of duct tape from his back pocket. He struggled to tear off a piece, tossing the roll aside.

Realizing his agenda now, Jazzmine began to panic. She didn't want him to tape her mouth shut. The next thing he would do was tie her up and hold her for ransom, if nothing even more so severe. Surely, he had no idea of her identity. If he didn't, she wouldn't foolishly *inform* him. He was making a huge mistake, and she would *show* him.

Jazzmine wiggled and squirmed, trying to free herself, but he was much too strong.

He leaned down to place the tape over her mouth, but she bit him. He yelped, cursing under his breath, as he attempted to shake the pain from his finger. When his guard was down, Jazzmine was able to wiggle her hands free. With a hard shove, she pushed him off of her and broke into a run.

Running fast, she screamed for help, but there wasn't a single soul in sight.

He was right behind her, keeping up with her fast pace.

Despite her tiredness, she kept running, panting.

Suddenly, he reached out and pushed her to the ground. She went down with a hard thump, hurting her chest and the side of her face.

He landed on her back.

Jazzmine screamed, begging him not to hurt her.

Despite her plea, he grabbed her arm and turned her to face him. "You are going to pay for running away," he hissed.

She swallowed hard, wanting desperately to get away. "Please!" she begged.

"Shut up!" he demanded, slapping her.

"No!" she yelled in her mind. He was not going to get away with that. If only she could free her hands, she would give him the fight of his life. No man would ever hit her and get away with it. She didn't care if he was as big as the tallest building in New York City. If she didn't tear him down, she would go down trying.

He tugged at the choker on her dress, almost choking her. He was hoping to break the snap, but he didn't.

"NO!" she screamed aloud this time.

He disregarded her objection and tugged at

the choker again. This time he hurt the back of her neck. When he pulled the choker, the back of her head jerked, and she yelped in pain.

He would not get her out of her clothes. She wouldn't allow it. She didn't care what she had to do, but she had to get away.

His hand went around her neck to the snap on her choker. Surprising him, she spit in his eye and mustered strength from nowhere to push him off of her.

He flew backward, landing against a brick wall. His hand was over his eye as he attempted to wipe away the spit.

Anger rose to the surface, overpowering her fear, which still remained in some form. Suppressing her fear, Jazzmine calmly walked over to him. Without warning, she kicked him in the stomach with her heel. "Don't you **ever** touch me again!"

He didn't respond, and she kicked him again even harder. He fell to his face. When his back was to her, she stomped him into the concrete three times, and then she kicked him over onto his back. Although he was wearing the mask, she could tell his face was hurt underneath. Blood was seeping through the mask.

She felt like smashing his head into the wall, but she didn't want to go too far. All she wanted to do was teach him a lesson. Believing that she had done so and not wanting him to come after her again, she turned and broke into a run.

Jazzmine did not stop running until she was back at the hotel. Even then, she raced the stairs to her suite. She didn't have time to wait for an elevator. She didn't know if the man was following her because she never looked back. She wanted to be in the safety of her own hotel suite where she could call security if necessary.

Breathing deeply, she prepared to slip the key into the lock, but the door to Levi's suite opened. Startled, she jumped.

He, wearing a robe and slippers, stepped out with wonder in his eyes. Seeing Jazzmine leaning against her door as if she were trying to hide from someone, he arched his eyebrows at her. Her nose was bleeding, and she looked like she had just seen a ghost. "Jazz? I thought I heard someone running down the hall..." His sentence faded as he realized that it must have been she who was running down the hall. "What happened? Are you ok?"

Swallowing hard, she shook her head. No, she wasn't all right. She probably wouldn't be for a long time. Had she not gotten away, she could have been a rape victim or even worse, *dead*! That psycho could have raped and killed her!

Pushing the door to his suite open, Levi invited her in. "Come in. Tell me what happened." The concern in his voice was genuine.

Jazzmine slowly stepped forward. When she moved, she felt the blood drip from her nose for the first time, and her hand went to the dripping blood. She didn't even know she was bleeding until now. Shaking her head, she moved past him into the suite.

He stepped inside and closed the door.

After Jazzmine explained the whole story to him, Levi, who was on his knees in front of her as she sat on the sofa, was overwhelmed with disbelief. He had known something terrible would happen. If he could have, he would have forbid her to go to the club, and she would never have gone through such a terrible ordeal.

Vanessa's twisted mind just never stopped working. Speaking of the *Devil Sister*, where was she now anyway? Then again, he knew she was smart enough not to show her face around again until tomorrow when she was to show up at the hospital. He expected that she was going to act innocent and pretend she knew nothing about Jazzmine's brutal attack. She couldn't fool him. He knew she was the culprit.

Looking up at her as she held her head down, Levi asked, "Did you see his face?"

"No. I told you he had on a mask."

He lowered his eyes, wishing she had taken the mask off when she had him pinned down to the concrete, but he knew she probably wasn't thinking at the time. He went on to ask, "Are you ok? Is there anything I can do for you?"

She shook her head, not wanting anything. "I'm fine."

She was already upset. There was no need to add to her anger or stress. Levi decided against asking her where Vanessa was or what happened to her. If he had to, he would take care of her personally. They didn't even have to talk if she didn't so desire. He just wanted her to know that he was there for her.

Jazzmine sniffed, wiping her eyes as she was crying. The experience had been too much for her, leaving her traumatized. Lifting her head, she cleared her throat. "Levi, I think I'm just going to go to bed now."

He stood up when she stood up. "Well, do you want me to come with you?"

She walked pass him to the door. Holding up a hand, she answered, "No, I'll be all right."

Not protesting her leaving, Levi turned to watch her go. If she didn't want him there, he would leave her alone.

Vanessa would get exactly what was coming to her. When it hit her, he hoped it would hit her hard!

Screaming, Jazzmine woke up from a nightmare in a panic. She sprang upright in the bed. This was the third nightmare she had tonight. She couldn't get over what happened to her. It was horrible.

Stretching out again, she turned over on her side and tried to settle down under the cover.

Although it was her imagination, she kept hearing strange sounds and her eyes kept darting around the room as if she thought someone else was there. *"Oh, my God!"* she thought, sitting up in bed again. *"I'll never be able to sleep at this rate!"*

Thinking that she heard something outside her window, she sprang out of bed and dashed to the door separating her suite from Levi's. She burst into his room unannounced.

Levi was sound asleep, tucked under the covers. He heard nothing.

Jazzmine went to the bed and lightly shook him.

Slowly coming out of his dream, he moaned with his eyes still closed. "Hum?"

"Levi," she whispered. He didn't wake up completely. "Levi!" she called louder, and he finally opened his eyes still feeling a little drowsy.

Thinking that he was imagining Jazzmine standing beside his bed in the pink silk pajamas, Levi blinked and rubbed his eyes. "Jazz? Is that you?"

"Yes," she whispered. "I couldn't sleep. May I please sleep in here with you?" She knew it was a lot to ask, but he was her friend. He understood that she needed his comfort.

Levi didn't even have to think about it. Tossing back the cover, he invited her into his bed. Of course she could sleep with him! He would love to have her in his bed, to wake up with her next to him. That was a dream come true. He probably should pinch himself to be certain he wasn't dreaming.

Jazzmine climbed into bed with him, and he covered her up. Knowing that she would feel safe next to him, she slid close to him, asking, "Levi, would you *please* hold me?" The security of his arms was exactly what she needed. It would allow her to rest more easily and feel protected as she always felt safe with him.

That was another question he didn't need to consider. It would be his pleasure to hold her. Opening his arms to her, he allowed her to slide into them, and he encased her. Knowing that she needed his comfort, he talked to her about whatever came to mind until she drifted off to sleep. He shortly fell asleep afterward.

CHAPTER EIGHT

Saturday morning, Vanessa sat in her father's room with a huge frown on her face. Her arms were folded across her chest as she pouted. Tapping her foot with anger, she shook her head with narrowed eyes.

It was just remarkable to know that Jazzmine, her scary sister, was able to tackle someone as large as Larry, Sam's older brother. She hired Larry to do as much damage to Jazzmine as humanly possible. Instead, it was the other way around. It was upsetting to discover that she didn't get her money's worth.

How did it happen anyway? Jazzmine had always been scary, the first person to run, and last night, she had to find courage to stand up for herself. What triggered it?

With a sigh, Vanessa sat up straight, dropping her arms. Her eyes went to her father, who was still asleep. Everything was going to be all right. She still had a few tricks up her sleeve. Her poor father was going to be hurt when Jazzmine left New York City for good this time, but he would be all right. She would make sure of it. He would be sad for a while, but she wouldn't let him get as depressed as he was before. That was how the accident resulted in the first place because he buried himself in his work. She was going to be taking over for him now. So, there was no excuse. He was going to have to face reality. Jazzmine wouldn't be around forever.

Vanessa glanced at her watch.

Jazzmine was due to be arriving at the hospital soon.

She sighed to herself, hoping her plan didn't fail this time. If it did, she didn't know what it would take to get rid of Jazzmine. She had a strong feeling this plan wouldn't fail because it was sure to be full proof!

Jazzmine rounded the corner on her way to her father's room. Unexpectedly a hand snaked out and grabbed her arm. In a panic thinking it was her attacker from the previous night, she jerked her arm away and balled both fists. She was ready to pounce on whoever it was.

He held up both hands in surrender as he had never seen her so up on her defenses. This was so unlike her. "Sorry!" was all that could be said at the moment.

Relieved that it was only Bartu, Jazzmine's hand rose to her heart in attempt to bring her heart rate back to its normal pace. After a second, she blinked with surprise and looked at him again. *"Bartu?"*

What was he doing in New York City? How did he find her at the hospital? Astonished, she took a step backward.

Bartu laughed at the surprised look on her face. It almost looked as if she didn't even know him, and she was surprised that the stranger had approached her. He could just as easily have been a fan. She wouldn't have treated a fan that way. At least, he hoped she wouldn't. "I guess I better stop sneaking up on you like that, huh?"

"I guess you better explain your presence in this hospital!" Jazzmine said. This explanation had better be a good one. If he didn't have a sick relative in this hospital, she might be tempted to report him as a stalker.

"What?" Bartu was actually surprised by the statement. She was being ridiculous. His presence in the hospital should need no explanation. He received an E-mail message from her telling him that she missed him, and she was ready to reconcile with him. It specifically stated that if he really wanted to be with her, he had to come and get her. She was the one who told him where she was and what happened with her father. Why was she playing dumb? Did she not expect him to come? He told her he had no intentions of giving up on her. She shouldn't have expected anything less than his guest appearance.

He returned her E-mail message, telling her that he had to finish the job he was working on, and he would be on the first flight to New York City, which was scheduled to land this morning. Naturally, he assumed she received the message. Obviously, she didn't. If she wasn't going to read her messages, why did she send him one?

"You heard me. I want to know what you're doing here," Jazzmine arched her eyebrows, waiting for his response. "How did you find me?"

"You have to be kidding!" Bartu didn't like this game she was playing. If he didn't want to be with her, he wouldn't have moved so abruptly. What more did she want from him? There wasn't much more he could do to prove himself. He was there in the flesh.

"I know Mrs. Trenton didn't tell you where I was going because I asked her not to. How...?"

"I got your E-mail," Bartu answered.

"E-mail? I never wrote you any E-mail!" Jazzmine replied with a frown. "What are you talking about?"

This was ridiculous! She called him all the way from California, telling him there was a chance of reconciliation. Now she was playing games. He didn't have time for this. She knew exactly of what he was referring. He wasn't going to play this game with her. Did she write the message to see how far he was willing to go to be with her? If she did, he hoped he proved himself because he wasn't going home without her.

Bartu waved a hand, dismissing the E-mail situation completely. "Look, Jazz, I didn't come here for this. I came here because I know that we belong together. I know you feel it, too. You have to. I know you can't just forget what we had."

Jazzmine lowered her eyes. It was true. What they shared was beautiful. She would never forget the countless nights they walked along the beach barefoot, and the way they cuddled up on rainy nights. She would, also, never forget the way he tried to pressure her into sleeping with him.

Having a terrible flashback, she lifted her eyes. That was all part of the past, and she had to move on. He hadn't changed, and he couldn't make her believe he had. "No, Bartu, I can't forget," she answered truthfully, which caused him to smile. "I can't forget the way you tried get me in bed with you, and..."

He held up a hand to silence her, the smile fading. She had to get over that. They would sleep together when the time was right, but it would never happen if they didn't stop feuding. He wanted to make things right with her. That would never happen as long as she couldn't get pass him wanting to sleep with her. Of course, he did! It was an undeniable fact. What man wouldn't want to sleep with her? It was a part of life. He didn't know why she was making such a big deal out of it. "Jazz, would you please just let that go?"

Ok. She could do that. "Fine." Jazzmine turned and prepared to walk away, but he grabbed her arm, again. Turning her to face him, he grabbed both of her arms, shaking her lightly.

Before either of them knew anything, Levi was between them. He knocked Bartu's arms away from Jazzmine and pushed him into the wall with a hard shove. His arm went back, and he made a fist, prepared to punch him if he made one wrong move.

Jazzmine screamed when Levi pushed Bartu. Not wanting him to hurt him, she grabbed his arm before he could land the fist in Bartu's face. It was so barbaric to fight, and she wouldn't allow either of them to do so, not in her presence. Levi came along at that wrong time, but she appreciated the fact that he was willing to fight for her honor, and he would accept nothing less than respect for her. "Levi, no," she pleaded in a panicky voice.

Jazzmine's scream disturbed several patients. Some of their relatives opened their doors and peeped into the hallway. Several people came out to check on the disturbing commotion.

Vanessa, hearing Jazzmine's scream, knew she must have gotten her surprise. She went to her father's door to peep out. She was anxious to see what was going on. The scene before her was shocking, however. Things did not look good from where she stood. Hoping that things would turn around, she stood at the door and observed.

Levi, who was holding Bartu to the wall with one hand, released him and took a step backward. He kept his eyes on him.

Jazzmine sighed with relief. She didn't want Levi to do anything he would regret later.

Bartu straightened up, fixing his shirt. He turned a hurt expression on Jazzmine. *"Levi again!"* he thought. He should have expected as much. Truthfully, he didn't expect to see Levi, and it hurt him to actually stand face to face with him at the hospital. Reality settled in, and he realized that he had probably been there by her side the entire time. It was painful because he had to receive the news about her father in an *e-mail*! Perhaps, there was more to the story than Jazzmine was letting on. If she was and Levi were just *friends*, an outsider would definitely be deceived. Now, even he was skeptical about the actual nature of their relationship. If she turned to Levi *first* for *everything*, there had to be something deeper than friendship.

"I should have known *he* would be lurking somewhere nearby," he spoke his thoughts. His tone was none too pleased.

Insulted by the comment, Levi leaped forward, ready to pounce on him again, but Jazzmine grabbed his arm a second time to stop him. Bartu had no reason to drag him into their affair as he was just an innocent bystander. Obviously, their feelings toward each other were mutual. He didn't care to be graced with his presence either.

"Levi, it's ok," Jazzmine insisted, feeling that she could handle the situation.

When Levi leaped, although he didn't attack, Bartu flinched and took a step back. Levi nodded with satisfaction at Bartu's reaction. He should be afraid because his desire was to tear him apart. However, if he didn't want any static, he shouldn't play with electricity!

"Of course Levi was going to be here. He is my best friend, Bartu. You know that," Jazzmine defended.

"Jazz, we have had this conversation before, and you know how I feel!"

"Yes, and you know how *I* feel."

Bartu sighed. He needed to speak to Jazzmine in private. He wasn't sure Levi was going to let her out of his sight. He was sure she told him what happened between them anyway. "Jazzmine, I came here to take you back to California with me, and I don't intend to leave without you," he blurted.

The look in Bartu's eyes told her he was serious. Jazzmine had no idea how to respond. She was actually stunned by the comment. Why he thought she would go anywhere with him was beyond her. She did not ask him to come to New York City. She did not tell him that there was any chance of reconciliation, and she did not want to continue this conversation. As far as she was concerned, it was done! Laughing with amusement, she shook her head and turned away.

"Jazz, I am serious," Bartu pleaded as she slowly walked down the hall. "I'm willing to give you what you want!" he yelled after her when she didn't stop.

At his words, Jazzmine froze. He was willing to give her what she wanted? What did that mean? How did he know what she wanted? He couldn't possibly know because she didn't know anymore. She was just so confused at this point. Nothing that was happening made any sense right now.

Bartu had to mean that he was ready to settle down with her. Her heart was pounding as she slowly turned back to face him, wondering if that was even what she wanted from him anymore. She didn't think it was because she wasn't a hundred percent sure she could trust him. He tricked her once, and she wouldn't allow him to do it again.

Swallowing hard, she looked at Levi, who was still standing in the same spot with his arms folding across his chest. He wasn't going to budge as long as Bartu was there. Clearing her throat, she called him to her. "Levi, could I please speak with Bartu alone?"

Levi eyed Bartu, not wanting him near her or to be alone with her. "Jazz," he pleaded.

"Please, Levi," she pleaded, as well. "I can handle it." She nodded.

Levi dropped his arms and walked pass Bartu on his way to James's room. As he passed Jazzmine, he stopped long enough to whisper in her ear, "If you need me, you know how to find me."

Seeing Levi coming her way, Vanessa closed the door and ran back to her seat. She got there just before Levi entered the room.

When Levi was gone, everyone standing in the hall went back into their rooms, closing the doors.

Jazzmine sat across from Bartu in the snack room at a small table. Her heart was pounding as she was wondering what he was going to say. "Ok, Bartu, why should I believe that you have changed?"

"I told you before, Jazz, I didn't come here to argue with you. I just want to rekindle our romance. I know it's still there. I've missed you dearly. I want you in my arms again. I want you..." his sentence faded, and he reached across the table to take her hand. "I want you in every sense of the word, Jazz."

Her eyes widened as she looked at him. What was he saying? "Bartu, what are you saying?" she asked the question on her mind.

"I'm saying that I'm willing to do whatever it takes to be with you and to keep you happy."

She frowned. She wanted him to do what it took to keep both of them happy. He didn't have to do anything out of obligation to her. He didn't owe her anything. If he was going to do something just to shut her up, she didn't want him to do anything at all. "And what is that, Bartu?"

"Jazz, I realize that you're not ready to be intimate with me until I can prove myself worthy of you, and I believe that I have done that. I flew all these miles just to be with you, and to give you this," he reached into the inner breast pocket of the blazer he wore to pull out a small, black velvet box.

Jazzmine's heart leaped to her throat as she stared at it. She was positive that she knew the contents of the box, and she didn't know what to do. *"YES!"* her heart sang before he even asked the question. She wanted this. She wanted this so badly, but then her heart sank as she considered it.

She didn't know if she wanted this now, from him. Before they broke up she had been positive that she wanted this from him. Now things had changed. Her feelings had changed, and she didn't want to lead him on. He tricked her once before, and if the box didn't contain what she was expecting, she would be more hurt than ever. She wasn't sure she even wanted to open it.

Her eyes lingered on the box for a moment, and she tried to find her voice, but it was gone. She couldn't speak.

Bartu opened the box for her, and her eyes widened.

Her mouth dropped with astonishment. She was almost drooling. The huge diamond ring was marvelous! The diamond baguettes sparkled as they rested in the center of the platinum band. They had to be at least two carats. The gorgeous ring almost took her breath away! She lifted her eyes back to him. "Bartu," she began, finally finding her voice, "are you..."

"Yes, Jazz, I am. I want you to marry me." He had intended to propose that last encounter they had when he asked her to let him show her how he felt about her in his own little way. She just hadn't been patient with him. Since their break up, he recognized his mistakes. He, also, realized that he didn't have a future without her in it, as Mrs. Flexler!

Her voice failed her, again, and all she could

do was stare at him. Her eyes dropped to the ring again and lingered on it for a moment. It was a gorgeous ring!

Marriage was a major commitment. Was she ready for it? Did she *love* him?

She lowered her eyes, knowing that she didn't. They had been together for five months, and not once in the relationship had either of them confessed their love for the other. Her feelings weren't that deep for him, and she couldn't pretend that they were. The most he ever said was that he *cared* for her. That wasn't enough to build a marriage on. That was just like marrying for money. It wouldn't last! There was no need for her to put herself through that.

"Maybe I'll grow to love him," she thought, looking at the ring again. She needed to talk to Levi. *"Levi,"* she thought, lifting her eyes back to Bartu's face. To be sure Bartu was serious and to get a reaction, she said, "Levi and I..."

He reacted the way she expected, by rolling his eyes and looking away. He didn't want to hear about Levi, and he hadn't accepted their relationship. That much hadn't changed, and she couldn't marry him if he wasn't willing to accept her *friend*.

Standing up, she pushed her chair back. The conversation was null and void.

Bartu looked up at her with hope in his eyes.

Jazzmine shook her head. "I'm sorry, Bartu, but I can't marry you." On that note, she turned and walked away.

When Jazzmine pushed the door open to her father's room, Vanessa looked up to see her entering. When she came in alone, her mouth dropped, and she almost frowned. She was supposed to be entering with her new fiancée, Bartu Flexler. After a second, she pulled herself together, thinking that perhaps Jazzmine was going to tell her father about him before she brought him in. That had to be it. If it was, she was going about it in the right way.

When Jazzmine stepped into the room, Vanessa's eyes went to her hand to check for an engagement ring. She gritted her teeth when she saw that she wasn't wearing one. *"Damn!"* she thought. *"I bombed again!"*

How did she fail this time?

Pretending to be Jazzmine, Vanessa sent Bartu an E-mail message telling him everything that happened with her father, where she was, and that she missed him. She told him that if he really wanted to reconcile, he had to prove his love for her. She did everything she could to lead him to believe she wanted him to ask her to marry him.

In his return message, he told her he was flying to New York City today, and he had something very important to ask her. Naturally, she assumed he was going to ask her to marry him. What happened? Bartu was such an idiot Vanessa concluded.

When she entered the room, Levi tossed her a sympathetic glance. "Are you all right?" he needed to know.

Jazzmine nodded. "I'm fine."

James looked at Jazzmine, wondering what Levi meant. "Jazzmine, what's wrong, baby?"

She shook her head, not wanting to discuss the situation. "There's nothing for you to worry about, Daddy. I'm fine."

Vanessa, wanting her father to press the issue so that she could find out what happened, glanced at him with hope in her eyes.

"Are you sure, honey?" Her eyes darted to her sister.

Jazzmine half smiled. "Yes, Daddy, I'm sure."

James said nothing else on the matter, upsetting Vanessa. Now, she had to come up with a whole new scheme. Nothing seemed to work. Jazzmine overpowered everything she tried.

Friday when Vanessa got to the hospital, Dr. Larch told her the best news she received in weeks. She and Jazzmine could take their father home. He was getting James's release forms just as she was walking through the door.

Happily, Vanessa followed the doctor to her father's room.

Finally, her problem with Jazzmine was about to be over! Surely, Jazzmine was going to go home now. Seeing that their father got out of the hospital all right was her only concern anyway. Vanessa entered her father's room with the biggest smile on her face. The fact that her father was in a wheelchair didn't seem to bother her.

Jazzmine was standing behind James's wheelchair with her arms folded around his neck. "We're taking you home, Daddy," she was saying when Dr. Larch and Vanessa entered the room.

James placed his hand on her arm with a loving pat and smile. "I know, baby, and I'm ready to go home."

"Hi, Daddy!" Vanessa smiled, feeling great.

"Hi, baby." James returned the smile.

"Well, Mr. Thomas, if I can get you to sign

these papers, you, your daughters and..." his eyes went to Levi, who stood at Jazzmine's side, "your... *son*?" He hoped he got it right. When no one objected, he nodded and continued, "can go."

James didn't mind Levi being called his son at all. He had grown quite fond of him in the past few weeks. He was starting to think of him as one of his own. He cared just as much about him as he did his own daughters. "All right," James said, holding his hand out for the clipboard and pen.

The doctor moved forward with the clipboard and pen, extending them to James. As soon as he signed the paper and handed the clipboard and pen back to the doctor, Jazzmine wheeled him out the door.

Dr. Larch followed them down the hall to the elevators. When they stopped, he asked to speak to James's daughters in private.

"Sure," Levi said just as the glass door of the first elevator opened. "We'll meet you out front," he told Jazzmine as he took her place behind her father's wheelchair. He pushed the chair into the elevator, and the door closed.

When the elevator went down, Jazzmine and Vanessa turned their attention to the doctor.

Having their full attention, Dr. Larch cleared his throat and removed the top sheet from his clipboard, holding it in his hand. Lifting his eyes back to the two sisters, he said, "I didn't want to frighten your father. So, I opted to talk to the two of you. His legs are getting stronger by the day, but they aren't strong enough for therapy, yet. It may take a few weeks. So, he'll need the wheelchair. He'll need lots of bed rest, and he shouldn't be allowed to try to stand up by himself. He may feel that he's capable from time to time." His eyes went back to his clipboard.

Clearing his throat again, he removed the top two sheets of paper and handed them to Vanessa. "Here is his prescription. I've already called it in for you. The nurse at the window will tell you how often the medication should be given."

Vanessa accepted the papers with a nod of comprehension. "Thank you, Doctor."

Dr. Larch walked away.

Vanessa turned her attention to her sister with a smile. "Well, let's go down and get Daddy's prescription so we can get him home. I'm sure he's anxious to get back there by now."

Jazzmine nodded with agreement. She started forward and then stopped. "Oh, wait!" She reached into her purse and took out her cell phone. Quickly dialing Levi's cell, she told him that they were on their way to the pharmacy, and they would be with him as soon as they picked up her father's medicine.

Vanessa took the small white bag with her father's medication in it from the nurse in the pharmacy window.

As the nurse began informing Vanessa of the necessary information about the medication, Jazzmine took the bag from her sister and peeped inside curiously.

Taking the medicine out, she examined the labels of each bottle carefully.

Vanessa turned from the window just in time to catch Jazzmine's frown. "What's wrong, honey?" she was anxious to know.

"I'm glad I'm not in Dad's shoes because I

probably wouldn't get cured. I can't take powdered sulfur. I can't take any kind of sulfur for that matter."

Vanessa didn't quite comprehend. "Why?"

"If I got too much of it, it would kill me! Just a little is enough to do a lot of damage! I'm allergic to it," Jazzmine explained.

"Oh!" Vanessa's hand rose to her heart, and she inhaled a deep breath. She wondered if there was any medication to which she was allergic. There was none to her knowledge. "Well, we don't want that to happen. You had better give me that." She took the medication bottles and put them back in the bag. Wrapping her arm around her sister's shoulder, they headed for the exit together.

Jazzmine and Vanessa surrounded their father's wheelchair as he sat by the fireplace with a blanket in his lap. Vanessa sat in the easy chair closest to the fireplace, and Jazzmine sat on the end of the love seat. Levi sat next to her.

"Oh, Daddy, it feels so good to be home," Jazzmine told her father as she looked about the living room of the house she lived in during her entire childhood. Nothing had changed. Everything was just as it always had been. She smiled as her eyes landed on the gigantic picture of her father, sister and herself as it sat over the mantle in the sterling silver frame. She recalled the exact day the picture was taken eight ago. Remembering that things weren't the same anymore, she lowered her eyes. This was no longer her home. She lived in Beverly Hills, California now.

James reached out and placed his hand on his younger daughter's leg. Smiling at her, he said,

"It's good to have you home."

Vanessa faked a smile, wanting her sister to hurry up and get back to her perfect life in Beverly Hills. "It sure is!"

Levi rolled his eyes at Vanessa and her false smile. He knew she didn't mean that. The only problem was that Jazzmine couldn't see through her. She bought everything her sister said. It was as if Vanessa could do no wrong in Jazzmine's eyes! She still looked up to her even though they were adults now.

"Hey!" Vanessa exclaimed. "Why don't you and I camp out here on the living room floor tonight and catch up on old times. We can turn it into a slumber party. It'll be fun."

Jazzmine loved the idea. She hadn't done anything to that affect in years. "Sure!"

Levi looked around Jazzmine at James. "Well, Mr. Thomas, it looks like it's going to be ladies' night tonight right here in your living room."

James smiled at both of his daughters. He adored the idea personally. Levi had no idea. It would be like old times. He longed to have his daughters back at home, getting along so well, with him like the good old days. "Yes! I'm glad to have both of them here at home with me. Speaking of that," he turned his eyes on Jazzmine. "How much longer are you going to be here with me, honey? I know you're anxious to get back home."

At the question, Vanessa sat up straight, anxious to hear her sister's response. Surely, it wouldn't be much longer now.

"Oh, no, Daddy! You're not going to get rid of me that easily. I'm going to see you walk again before I leave."

"Oh no!" Vanessa thought, horrified by the response she didn't expect. She assumed Jazzmine's goal was to be by their father's hospital bedside. This was ridiculous! He wouldn't be able to walk for weeks! Jazzmine had to go now! Her eyes widened with the realization that, if their father never walked again, Jazzmine could be there permanently!

James reached over and patted Jazzmine's knee. "Thank you, honey." He had no objections as she was welcome to stay as long as she liked. He was in no hurry for her to leave.

"You're welcome, Daddy. I'm here for you!" He had to know that.

"We both are," Vanessa was inclined to include herself. All the while, her mind was strategizing to do her worst!

At ten o'clock after James was put to bed in the first bedroom downstairs, Jazzmine went upstairs to take a bath.

Vanessa showered in the downstairs bathroom.

Levi used the bathroom in James's master bedroom upstairs.

Leaving the bathroom, wearing flannel pajamas and slippers, Jazzmine went down the hall to the first guest bedroom. Knocking on the door, she waited for Levi's command to come in. Upon entering, she found him standing beside the bed taking clothes out of his suitcase.

He was only wearing pajama bottoms, and she found herself ogling his sexy bald and muscular chest. Her heart was racing as her eyes were glued to it. She never imagined him to be so sexy!

He was so enticing that she wanted to reach out and touch it, massage his muscles. His manliness was exposed, almost welcoming her. Something stirred deep within her, a strong arousal. *"What are you doing?"* she asked herself. *"This is Levi!"* She shouldn't be thinking of him in such a manner. It was as if she *wanted* him. The arousal he stirred within her was something she had never before experienced. Not even Bartu made her *want*, actual *desire*, him!

When he looked at her, Jazzmine swallowed hard and lowered her eyes as she tried to maintain the little control she had. "Um..." She forgot what she wanted to say. "I... I..." Her eyes went to his chest again, and she licked her lips, clearing her throat. It was funny. They had known each other for years, and it never occurred to her that he was such a *delicious* looking man. He had been under her nose all along, and she never noticed him.

Now, as he stood before her half naked, she was noticing! If he got too close to her, she would probably melt away.

Levi stared at her for moment. She was just looking at him. He couldn't even guess what was on her mind. Arching his eyebrows at her, he nodded with the expectation that she would say whatever was on her mind. "You...?" he encouraged, wanting her to make a complete statement.

It all came back to her, and Jazzmine composed herself. "I just came to say good-night."

"Good-night," Levi returned with appreciation. "Have fun with your sister."

"I will." Jazzmine closed the door and exhaled. She had no idea what had gotten into her. She had seen Levi's chest plenty of times. They had gone swimming together several times. He had even used her shower at home a few times. *"Oh well,"* she thought, shrugging off the idea. Then, she started for the stairs.

Approaching the last step, she discovered two sleeping bags on the living room floor in front of the fireplace. Smiling, she climbed down the stairs and walked over to the fireplace.

Standing at the kitchen counter in the pink robe, which was open to expose the pink silk pajamas, Vanessa shook her head as she fixed her father's medicine for him. "Jazzmine, you have to go," she whispered to herself as she poured hot soup into a bowl and placed the bowl on a breakfast tray.

Reaching above the counter, she grabbed the first tall glass she saw from the cabinet. Moving to the sink with the glass, she got some water from the faucet. The water in the refrigerator was too cold. Going back to the counter, she sat the glass on the tray and picked it up, knocking a medicine bottle off the counter. Putting the tray down again, she leaned down to collect the bottle. Lifting it, she caught a glimpse of the label, which read powdered sulfur.

"I can't take any kind of sulfur." The words Jazzmine had spoken to her earlier at the hospital rang in her head as she straightened up with the bottle in her hand. *"If I got too much of it, it would kill me! Just a little is enough to do a lot of damage! I'm allergic to it."*

Vanessa clutched the bottle tight. An idea popped into her head. She knew exactly how to get rid of Jazzmine for good! A mischievous smile spread across her lips as she looked down at the bottle and read the word, *Refill*. Her plan would work this time. There was no way it could fail. Perking up, she slipped the bottle into the pocket of her robe and picked up the tray. "This is it, Jazz," she whispered to herself with a happy smile. "No one will ever know!"

Leaving James's room, Vanessa returned to the living room. Looking at Jazzmine, who was sitting next to the fireplace hugging her knees, she patted the bottle in her pocket. "Hey," she called to her sister.

Jazzmine, who was staring into the flames wondering why she was having such strange feelings about Levi lately, blinked at her sister's voice. She glanced up at her.

"I'm going to get something to drink. What will you have?" Vanessa asked, hoping she was thirsty.

"Oh, I'll take an ice tea."

"Good choice," Vanessa thought. "One ice tea coming up." She went off to the kitchen. Moving about the kitchen swiftly, she fixed herself a glass of lemonade to be sure she didn't get the two beverages mixed up. She couldn't have Jazzmine getting the wrong drink. Fixing Jazzmine's tea, she poured two tablespoons of the powdered sulfur in the glass and a pinch of sugar. Hopefully, she had put in a sufficient amount of sulfur to do the job, which was to *kill* Jazzmine!

Rubbing her hands together anxiously, she picked up both glasses and went back to the living room. "Here you are," she told her sister as she moved closer into the room to extend the glass to her.

Jazzmine accepted the glass. Placing it on the floor beside her, she looked up at Vanessa, who almost frowned. "Why don't you come over here? Let's talk for a while. I have a lot on my mind, and I need to release it. I don't want to disturb Levi if he's sleeping."

"Why don't you drink the damned ice tea?" Vanessa asked mentally. "Sure, honey," she said. She sat on top of the sleeping bag in front of Jazzmine's. Facing her, she smiled. She sipped from her glass, hoping Jazzmine would sip from hers, as well.

Jazzmine switched to an Indian style position and picked up the glass, which caused Vanessa's smile to widened. She shook her head. "You know, I just don't know what's wrong with me these days. I just don't seem to be myself. I mean there's my job, and I love it. Then there's Bartu," she shook her head, again. "I can't believe he came all this way thinking he could force me to go back with him. I do care for him, but he can't accept my relationship with Levi. Do I forgive him and give him another chance or do I just forget about him and move on? He could be the one."

Vanessa's eyes went to the glass in her sister's hand. "Honey, you really should drink your tea." She sipped from her glass, again.

Jazzmine nodded with agreement. "I will. You know, the truth is I'm afraid. What if I do forget about Bartu and move on? If I can't find anybody else, I'll be lonely forever!"

Vanessa shook her head with disagreement. "No, you won't have that problem. I'm sure there are plenty of guys out there dying to be with you. Drink your tea," she insisted.

Jazzmine arched her eyebrows at her sister. "Do you really think so?"

"Yes! You're young and beautiful! What guy wouldn't want you? You..."

"I'm not sure I would know how to act around anyone else."

Vanessa shook her head with confusion and anger, more anger than confusion. What was Jazzmine's real concern? All men were basically alike. If she knew how to act around one, she knew how to act around them all! Why was it so hard to get her to drink the tea? She wanted to get it over with as quickly as possible. If Jazzmine never drank the tea, it would be impossible to get rid of her. "Why do you say that?" She had to pretend she was interested for her sister's sake.

Jazzmine lowered her eyes. "Well, the truth is..." she sighed, feeling embarrassed about telling her sister, the men magnet, something so severe. "Well, Bartu was my first boyfriend." She raised her eyes and met her sister's gaze.

"The ice cubes are going to melt if you don't drink..." Vanessa's voice trailed off with the realization of what her sister said. Bartu was her first boyfriend *ever*? There were none before him? That was hilarious, and she wanted to laugh in her sister's face! Jazzmine just admitted that she didn't go on her first real date or get her first kiss until she was twenty-three. What if people made that discovery? She would sure to be the laughingstock of the city! That was ridiculous! Jazzmine was a beautiful model, always in the lime light. How had she avoided dating before now? Not even *Levi* crossed her mind as a possible prospect? This was so succulent and hilarious to Vanessa. "Did you say Bartu was your *first* boyfriend?" She had to be certain she heard correctly.

Jazzmine looked away with a nod. "Yes," she confirmed. "I wanted to date plenty of guys sure, but I was too afraid of how they would react to me."

"Even after you became a model?"

"Yes! I was even more afraid then. I don't want someone to want me just because I have a pretty face. I want someone to want me because I have a good heart." Her eyes returned to her sister. "I was, also, afraid because..." her eyes dropped. "Well, you know, most men want to..." She laughed at herself and shook her head. "Forget it." Having this conversation with her sister was uncomfortable for her. She hadn't even had this discussion with Levi.

CHAPTER NINE

*V*anessa searched her sister's face for the answer to the unfinished statement with interest. "No. Most men want to what? Sleep with a woman?" She shrugged her shoulders. Of course that was true. Everyone knew that.

Unable to give her sister eye contact, Jazzmine swallowed hard with a nod. "Yes."

Vanessa laughed, tilting her head. "Ok. Well, after you and Bartu slept together for the first time, everything was ok, right? You aren't afraid of that anymore, are you?"

Jazzmine sucked in her bottom lip with her head down. "Vanessa," she lifted her eyes, "let me tell you my biggest secret. No one else knows this, not even Levi. If anyone finds out, I'll just die! It's really embarrassing when you're around a lot of people who don't know how you feel."

"*A secret?*" Vanessa perked up, anxious to hear. This could be good. Maybe, she could kill Jazzmine with words and watch her suffer rather than for her to go all at once. That would be fun to watch. If she revealed Jazzmine's biggest secret, and everyone laughed at her, she would get exactly what she deserved. "What is it, honey?"

"Well," Jazzmine swallowed hard and blurted, "the reason Bartu and I broke up was because we *never* slept together. I couldn't. I don't love him. I want my first time to be with someone I love, preferably my husband, if I ever get married."

Vanessa cleared her throat to keep from laughing aloud. If Jazzmine and Bartu never slept together, that meant she was still a virgin! Oh that was great! She couldn't wait until everyone discovered the truth. Once everyone found out that their favorite *Beauty Queen* couldn't keep the only man she ever had because she was too afraid to sleep with him, everything would go haywire. She was too anxious. "Are you saying that you're still a *virgin*?"

Feeling rather embarrassed, Jazzmine inhaled a deep breath. No one else knew the truth, not even her best friend. It was painful to admit, but in actuality, she was a *virgin*, probably the last in existence. Everyone was having sex except her. Even teenagers were enjoying themselves sexually. "Yes."

Vanessa pulled in her bottom lip to hold her tongue. This was fabulous, very succulent gossip! It had to be spread around the city. She didn't know anyone who wouldn't want to hear this gossip!

Jazzmine Thomas, the celebrity model, was a twenty-three-year-old *virgin*! She was as pure as the freshly fallen snow.

"Well, honey..." Vanessa stopped when the red light on the intercom, which was above Jazzmine's head on the wall, popped on.

When her eyes moved, Jazzmine looked up, as well.

"Yes, Daddy?" Vanessa called as her father was buzzing the room. It certainly wasn't Levi. It was an excellent idea to install intercoms in every room years ago. They were very useful.

"Could someone please help me?" James asked in a polite voice.

Vanessa stood up and went down the hall to his room.

When Vanessa was gone, Jazzmine turned her attention to the tea and drank it all without taking a breath. For some strange reason, the tea tasted sour and left a bitter taste in her mouth. She pursed her lips, wondering why it tasted so funny. Vanessa usually made the best ice tea. That was a long time ago, however. Maybe, she lost her touch.

Footsteps could be heard on the stairs.

Jazzmine looked up to see Levi coming down the stairs in his robe. Suddenly, his frame became a blur, and she could barely see him. She blinked, hearing his voice.

"Jazz? Where's Vanessa? Mr. Thomas..." he stopped himself when he noticed the expression on her face. Something was wrong.

"Levi," Jazzmine began, standing up. What was happening? She felt dizzy. The room was spinning. She saw Levi. No. There were two of him.

She attempted to move toward him, but she found herself staggering. "Oh, Levi!" she cried his name as a plea for help. Bending over in fear of losing her balance, she placed her right hand on her forehead as a sharp pain stung her right between the eyes. She screamed, and her vision went black. "I can't see! I can't see!"

Levi rushed to her, but it was too late. She hit

the floor in a cold faint.

The glass hit the floor as well, shattering to pieces. Ice cubes spewed everywhere.

Levi dropped to his knees beside her, wondering what happened. *"Oh, Lord,"* he thought. *"This is Vanessa's doing! What has she done to her?"* Whatever happened was Vanessa's fault. She and Jazzmine were the only two people downstairs. James couldn't have done anything. He couldn't even walk.

Taking Jazzmine's hand, he patted it, calling her name.

Vanessa rushed into the room. She heard a crash, and she had come to investigate. "Jazzmine!" she screamed at the sight of her sister lying on the floor. What happened?

Hatred for Vanessa surfaced as he could no longer suppress it, and he turned anger eyes on her. How dare she play the innocent role? Her sister was out cold because of something she did, and she was standing there pretending to care. "What did you do to her?" he hissed without thinking. He didn't mean for James to hear. Hopefully, he hadn't heard.

Vanessa's eyes went to the pieces of glass, and she remembered the poison. *"Oh no!"* she thought. She completely forgot. She was so wrapped up in Jazzmine's secrets that the sulfur slipped her mind. If anything happened to her, it would be all her fault. Their father would never forgive her. If Jazzmine died, she would be a murderer! *"Oh God! Please!"* she begged in a panic. *"Don't let her die!"* Rushing for the phone, she chanted, "I have to call 911!" in a panicky voice.

Levi watched Vanessa move about with suspicion. Her fear and concern seemed to be genuine, but he didn't trust her. It could be a front for his benefit. If anything happened to Jazzmine, he would hold her solely responsible, and he would make her pay with her dear life. She could count on it!

The following morning, Jazzmine opened her eyes feeling absolutely dreadful! Her entire face hurt, and it felt weird.

She looked about the room to discover that she wasn't at her father's house. It looked as if she were in a...

Her eyes dropped to the hospital bracelet and the IV in her arm. She *was* in a hospital! Why? What happened to her? She opened her mouth to speak, but her throat was sore, and no words came forth. She couldn't even moan.

Optimistic, Vanessa stood by Jazzmine's bedside, watching her sleep. Silently, she had been praying for her sister as her conscience was nagging her. When her eyes opened, she inwardly exhaled with relief. "Levi," she whispered happily, calling for his attention to let him know that Jazzmine was awake.

Levi, who had his head down as he sat in the chair on the opposite side of the bed, looked up at the sound of his name. Seeing Jazzmine's eyes open, he stood up and took her hand with a broad smile. "Hey, Jazz! How do you feel?"

She swallowed hard, stuttering, "I... I... hurt." The words didn't come out correctly, and she felt retarded.

"Oh, honey," Vanessa caressed her cheek, seizing her attention. "I'm so glad you're ok. You gave us quite a scare."

"What's... what's wrong... with me?" the words came out slowly, scratching Jazzmine's throat.

"Do you remember anything that happened last night?" Levi encouraged.

Jazzmine strained her brain to remember. She didn't remember anything. Slowly shaking her head, she said, "N... no."

"That's ok, baby." Levi didn't expect her to remember. The doctor said that it was normal for a patient not to remember a painful part of their past right away. "It'll come back to you gradually." Hopefully, he could explain things to her before it all came back to her as a shock. For now, he only wanted to concentrate on helping her get well.

"Why do I feel so puffy in the face?" Jazzmine wondered. She felt so awful. "M..." She swallowed hard. "Mirror."

Levi and Vanessa exchanged glances. The one thing she didn't need was to glimpse herself in the mirror. She didn't look at all herself right now, and they didn't want her to get upset or to get sick.

"Um... Hey, Jazz, why don't we call Dad, and say hi? Don't you want to hear his voice?" Vanessa encouraged, hoping she would forget about looking in the mirror.

Jazzmine shook her head. She didn't want to talk to her father right now. Her throat hurt as it was hard enough to speak. She wanted to consult a mirror as her desire was to see if she was all right. She didn't feel all right, abnormal to be exact. "Mir... mirror."

Vanessa glanced at Levi in hopes that he had an answer of how to handle the predicament. She had no idea. He knew her better than anyone.

"Later, ok, Jazz? Right now let's get you something to eat." Levi dismissed the whole topic of the mirror.

"Good idea!" Vanessa agreed, and she buzzed the nurse.

That evening, Vanessa went home to check on their father, whom she had called three times that day.

Jazzmine, whose throat finally stopped aching, realized that Levi and Vanessa were trying to keep her from looking in the mirror. Every time she asked about it, they came up with something for her to do and a reason why she shouldn't look in the mirror. Naturally, she suspected that if they didn't want her to look in the mirror, she must look horrible!

When her speech was restored, she sat silently with her arms folded across her chest for the remainder of Vanessa's visit. Levi and Vanessa talked to her and made jokes, but she refused to respond or even crack a smile. She rarely even blinked.

When Vanessa left, Levi stood up and stretched just as a nurse was coming in to check Jazzmine's blood pressure. "Excuse me, Jazz. I'm going to run to the bathroom," he whispered.

She excused him with a nod, turning her attention to the nurse.

When the nurse was done and on her way out, Jazzmine called her back, asking for a mirror. If Levi wouldn't give her one, she would get one from someone else.

"Oh, sure," the nurse answered, returning to

her beside. She opened the top drawer of the nightstand and took out a circular hand mirror. "Here you go." She handed her the mirror and left.

Seeing her reflection, Jazzmine could do no more than scream. It was no wonder Levi and Vanessa didn't want her to see her reflection. She was hideous!

Her entire face was swollen and puffy. It looked as if she had been punched in the face with boxing gloves a million times. Tears streamed down her face and her mind flashed back six years when she had been called *ugly*. That was exactly how she felt now.

Levi returned to the room with a smile, which quickly faded when he saw Jazzmine holding the mirror. Moving closer to her, he saw her tears. A pang of sympathy stabbed him in the heart. He hadn't intended for her to find out this way. He expected her to react with tears, however. Her appearance was none too flattering.

"Oh, Jazz," he sighed, wishing she hadn't found the mirror. His desire was to take her into his arms and caress away all of her sorrow.

"Levi, I'm *ugly*! Is this the face of a model?" she sobbed.

Levi took the mirror from her and placed it on the nightstand face down. "Don't say that," he whispered. She could never be ugly to him.

"How could you say that? Look at me! I *am* ugly!" Jazzmine cried.

Levi caressed her cheek, whispering, "You'll always be beautiful to me."

His words were shocking and pleasant at the same time. However, she knew he only made the statement because he was a *true* friend. Anyone else would have run out on her by now. "You're just saying that," she sniffed.

"No," he whispered with a shake of his head as he caressed her tears away. "I wouldn't lie to you. Don't worry. In a few days, you'll be back to normal."

Jazzmine sniffed again, hoping he was right. She couldn't go around looking like this! If Mrs. Trenton saw her now, her career would be terminated. "What happened to me anyway?" She needed to know because she couldn't remember a single detail.

"The doctor found traces of powdered sulfur in your system," Levi explained.

Jazzmine was shocked. How in the world did that happen? "Powdered sulfur?" Levi nodded. "I'm allergic to sulfur!" Her hand went to her forehead in a panic. "Levi, I could have been killed! How did this happen? How did the sulfur get in my system?"

He shook his head, unable to answer her question. "It's unknown at the moment."

"Wait a minute," Jazzmine thought of something. "My father has to take powdered sulfur. Maybe, I accidentally..."

Levi shook his head, knowing what she was thinking. He didn't know how to tell her he suspected that her sister tried to poison her. He wouldn't allow her to blame herself. "Jazzmine, I think..." He couldn't do it. She wouldn't believe him anyway. Now was not the time. "Never mind. It wasn't you. You didn't accidentally take the medicine. I'm sure of it."

"How do you know?"

"Get some rest." Levi leaned forward and

kissed her on the cheek, ignoring the question. He couldn't tell her now. He would tell her in due time.

A week and a half later when Jazzmine's face was back to normal and her body was functioning normally again, Levi decided to treat her to lunch at one of the most elegant restaurants in town.

As they sat at a table for two across from each other, Jazzmine found herself laughing at all of his jokes. She, also, found him attractive, more so desirable than ever. His eyes were gorgeous as they sparkled when he looked at her. His lips were tempting as she watched them move with every word he uttered to her. When he reached across the table and took her hand, she could have fainted! His touch was so electrifying! Her heart was racing, and she could hardly control her thoughts.

In her mind, she wanted him to do more than hold her hand. She wanted him to hold *her.* She desired the touch of his beautiful soft lips, which he could place anywhere he so desired! He could kiss her lips and moved down farther to her...

She blinked back to reality as he was speaking to her.

"See, Jazz!" He smiled across at her as he held her hand in his own. "I told you everything would be ok. Your father is going to be fine, and you're looking as fabulous as usual!"

Jazzmine blushed. "Thank you!"

Releasing her hand, Levi pushed his chair back and stood up. "If you will excuse me, I need to..."

Jazzmine raised a hand, dismissing him. She

knew exactly what he needed to do. "Yes, I know." She smiled broadly and winked at him. "Go ahead," she said in a low voice.

Levi returned the smile and walked away.

Jazzmine lowered her head with a shake. Oh, that Levi was a character. One couldn't help liking him. In fact, she was beginning to like him more and more. Perhaps... her concentration was broken by the sound of masculine voices, and she lifted her head to find two handsome men standing two tables away deep in conversation. Their voices were louder than they intended.

There was something so familiar about one of the men. The other she was positive she didn't know. What was it about the man? Was he an actor, perhaps a friend of Levi's, or a singer? Her mouth dropped when he quickly glanced back at her and then back to his associate.

She did recognize him! He hadn't changed a bit! It was Keith Bedly, and he was looking quite distinguished in the gray business suit and tie. Nothing had changed about him, nothing at all. He was still the same height. His hair was still the same. The only thing that was different about him was the way he made Jazzmine feel. Her heart didn't skip a beat at seeing him again. She was happy to see him, however. She hadn't seen him in years. *"What is he doing with his life these days?"* she wondered. She knew he would be fascinated to know what she was doing with hers.

As quickly as he glanced away, Keith turned back to stare for a moment.

Jazzmine smiled.

Keith smiled in return. The man to whom he was speaking called for his attention, and he tore his eyes away from the beautiful model.

Wondering if he recognized her, Jazzmine dropped her eyes. If he did, wouldn't he have waved? Of course, he didn't recognize her! She had changed so drastically, and they hadn't seen each other in years. She promised him she would never try to contact him if she ever returned to New York City. Thus far, she kept her word. He seemed to be doing fine without knowing where she was or what she was doing with her life. He hadn't even asked about her in all this time. Had he, her father or Vanessa would have told her. He wasn't interested in...

She raised her eyes when someone cleared his throat to get her attention.

It was Keith. He was standing behind Levi's chair with a broad smile on his face. "Hel-lo there!" he said in a flirtatious voice. She smiled, not saying a word. "I was standing over there," he pointed to where he and his associate were standing, "and I couldn't help noticing how beautiful you are."

Keith had no idea who she was, and Jazzmine was positive of the fact now. He would never have called her beautiful years ago.

Jazzmine nodded. "Thank you."

Keith cleared his throat. "I am..."

"Keith Bedly," she finished for him.

His eyes widened. "You know who I am?" Then, he pulled a straight face. That wasn't too hard to believe. He had made quite a name for himself. He did own the top bank in the city.

Jazzmine nodded again. "Yes, I'm quite aware of who you are." She arched an eyebrow at him. "Are you sure you don't know who I am?"

Keith placed his hands on the back of Levi's

chair and looked at her for a moment, trying to figure out her identity. She talked as if they knew each other. Puzzled, he shook his head. "Yes, I'm sure. I would never forget a woman with a face as gorgeous as yours! Do I know you?"

"Sure you do, Keith." Jazzmine sighed. "Before I tell you who I am, let me ask you a question. Do you believe that looks can be deceiving?"

He considered the question. "Well, I suppose so."

"Good." She nodded with satisfaction. "Six years ago you called me ugly and scarred me emotionally."

The expression on Keith's face was that of disbelief. "Why would I…"

"You, also, called me fat, and you said that I was not fit to be taken out in public. You did have a fancy for my sister, though."

Keith didn't quite comprehend as he was sure she had him mistaken with someone else. Why would he say such horrific things about a woman as beautiful as she? The only person he remembered calling fat was Jazzmine Thomas, and that was because she was fat! Vanessa had been…

When reality hit home, he blinked and looked at her with wide eyes and an open mouth. It was remarkable! It couldn't be! **This** woman was **Jazzmine Thomas**? Was this the Jazzmine who had been valedictorian of her class? The fat, ugly girl with bad acne? Where did her acne go? She wasn't fat, and he would never call her ugly now.

"Jazzmine?" he asked with disbelief in his voice. His eyes went over her body and the tank dress she wore. She looked excellent in it. He never thought he would say Jazzmine Thomas looked nice in a tank dress. That was the one thing he thought he would never want to see her in.

Jazzmine applauded him. "Glory! You've got it!" She had hoped her little hints would jog his memory.

"What happened? You..."

"Look different?" Jazzmine laughed. "Yes, I know. I'm a model now. I'm just here visiting my father."

A model? Jazzmine Thomas? Well, he could see why. Keith felt so awkward now. He didn't know what to say or how to act. If he had known that she would turn out this way, he would never have talked about her the way he did. He didn't have an interest in her then, but he wouldn't mind at all starting a relationship with her now. "Well," he sighed, "are you dining alone?"

"Actually," Jazzmine began, wondering what was taking Levi so long to use the phone, "I..."

At that moment, Levi returned to her, interrupting her statement. He stopped behind her chair and placed a hand on her shoulder. She looked back at him. "Sorry I took so long. Bradley can talk forever!" He shook his head and raised his eyes to Keith.

Jazzmine placed her hand on his and held it lightly. Her eyes going back to Keith, she began, "Oh, Levi, this is an old friend of mine, Keith Bedly. Keith this is..."

Keith nodded, knowing exactly who the man was. Everyone knew Levi. He was a great actor. "Levi Proctor." He moved a little closer to extend his hand to him. "Pleased to meet you. I'm a huge fan!"

Levi firmly shook his hand with his free hand. "Same here. Thank you!" He was pleased to meet another one of his many fans.

Keith dropped his eyes to Jazzmine. "You have a great woman there." He raised his eyes back to Levi. "Don't let her get away. I made that mistake once." Without another word, he walked away.

Jazzmine opened her mouth to tell Keith that she and Levi weren't dating, but it was too late. He was gone. Oh, it didn't matter. He could think whatever he wanted. They wouldn't see each other again anyway.

Levi frowned as she released his hand. Walking around the table to his own seat, he sat down. "What was that all about?"

Jazzmine glanced back at Keith with a shake of her head. Turning her attention back, she smiled. "Oh, nothing. Never mind him. What did Bradley say?"

"Nothing much. He just went on and on about how much Leila enjoyed working with me. I think he's trying to play matchmaker and get us together."

Jazzmine almost frowned. The idea of Levi dating Leila Brewer didn't thrill her. It could complicate their friendship. What if Leila wanted him to move to New York City permanently? What would she do without him? Lowering her eyes, she said, "I thought you liked her. I mean, she is attractive."

Levi agreed. "Yes, she is, but while we were working together on the set, I found her impossible to get alone with. She always wants everything to be her way. She's ok, but she's not my type."

Relieved, Jazzmine exhaled silently. That was good news.

Friday night, Jazzmine sat in her old bedroom thinking of old times. She missed the good old days and doing things with her sister. They used to have fun together. Perhaps, there was something they could do together for old times' sake. After a moment of thought, she had a brilliant idea.

If there was one thing the two sisters had in common, it was their love of nature. Jazzmine knew the perfect place where she and her sister could go to enjoy nature and spend quality time together. With a smile on her face, she reached over and picked up the telephone. Speed dialing her sister, she waited for an answer.

"Hello?" Vanessa picked up on the second ring.

"Vanessa, hey! It's me. Let's do something tomorrow. You know, just you and me."

Vanessa was weary for a moment. The last time they tried that, Jazzmine didn't cooperate with her and everything was backwards. But, what did Jazzmine have in mind? She didn't have time to waste. If Jazzmine didn't say something worth her while, she wasn't going. After a moment, she asked, "What did you have in mind?"

"I was thinking maybe we could go up on *Crest Mountain* for old times' sake. It will be fun. We can view the city just like we used to do. What do you say?"

A smile spread across Vanessa's lips. That did sound like fun. They shared a lot of great times on *Crest Mountain*. It had been the one place she had been able to go with Jazzmine and no one else knew. When they were on *Crest Mountain*, Vanessa actually enjoyed Jazzmine's company and being with her in private. "I'm game. Let's do breakfast first, my treat." She was so excited.

Jazzmine nodded, liking her sister's idea. "All right. The nurse will be here early. So we can go when she gets here."

"See you then, honey."

"OK."

They hung up and Jazzmine heaved a sigh of happiness. Vanessa worked too hard and too much. They were finally going to get a little time together and do something they both enjoyed as opposed to the club thing they tried. That didn't work out at all, and she didn't want to go through it again.

"I'm going to *Crest Mountain* with Vanessa," Jazzmine explained to Levi as he followed her down the stairs the following morning.

"Where is *Crest Mountain*?" he was anxious to know.

"Levi," she glanced back at him. "It's the only mountain around here." Turning her attention back, she stepped down to the living room floor.

"Are you sure you're dressed properly? It could get chilly." He had to think of an excuse to get her to stay. The last time she went out with Vanessa, he remembered what happened, and it wasn't a nice thought. He stopped on the last step and leaned against the banister. His arms were on the rail and his hands dangled down.

Jazzmine's eyes dropped to her outfit. She wore a long sleeve blue jean shirt with a black collar. The edges of the sleeves were black, and the name brand was in black print in the top left hand corner. She wore the matching jeans with a black belt and shoes. She thought the outfit was fine. It was warm. Perhaps, she would need a jacket, but she didn't think so. The sun was shining brighter than ever outside. Levi was just being his usual cautious self.

Lifting her eyes, she asked, "What's wrong with this?"

"Well nothing if you think you'll be warm," Levi answered, knowing that he was failing at his mission. It wasn't cold enough for a jacket, as of yet.

"Oh, Levi," she waved a hand at him, dismissing his comment. Her eyes went to his outfit. He was wearing a short sleeve blue shirt, which zipped at the top with pouch pockets at the bottom and jeans. "Don't you think you might get cold in that?"

He winked at her. "If I go anywhere, I'll wear a jacket."

"Miss Thomas," the nurse called as she was entering the room from the hall.

Jazzmine switched her attention to the nurse, who had finally arrived.

The idea of Jazzmine being alone on some mountaintop with that wicked sister of hers didn't set too well with Levi.

He paced the floor for nearly an hour wondering what they were doing up there. He had a bad feeling Vanessa was going to try to pull another stunt to hurt Jazzmine, and he couldn't let that happen. He would never forgive himself if he did.

He couldn't go up on the mountain, however. Jazzmine would think he was a complete idiot for invading her time with her sister. She did deserve it after all this time, but why now? Couldn't they go to a movie where it would be safer for Jazzmine. Who knew what Vanessa had planned for that mountaintop? There were no witnesses for miles and...

Shaking the thought, Levi grabbed his brown leather jacket from the bed, and he was out the door.

Whether Jazzmine wanted him to or not, he was going to *Crest Mountain*!

Jazzmine stood at the edge of the mountaintop, looking down at the entire city. The view was as wonderful and lovely as she remembered. With a sigh, she closed her eyes, enjoying the cool breeze as it hit her face and blew through her hair.

Seeing Jazzmine standing there with her face lifted to the air and her eyes closed, hatred overpowered Vanessa, and she couldn't control herself. They were all alone on the mountaintop, just the two of them. No one else was around for a far.

Vanessa looked around, glancing over her shoulder as if she expected someone to be there. Yes, they were in private. This was the perfect opportunity for her to eliminate Jazzmine from the equation. With a wicked smile on her face, she eased forward and poked her in the back.

Feeling a sharp pain in her back, Jazzmine jumped, frightened. She could have fallen off the mountaintop. Her heart was beating rapidly as her life almost flashed before her very eyes. Glancing back with fear in her eyes, she swallowed hard.

What was that?

Looking around innocently, Vanessa frowned at her sister's expression. "What's wrong?" she asked, pretending to be concerned.

"I don't know. It felt like something just stung me in the back."

Vanessa laughed. "You must be imagining things. I didn't see anything, and there's nothing flying around." She wanted her to feel stupid.

Jazzmine slowly nodded and looked back down at the city. "Maybe, you're right."

Vanessa smiled mischievously to herself. She was going to push her sister this time, and she wouldn't miss. It would be a pleasure to watch Jazzmine fall off the mountain and plunge to her death. No one would ever know she pushed her. She would cry and tell the police she didn't know what happened. She definitely wouldn't feel guilty this time.

It would be hard on their father, but eventually, he would get over it.

Vanessa would be an only child! Loving the very idea, she positioned her hands at Jazzmine's back to push her, but she froze and snapped her head around when someone called Jazzmine's name from a distance.

She should have known! It was stupid Levi! Why did he always...

How much did he see? Had he seen everything? *"Oh no!"* she thought. If he got to Jazzmine before she did, he could destroy everything. What was she going to do?

At her name, Jazzmine snapped her head around, as well, wondering who knew where to find her.

When Jazzmine looked around, Vanessa reached out and hugged her sister from behind, pretending to protect her from the intruder.

Levi, witnessing everything from his distance behind a huge boulder, stepped forward. He knew Vanessa couldn't be trusted. He actually witnessed her trying to push her sister off the mountaintop! Did she hate her that much? Why? He just could not understand it. *"I knew something was wrong with that woman!"* he thought. He was glad he arrived in time to save Jazzmine's life. Vanessa's actions only confirmed his suspicions that she tried to poison her sister with the sulfur. He had known as much.

He had to wonder what was in store for Jazzmine next. Surely, Vanessa had something else up her sleeve if this didn't work. He couldn't allow anything else to happen to Jazzmine. He **wouldn't**. If Vanessa didn't love her sister, he sure did!

When he moved forward, Jazzmine saw him clearly. Recognizing him, she frowned with dismay. "Levi! What are you doing up here?" He didn't have to come all the way up to *Crest Mountain*. Was he…? What *was* he doing on the mountaintop?

"Rescuing my beautiful princess," Levi answered in his mind, wishing he could tell her. He was quick to bring the hand he held behind his back around to show off the brown leather jacket he had bought her for Christmas. It was the same as the one he was wearing. "I thought you might need this."

Jazzmine sighed. "That's sweet, but it's not that cold."

Vanessa smiled at Levi. "That's sweet and cute!"

Levi gave her a cold stare and moved forward to extend the jacket to Jazzmine. "It's chilly enough for a jacket to me."

Jazzmine snatched the jacket playfully and walked away.

Vanessa turned to face Levi, who gave her another cold stare. At the expression on his face, fear washed over her, causing her to feel a chill. She swallowed hard as fear rose to her throat, almost choking her. If he saw any of what she did to Jazzmine, he could destroy her. She could not allow that to happen. Hoping to find out how much he had seen, she opened her mouth to speak, but he was quicker to speak, whispering, "You're going straight to hell!" Shaking his head, he followed his best friend.

Vanessa stared after him. He had seen too much. Now she had to do something about him and fast! He couldn't be trusted. He was Jazzmine's best friend, and she was sure he could be very convincing at anything he said to her. He was the one person who could probably get Jazzmine to see the truth about her, and she was just too close for that now. How could she insure herself that he would keep quiet? Levi was nothing like Jazzmine. He wasn't easily intimidated, and whatever scheme she came up with would have to be superior and above his head.

CHAPTER TEN

As the first day of November arrived, which was Sunday, the weather began to change drastically.

That morning, it was warm, a gorgeous day for church and going to the park for a long stroll, which Jazzmine and Levi did.

That evening it cooled off a bit and rain fell unexpectedly, pouring down on their heads as they were walking through the cemetery, visiting her mother's grave. With every raindrop that fell, the wind seemed to blow colder until it was freezing.

"Great! The fire is lit!" Jazzmine exclaimed when she entered the house, dripping wet from head to toe. The warmth of the room met her at the door. Her eyes immediately went to the fire burning in the fireplace.

"Why don't you go upstairs and put on something dry?" Levi suggested as he closed the door behind him. Cold and wet, also, he was shaking.

"I'm going to check on Daddy, and then I will change."

"Ok. I'll meet you back down here when you're done. We'll warm up by the fire together."

Loving the sound of that, Jazzmine secretly smiled to herself and walked away.

Jazzmine returned downstairs wearing a black silk robe open to expose the sexy nightgown underneath.

Levi was sitting on the floor next to the fireplace in his pajamas wrapped in a blanket. He appeared to be deep in thought as he stared into space with a blank expression on his face.

She moved closer to him. "Penny for your thoughts!"

Hearing her voice, he blinked out of his trance and glanced at her.

The sight of her in the sexy gown was almost unbearable. Why must she tease him so? He didn't want to stare, but it was impossible not to ogle. Her full, bare breasts were quite visible as their nipples peeked through the thin lace. Her legs were gorgeous and sexy, very smooth. Even her blow-dried hair looked good pulled back in the straight ponytail.

Couldn't she have worn pajamas? That would have been more appropriate than driving him insane!

Levi lowered his eyes and swallowed hard as she moved even closer. He had to contain himself as his desire, which had to be repressed, was to take her in arms and pleasure her right there on the living room floor. He wanted to tease her body as she was practically teasing him with it, flaunting it before him. He would be gentle with every inch of it as his tongue tasted the softness of it, giving her everything he had to offer. Oh, how he desired her. If only she knew, she would go back upstairs and slip into non-revealing pajamas.

"Is there room in that blanket for me?" Jazzmine asked as she hoped he wouldn't say no. She needed to be next to him right now, in his arms.

The question caught him completely off guard, and he quivered under the blanket. He wanted more than anything to answer that question in a different way than she intended. Of course, she wanted to hear *yes*, but he wanted to show her **yes**! "*Oh Lord!*" Levi thought. "*Why now? Why tonight?*" If Jazzmine got too close to him or he touched her, he would lose his mind!

However, he would take advantage of the situation as she was offering. He would love to hold her, having her warm body next to his. Looking up at her and wanting her near him, he nodded. Opening the blanket, he beckoned her to come closer with a nod of his head.

Jazzmine, shivering with anticipation, hurried to sit between his legs, which were propped in the air, in front of him. He closed the blanket around them, encasing her in the security of his arms. All thought of any kind left her mind as she enjoyed the feeling of cuddling up to a warm fire with Levi.

It was so nice and romantic. It was something she had only read about in romance novels or seen on television. She never imagined it would happen to her. Having Levi's strong arms around her was blissful. She never dreamed being in someone's arms could feel this way. It hadn't felt this way with Bartu, and he held her countless times, more often than not. Why? What was so different about Levi?

Levi strained with every fiber of his being to control his urges, which grew stronger with every passing second. When he could no longer do so, he shook his head and stood up. Turning to face the fire, he stared down into it.

Confused, Jazzmine looked up at him. What was wrong? Did he not want to be close to her? Did he wish she were someone else? She had to know. "Levi, what's wrong? Did I upset you? I didn't mean to. I..."

"No," he turned back to her. "It's not you. I just..." He shook his head and lifted his eyes to the ceiling. He didn't know what was going on himself. All he knew was that he was madly in love with her, and he was afraid of how she would react to him. He couldn't afford to lose her friendship.

Jazzmine stood up, as well, and looked him in the eyes. "What? You what?" She was anxious to know what was holding him back.

Gazing into her eyes, he couldn't help loving her. She was a beautiful woman with a beautiful heart. How could he not? She was the woman men had been searching for an entire lifetime with no success. He was standing before his sole mate, an angel sent from God, and she probably had no thoughts of him in the romantic sense.

"You what?" Jazzmine urged again with wonder in her eyes.

"I... Oh, what the hell..." Levi dropped the blanket and took her into his arms, kissing her with all the passion he possessed inside.

"Finally!" Jazzmine thought, her insides doing major cartwheels. She thought he would never kiss her. For a moment, she wondered if she had to grab him and kiss him.

Enjoying the warm sensation of his lips, she returned the kiss, locking her arms around his neck. He teased her lips apart so that he could deepen the kiss. *"Wow!"* she thought. It was even better than she imagined. It was magnificent to be exact! The way his tongue lavished her mouth, shocking her with pleasure, was a forbidden deed between two friends. She loved it!

When she responded to him, Levi pulled her even closer, adding more passion to the kiss. When he finally pulled back, he whispered, "That's something I've wanted to do for a long time."

She smiled into his eyes. If he could kiss like that, there were so many other things he could probably do so well! "You should have done it a long time ago!" she whispered back.

Her words shocked him, and Levi was speechless. He wasn't exactly sure what she was telling him.

Taking his hand, Jazzmine led him to the sofa, and they sat down. Standing on her knees behind him, she found herself massaging his shoulders and kissing his neck.

That within itself was a statement that needed no explanation! Joy and happiness sprang to Levi's heart, and he had to tell her how much he was enjoying the massage. He, also, told her how wonderful her lips felt against his skin.

Before long, Jazzmine found herself lying beside him in his arms. He whispered sweet nothings in her ear, and she enjoyed every word. He kissed her whenever he felt the urge, and she gave back to the kiss, appreciating his lips.

They laid together in each other's arms all night on the sofa, drifting off to sleep together.

Monday evening, after work, Vanessa went directly to her father's. She let herself in without knocking. At the door, she stripped from her fur coat and the leather gloves. Stuffing the gloves in the coat pocket, she hung it up on the coat rack and closed the door.

The house was peaceful and quiet.

Assuming that her father was resting as Jazzmine and Levi were off together somewhere, Vanessa tiptoed down the hall to her father's room, hoping to sneak up on him. Instead of surprising her father, she was surprised to hear voices in his room.

The door was slightly ajar.

Tiptoeing to the door, Vanessa peeked inside.

Jazzmine was standing at their father's bedside with her back to the door.

James was looking up at her with a loving expression on his face as he listened to her.

Not wanting to interrupt, Vanessa started on her way again, only to stop when she heard Jazzmine's statement to their father.

"Daddy, I don't know what to do! It's all happening so fast. I really do think I'm falling in love with Levi."

Vanessa's mouth dropped with sheer surprise. What? Jazzmine was falling in love with Levi? That just couldn't happen. If they fell in love, she would trust him completely and probably believe every word he said. If that happened, he would be free to tell her *everything*!

Worried, Vanessa bit her bottom lip. She just could not let that happen. Levi couldn't get to Jazzmine before she did. What if he was already filling her head with bits and pieces of the truth about her? He could be slowly preparing her for the major things like how she tried to poison her with the sulfur. Surely, he figured it out. She distinctly remembered him asking her what she did to her sister that night she entered the room and discovered that Jazzmine drank the tea. If he told her that she tried to push her off the mountaintop, it would be inevitable that Jazzmine would figure everything else out for herself. Levi witnessed it with his own eyes!

"Well, baby, after what you said happened last night, maybe you should just tell him," James encouraged. Actually, he believed that Levi already knew. He knew that Levi was in love with his daughter. He gathered that much upon his first visit to Beverly Hills. Levi never once tried to hide his feelings, and James picked up on that on day one!

"Something happened between Levi and Jazzmine last night?" Vanessa wondered. *"What happened?"* She shook her head, dismissing the question as she didn't care to hear the answer. She didn't have time to worry about it. They couldn't have slept together because that wasn't the type of thing a woman openly discussed with her father! She had to do something before Jazzmine told Levi she was falling in love with him.

After a moment of worrying and plotting in her mind, the perfect idea came to her. She knew exactly how to stop everything before anything got started. She had to find Levi. Obviously, he was in the house somewhere. His rental was parked in the driveway. Besides, he didn't stray too far from Jazzmine. He was practically her shadow. Hopefully, he was in his room.

Not having time to waste, she raced the stairs to Levi's room, bursting in.

When the door burst open, Levi, lying flat on his back at the foot of the bed with his feet planted on the floor, arched up on his elbows. Surprised that someone would burst in on him that way, he frowned. Seeing that it was Vanessa, his frowned deepened. What did she want? "What's the matter with you?" he asked curiously, wondering if she had lost her mind.

"No time to talk," Vanessa explained as she hurriedly unbuttoned the navy top she was wearing, which she stripped from and tossed to the floor.

The appalled look on his face did nothing to hide Levi's feelings. She *was* crazy! He had no idea what had gotten into her. All he knew was that he wanted her to put her top back on and get out of his room. His eyes moved from her face to the navy lace bra covering her medium sized breasts. "What...?"

Before he could finish his statement, Vanessa rushed to the bed and jumped on top of him, kissing him wildly. "Oh, Levi," she moaned and busied herself unbuttoning his crisp white shirt. "I want you too!" She kissed him again and lowered her mouth to his neck.

"Vanessa..." Someone clearing her throat cut off Levi's statement.

Vanessa and Levi both looked around at the same time to find Jazzmine standing in the doorway with her arms folded across her chest. An angry expression was on her face.

Seeing Jazzmine, Levi immediately figured out

Vanessa's agenda, and he felt like a fool. He should have known! Jazzmine was naturally going to believe her eyes and not her heart. In her heart she knew that he would never do what it looked like he was doing to her, but of course, it looked much differently. To say, *"This isn't what it looks like,"* would sound so typical.

Pretending to be embarrassed, Vanessa rolled off of Levi and landed on her back. "Jazzmine!" she sounded surprised to see her. With a sigh of embarrassment, she hopped up from the bed and scrambled about to find her blouse. Collecting it, she hurried from the room, pretending to be too embarrassed to talk.

Levi sat up. He knew exactly what was coming next. "Jazz, I know what you're thinking, and I'm sorry..."

Jazzmine held up a hand to silence him. The scene before her devastated her. She was overwhelmed with anger and guilt. The things she wanted from him and the things she wanted to do to him faded away with a simple snap of a finger. How could he do this to her? She had actually come up to his room to confess her love for him. It was just luck that she walked in before anything major happened. She wouldn't have been able to handle that. "I don't want to hear it! You think you can have my sister and me, too? Levi, how could you hurt me like this?"

"Jazz, please let me explain," Levi pleaded.

Too angry with him to listen to anything he had to say, Jazzmine walked away, turning her back on him. "Don't," she told him in a cold tone. Turning back, she said, "I want you to get out of my father's house! I want you out **NOW**! When I come back up here, I don't want you here!" On that note, she left the room.

When she was gone, Levi dropped his head with anger and disappointment. He was angry with Vanessa for the wedge she just drove between him and the woman of his dreams. He was disappointed with Jazzmine for not allow him to tell his side of the story. They had been best friends for six years! One moment of madness shouldn't be able to destroy that!

"Damn you, Vanessa!" he thought. She had to go and take the one thing that meant the world to him just to assure herself that her secret would never be revealed. That was very clever of her, eliminating him from her sister's life. Obviously, if Jazzmine wouldn't listen to him, he couldn't tell her about her evil sister's plot to destroy her! Well, he had news for Vanessa. He would expose her secrets whether Jazzmine wanted to listen or not. When the truth came out, she would have to listen because she would have no other choice.

Jazzmine laid on her side next to her father with her head on his chest. His arm was around her as he tried to comfort her even though she wouldn't tell him what was wrong.

Understanding that she didn't feel like talking about whatever was wrong, he let her be. He kissed her hair, and he told her he loved her.

Jazzmine stared at the wall, feeling hopeless. It was just unbelievable that Levi would do this to her. The way he kissed her last night, he was so convincing. He made her believe that he really did care for her, and today she found out that it had all been to see if he could have her and her sister!

It just wasn't fair! She had known him for years, and she couldn't believe he would act this way. What had gotten into him? Why had he done this to her? Well, of course this wasn't the first time this happened to her. Vanessa was always getting the men she wanted.

Jazzmine still couldn't compete with Vanessa when it came to men. They would always want Vanessa more whether they wanted her or not, and that was what hurt the most. She had actually given Levi her heart, and he stomped all over it! She would never fall in love, again. If she did, it would be as far away from Vanessa as possible. She just wondered why Vanessa wanted *Levi* of all men. She had men of her own. Perhaps, the men she dated weren't enough. She had to have all the men!

"Levi is mine!" she told Vanessa mentally. Even though her mind was telling her to let Levi go, her heart was still telling her that she loved him. She did, and there was no way to run from that. It would just take her a little time to get over him. How could she get over him? They lived right next door to each other in Beverly Hills, and she couldn't just pick up and move. She loved her house. She couldn't ask him to move either. He was a grown man, and he could live wherever he pleased. She would just have to avoid him as best as possible.

"Now, Daddy, you take your time, and don't fall," Vanessa encouraged her father as they were in the physical therapist's office, preparing for James to walk for the first time. She sat next to her father on the comfortable sofa in the waiting room.

Jazzmine stood beside her father's wheelchair. "Daddy, you can do it!" she exclaimed, placing her hand on his shoulder.

James's eyes went up to Jazzmine, and he frowned. "Where is Levi? Isn't he coming? I want him to be here as well as the two of you."

Vanessa looked around her father at Jazzmine to see the expression on her face when their father asked her about Levi. She smiled to herself and sat back again when Jazzmine appeared to be upset by the question. That was just for what she was hoping. The two of them hadn't spoken to each other in almost a week. She had been delighted to find out that Jazzmine put him out of the house, forcing him to move into a hotel.

"Um, Daddy," Jazzmine dropped her eyes, not wanting to talk about Levi. "Levi is..."

"Right here," a masculine voice came from nowhere, causing all eyes to go to the door. Levi, standing at the door, moved farther into the room. "Sorry, I'm late, Mr. Thomas. I didn't realize how late it was."

James nodded with understanding. "That's quite all right."

Seeing Levi, Vanessa was furious. He wasn't supposed to come! He was supposed to be somewhere else, anywhere else but there!

Levi's eyes went to Jazzmine, and their gazes locked.

Seeing him again for the first time in almost a week, the love she had for him rose to the surface, causing her to want to run to his warm embrace. She had known it would be hard to let him go. Dropping her eyes, she looked away.

"All right, Mr. Thomas," Nancy Warner, the therapist, said as she was entering the room. "Are you ready for this?"

James nodded eagerly. "I'm as ready as I'll ever be." His eyes went from Vanessa to Levi and then to Jazzmine. "I've got the support of my family. What more could a man ask for?"

Nancy laughed. "I suppose you're ready then."

Jazzmine smiled broadly, clapping, as she watched her father take slow steps down the long walkway. He was doing an excellent job for the first time. It seemed as if he had done this before. He hadn't fallen once.

Vanessa nodded anxiously with each step her father took. She was so proud of him. He was doing so well. Soon, he would be back to normal, and they could ship Jazzmine out of there!

Levi watched James move with admiration. He was happy for him. Soon, he would be able to walk as if nothing happened to him, and they could put this behind them.

"Jazz," Levi called to her in the crowded lobby as they were heading for the exit.

Hearing her name, Jazzmine stopped and slowly turned around. Not saying a word, she gave her former best friend a cold stare.

"We need to talk," Levi explained when he was finally at her side.

She tilted her head to the side, wondering why he felt the need to talk to her now. "Oh really?"

Levi was nervous as he stood face to face with Jazzmine. His feelings hadn't changed, and they never would. Her feelings for him might change, however, because he intended to hold nothing back. He was going to tell her everything about her rotten sister! If she didn't believe him or if she never trusted him again, that was fine. As long as he cleared his conscience, he could endure the consequences.

"Yes, really! I've tried everything I could think of to get your attention. I've called your father's house, and you've hung up on me. I've invited you out to dinner, and you refused to come. I've even sent you flowers, apologizing for what you think you saw. You sent them back." He wasn't Bartu, and he didn't deserve such treatment. Bartu might have deliberately hurt her, but he didn't, and he refused to allow her to believe he did!

Jazzmine laughed with amusement at his silly statement. She was no fool! She *knew* what she saw! "What I *think* I saw? Levi, I *know* what I saw, and it really hurt me."

Levi shook his head with disagreement. "I didn't do what you think I did. Vanessa threw herself at me. Before I knew anything, she was all over me. Before I could get her off of me, there you were entering the room."

Jazzmine glanced over her shoulder at her sister, who was pushing their father's wheelchair to the door. What Levi was saying didn't make sense. That couldn't possibly be true. Turning her eyes back to him, she asked, "So, you weren't the least bit tempted by her?"

"No! Jazz," Levi reached out and took her hand, but she pulled away. Accepting her action, Levi shook his head. "I was not, and am not, attracted to your sister." In fact, he could actually say that she repulsed him.

Jazzmine laughed and looked back at her sister again. Looking back to him one more time, she laughed, again. "Nice try. Vanessa is a very attractive woman, and I've always known I couldn't compete with her. You must have felt really awkward having both of us in one room today." She shook her head. "How can you live with yourself? That was really low." She nodded. "Really low!"

Levi sighed. "Jazz," he pleaded.

She shook her head again. "You know, Levi, I thought I knew you, but I don't know you at all. I can't talk anymore. I have to go!" Jazzmine turned to walk away.

"No, Jazz, it's Vanessa who you really don't know," he called after her, stopping her in her tracks.

She turned back to face him. What could he possibly think he knew about her sister that she didn't know?

Staying his distance, he continued, "I'm the same person I've always been. Vanessa is the one who is doing these things to you. *Above Beautiful* doesn't even exist! *She* called Mrs. Trenton and set the whole thing up to get you to go home. *She's* Charlene Barks. She doesn't want you here. That's why she never showed up at the airport to pick you up. That's, also, why she planted those pictures of you as a child everywhere. Yes, she did that too, believe it or not! *She* is the one who had that hit man come after you that night at the club.

"She tried to poison you with the powdered sulfur. I don't know how, but she did. She even tried to push you off *Crest Mountain*. She did these things to you, Jazz, and now she's trying to take away the one thing that you'll always have, *me*!

Believe me when I tell you that I'm not lying to you. I would never do anything to hurt you. You have to know that!"

Jazzmine cringed with disbelief, horrified at his words. She couldn't believe he was accusing her sister of such horrible things. Vanessa would never try to *kill* her. The suggestion was outrageous and utterly ridiculous! Did he think she was going to let him get away with that? Surely, he didn't.

Her first instinct was to slap him, but the second told her not to because she didn't want to hurt him just because he hurt her. That would be an eye for an eye, and she wasn't that type of person.

She didn't even have to deal with this. Holding up a hand in surrender, she shook her head. "Ok, Levi, I give up. You win. You can have Vanessa. I'll just get out of your way." She turned around and practically ran away this time.

When she left him, Levi dropped his head in shame. He failed again, and there was no way he was going to get her to believe him now. He had no more hope.

A full week passed, and Jazzmine felt more alone than ever. Her life was a complete mess, and she wasn't sure how to fix it. She wasn't even sure it could be fixed.

Nothing was going her way. She lost her best friend, her relationship with her sister had changed because of what had happened between her and Levi, and strange things had been happening to her, which she couldn't explain.

Secrets that she had never told a soul were flying around about her, and she had no idea how they were leaking. These were secrets even Levi didn't know about her. People were constantly calling her teasing her that she had only had one boyfriend in her entire life, and she wasn't even able to hold on to him.

No one had known that Bartu had been her first boyfriend. Even he didn't know. She had no idea how the discovery was made.

"Why does this keep happening to me?" Jazzmine asked herself as the tears continued to fall. "I just can't be happy."

Her eyes were on the tabloid she held in her hand as she sat on the edge of the sofa reading it. She was reading her life story as it was written in black and white from beginning to end.

Everything was there except the fact that she was a virgin. She had no idea how this had happened. She hadn't been interviewed. It was just impossible. Someone was out to destroy her, and she had no idea who hated her that much. Who could be so evil?

Tossing the tabloid to the coffee table, she rested her face in her palms and sobbed silently.

She wanted Levi!

"Oh God," she thought. *"I miss him so much!"* She wanted him to hold her and tell her that everything was going to be all right, but it wasn't. He couldn't do that because she couldn't trust him, and she couldn't forgive him for what he did to her. Her life was nothing more than a big joke for the world to laugh at, and that was exactly what they were doing, laughing at her.

Vanessa sat behind her desk, wondering how long it would be before Jazzmine decided that she had taken enough abuse, and she was ready to go home. Surely, it wouldn't be long. She didn't have any reason to stay in New York City. Their father was doing much better. Levi was no longer the person with whom she confided her deepest secrets. And the world was laughing at Jazzmine thanks to her! Why would she stay?

Cassandra entered the office unexpectedly, and Vanessa smiled as she crossed the room to her. "Hey, Vanessa, how's your father? I hear he's walking now."

"Yes, he is. They're baby steps, but he's walking!"

"Good! And how's Jazz?"

Vanessa lowered her eyes and looked away. "Um, Jazzmine... Well, I don't know what to say about her. She hasn't been herself lately. She has this attitude. It's like she thinks she on top of the world."

Cassandra's mouth dropped with disbelief. That didn't sound like the Jazzmine she met. "What? Jazz?"

Vanessa nodded. "Yes! Girl, do you know what she said to me about you the other day?"

Cassandra drew back in horror. Jazzmine had been talking about her behind her back? Why? What did she say? They didn't even know each other. Where did Jazzmine get off talking about her? "No. What did she say?"

"Well..."

Friday, Jazzmine decided that it was a good idea that she just go home the next day, and put all of this behind her. It wouldn't be easy, but she would do her best.

Deciding to leave as early as possible, she wanted to stop by the office and tell Vanessa good-bye.

To her surprise, when she got to Vanessa's office, it was empty. Wanting to see Cassandra to say good-bye to her, she started down the hall toward her office. Just her luck, Cassandra was coming out of her office when she got there.

Seeing Jazzmine, Cassandra narrowed her eyes with hatred. It was just impossible to believe that someone she believed to be so sweet was so rotten! It was childish to talk about someone behind his or her back!

"Cassandra, hi!" Jazzmine smiled at her innocently. "I just dropped by Vanessa's office to say good-bye, but she wasn't there. Do you know where I could find her?"

Cassandra gave her a cold stare. "Oh, are you leaving?" she asked sarcastically. "Well, good-bye, Miss Queen of the World!"

Jazzmine drew back in horror, wondering what her problem was. "Cassandra, what's the matter with you?"

"My problem is **you**! So, you think you're better than everyone else, do you? You think my face isn't pretty enough to be a model? Well, guess what! Before you moved to California, you weren't so hot yourself, Missy! I'm a little control freak, am I? I think I could run this company all by myself, do I? You know what I think? I think you were just trying to start trouble between Vanessa and me. I, also, think you had better get out of here before I tell you where you can really go, you little ***virgin***!"

At the word ***virgin***, Jazzmine's eyes widened. Her mouth dropped. Her heart almost stopped beating. How did Cassandra know that she was a virgin? Who told her that? What was she talking about because she had no idea? Why was she treating her so harshly? This wasn't like Cassandra at all. It seemed that the people she cared the most about were turning against her, and she had no earthly idea why!

"Vanessa went home for the day if you really want to know!" Cassandra went on to say. On that note, she walked away as it was apparent that she was furious.

Jazzmine turned to stare after her in total awe. She had no idea what was going on. Placing her hand on her forehead, she shook her head with confusion.

Suddenly, a vision of her and Vanessa sitting by the fireplace in their pajamas flashed in her mind. Trying to shake the vision, she blinked. Visions of the night she drank the powdered sulfur came flooding back.

"The secrets!" she thought, recollecting her conversation with her sister that night. It was quite comprehensible what was happening now. *"I confessed my secrets to Vanessa. I told her that I was a virgin, and Bartu was my first boyfriend. She must have turned Cassandra against me, but why? I've never done anything to her!"*

The day she watched her father take his first steps came crashing back, as well, and she distinctly remembered Levi saying, *"She doesn't want you here."*

Trying to shake the thought, his words rang in her ears, *"I'm the same person I've always been. Vanessa is the one who is doing these things to you. Above Beautiful doesn't even exist!* **She** *called Mrs.*

*Trenton and set the whole thing up to get you to go home. **She's** Charlene Barks. She doesn't want you here. That's why she never showed up at the airport to pick you up. That's, also, why she planted those pictures of you as a child everywhere. Yes, she did that, too, believe it or not! **She** is the one who had that hit man come after you that night at the club.*

*"She tried to poison you with the powdered sulfur. I don't know how, but she did. She even tried to push you off of Crest Mountain. She did these things to you, Jazzmine, and now she's trying to take away the one thing that you'll always have, **me**! Believe me when I tell you that I'm not lying to you. I would never do anything to hurt you. You have to know that!"*

"Levi," she whispered to herself, "if you are telling the truth," she shook her head, thinking of the things she wanted to do to Vanessa, "Vanessa is dead meat!" She balled a fist and slammed it into the palm of her other hand. She had to see for herself to be one hundred percent sure. Turning around, she continued down the hall.

Jazzmine let herself into her father's office and locked the door. She didn't want any disturbances.

When she turned into the room, her eyes landed on his computer.

She went to it, sitting down in front of it. She immediately logged on.

Her intentions were to use the Internet to search for all of the modeling agencies in New York City. If she could not find an agency with the title *Above Beautiful*, and, if no other model she contacted on line had ever heard of it, she would know that every word of what Levi told her was the complete truth. She had to know the truth.

Neither did she want to believe that her sister could be so evil nor that she would try to harm her. Yet, it was so hard to believe that Levi would make up all of those things. She couldn't believe that he would do anything to hurt her intentionally.

First, she had to check her E-mail because she hadn't checked it in quite some time. She accessed all the right codes and got into her E-mail account.

A frown of confusion darkened her features when the first thing she saw was an E-mail message from Bartu. She read it quickly. She gathered from his message that someone sent him a message telling him everything about her father's accident, and he needed to fly out to New York City immediately.

She snapped her head up remembering Bartu's words, *"I got your E-mail."* Someone, *Vanessa* particularly, must have E-mailed him a message, signing her name. It was the only logical explanation. Believing her assumption to be correct, she nodded and bit her bottom lip. She continued to go through her mail to find a message from Levi apologizing for everything that happened between them, but he was blunt in letting her know that he meant every word he said about her sister, and he wasn't taking it back.

She sighed to herself, lifting her eyes as she clearly remembered the passionate kiss they shared. The vision was vivid in her mind as she could almost relive the experience. Her hand rose to her heart as she went on to read how deep Levi's feelings were for her. She was touched.

Levi confessed everything in his e-mail. He explained that he had been madly in love with her since the first day he met her in his father's church years ago. He confessed that he had been jealous of Bartu and their relationship. He even told her that he wished she had let him punch him that day at the hospital, which made her smile. She didn't know he felt so passionately about her, and it was flattering.

He, also, confessed to finding out about every scheme Vanessa plotted against her and how he came about uncovering her secrets. He apologized for doing these things behind her back, telling her that he knew she wouldn't have believed him had he come to her with them first. She nodded at the message, knowing that he was right. She wouldn't have listened to him, and she knew it.

Concluding the message, he told her, despite everything that was going on between them, he would still be there for her when she needed him.

"Oh," Jazzmine moaned as she read, *"I love you! With all sincerity, Levi!"* from the bottom of the message.

He was so sweet, the total package, and she was sorry she ever doubted him.

"I love you, too," she whispered, wishing he were there with her now.

Getting out of her E-mail account, she surfed the Internet for *Above Beautiful Modeling Agency.* Discovering it to be nonexistent, she concluded that Levi had been correct in everything he said, and she regretted not believing him.

Standing up with anger flowing through her

veins, Jazzmine gritted her teeth. Vanessa was going to pay for what she had done to her, and she would pay dearly. "Vanessa!" she said aloud as if she were in the room with her, "I have a *big* surprise for you!"

Jazzmine clutched the steering wheel of her father's car tighter as she drove down the street toward Vanessa's house. She was angrier than ever. She could not get over the fact that her own sister could be so cruel! Levi had been right when he told her that she really didn't know Vanessa. She *didn't* know her anymore. She was so unlike the compassionate person she had been years ago.

Narrowing her eyes with every thought of her recent discovery, she bit her bottom lip. "Well, Vanessa, you once stole Keith Bedly from me, but I will not allow you to steal Levi! He is **my** man!" she hissed aloud as if Vanessa were in the car with her. Unconsciously, wanting to get to Vanessa as she was anxious to settle the score, she pressed her foot to the accelerator, going top speed. "Oh, no, sister! I am not giving Levi up without a fight, and you can believe that!"

She was breathing deeply now as her anger escalated to the highest degree. The way she felt at that moment, there was no telling what she would do to Vanessa if she crossed her again.

Vanessa had better watch out because Jazzmine was on a rampage. Even the people on the street needed to get out of her way!

CHAPTER ELEVEN

On Vanessa's doorstep, Jazzmine positioned her finger to ring the doorbell, and but she stopped herself. She didn't want to be *welcomed* inside. Vanessa had pretended with her too many times. Trying the doorknob, which turned easily, she let herself in. It would be better to sneak up on her sister. She would never suspect a thing. Perhaps, she would catch her on the phone telling someone else her secrets, and she would be glad to slap her in the mouth!

Stepping inside, she quietly closed the door behind her and tiptoed around the house until she heard Vanessa's voice in the den. Perhaps, she was on the phone gossiping about her or entertaining someone with more of her life story.

It was shocking and very surprising that *Levi* was the person with whom her sister was speaking. Jazzmine's mouth dropped, and her heart leaped to her throat as it beat rapidly at the sight of him.

Levi stood in the center of the room with his arms folded across his chest looking sexier than ever. There was a serious expression on his face as he stared at Vanessa.

Vanessa was standing at the window with her back to it, looking at him with amusement. Apparently, she wasn't taking anything he was saying seriously.

Seeing Levi for the first time in a week, Jazzmine's knees quivered. She shivered, wanting to run to the comfort of his arms.

He *loved* her. He actually loved her for who she was, and she appreciated that. He was a real man, the man for her. The way she felt about him just from seeing him was amazing. She loved him so much. She probably loved him more than he would ever know. Her feelings couldn't even be put into words.

Her heart was racing, her palms were sweating, and she could barely breathe. She had never felt so strongly about a man in her life. She knew that she wouldn't be able to hide her feelings from him for much longer.

Jazzmine stepped closer to the door, listening.

"Vanessa, I am tired of you trying to destroy your sister's life!" Levi was saying.

Vanessa laughed. "And just what are you going to do about it? Are you going to try to stop me?" She laughed again. "Oh, wait! You can't do that because Jazzmine hates you! She'll never believe a word you say. She thinks you and I are lovers!"

"We're not!" he hissed as if she didn't know.

Hearing his confession aloud, Jazzmine's heart melted, and she closed her eyes, exhaling inwardly with happiness. She couldn't bear the thought of Vanessa and Levi in bed together. It was just too much for her. Vanessa could *not* have every man. Levi was one she definitely couldn't have.

"That's just the point! Nothing happened that day! You set me up to get me out of your way because I knew too much."

"Correction! I got you out of my way!" Vanessa corrected him.

Jazzmine narrowed her eyes at her sister. *"That's what you think!"* she told her mentally.

Levi shook his head. "What's next, Vanessa? First, you spread that embarrassing picture of her all over town. Then, you had her attacked. You tried to poison her by putting powdered sulfur in her ice tea. You tried to push her off the mountain. You made her think there was something going on between the two of us, and then you had that crap printed about her in the tabloids! What's next?"

Jazzmine's heart almost skipped a beat as she had a feeling she knew the answer to Levi's question. She had a feeling that Vanessa was going to unleash her secret about being a virgin because it was the one thing she didn't want anyone to know. It would be the perfect way to destroy her. She wanted to save the best for last. At the thought of her secret being revealed, Jazzmine felt nervous because Levi didn't know. She didn't know how he would react if Vanessa told him right now. She wanted to be the one to tell him.

Vanessa was showing no mercy! She had no reason to believe that she wasn't going to spill her secret at any given moment. Crossing her fingers, she closed her eyes and prayed.

"Are you going to stab her in the back? Why not just shoot her and get it over with?" Levi went on. The minute the questions were out, he wished he hadn't asked them because he didn't want to give her any ideas. The next time she went after

Jazzmine, he wasn't sure he would be there to save her, especially since he and Jazzmine weren't on speaking terms. He wouldn't know Vanessa's next move and that frightened him.

Vanessa clapped her hands with a brilliant smile. So, he had figured her out. She assumed as much. He knew *everything* she did except for the part about Bartu. Obviously, he was an excellent observer and researcher. How did he miss that? Well, none of that matter now because he would never be able to use any of those things against her. Jazzmine no longer trusted him. She wouldn't listen to a word he said. He was no longer a threat to her. "Yes, I was clever to do all of those things, wasn't I? You're the only person who was smart enough to figure out that it was I who was behind the scene the whole time. If you hadn't been there to save Jazzmine on the mountaintop, I would have gotten away with it, and no one would have known."

Jazzmine's mind flashed back to the night she was attacked. Then, it flashed to the night she drank the tea. She remembered it clearly. It was strange how Vanessa kept insisting that she drink the tea, and now she knew why. She had poisoned it with their father's medication. She didn't know how anyone could have such a cold heart toward her own flesh and blood!

Finally, she remembered the day that she and Vanessa went up on the mountaintop. Now she regretted that she even made the suggestion to her sister. She didn't know she was making arrangements for her own funeral. If Levi had shown up a moment later, she would have been dead right now.

Vanessa confessed to doing everything! She tried to *kill* her! Her own sister tried to *kill* her! She felt like such an idiot now for confiding in Vanessa! She always knew her mouth would get her into trouble.

"I'm glad I was there!" Levi confessed. "I love your sister with all my heart, and I'm not going to let anything happen to her even if it means taking you down!"

Jazzmine's heart leaped to her throat, beating rapidly. All she could do was smile broadly. Levi didn't just say he loved her, he meant it. He was even proving it.

Vanessa laughed with amusement. "How are you going to take *me* down, Levi? Jazzmine will never believe you! I'm her sister! Sisters would never do anything to hurt each other!"

Not being able to take anymore, Jazzmine burst into the room, drawing all attention to herself. The angry expression on her face was enough to keep the room silent. "That may be true, but I'm about to hurt you, ***"Sister"***!" She walked up to Vanessa and slapped her hard across the face, knocking her to the floor. Climbing on top of her, she began choking her, banging her head against the floor. "You wanted me dead? You tried to kill me? Why did you do it?"

"Because I hate you!" Vanessa hissed as she reached up and clamped her hands to her sister's face, like a claw, to push her off.

Before either of them knew it, they were rolling around on the floor, punching, slapping each other, and pulling each other's hair. When Vanessa was finally on top, holding Jazzmine down by the neck, she took a moment to catch her breath. Smiling mischievously at her, she turned her eyes to Levi, who was still standing in the same spot waiting for Jazzmine to call him for help. She laughed loudly. Squeezing Jazzmine's neck as hard as she could, she told him, "Well, Levi, this is it. You had better say good-bye to her now because she's about to ***die***!"

"***NO***!" Levi exclaimed as he leaped forward.

Jazzmine, thinking quickly, reached over and shook the desk in the corner until the glass lamp on top landed on Vanessa's head, shattering to pieces and knocking her out cold.

Jazzmine kicked Vanessa off of her and stood up, rushing to Levi's open arms. "Oh, Levi!" she exclaimed. "I'm so sorry. I thought... Well, you know what I thought. When I overheard you two talking just now, the truth came out and," she shook her head, "I felt like a total fool. I should have listened to you. I was just so used to Vanessa taking the men I wanted that it just seemed to be happening again. Will you ever forgive me?"

In response to her question, Levi kissed her as if he never wanted to let her go. He held her close to his heart. "Does that answer your question?"

She kissed him in return and hugged his neck tighter. After a moment, she pulled back to look at him. "Levi, we need to talk."

Yes, they did.

"I agree."

Jazzmine looked down at Vanessa. "Let's get out of here before I throw up."

All for the idea, Levi wrapped his arm around Jazzmine's waist and escorted her out of the room.

Jazzmine and Levi walked hand and hand along the beach. She felt nervous at revealing her secret to him for fear that he would laugh at her. It was very rare to find a virgin her age. She was probably the only one. She was sure that he had been with several women, and he knew all about it. She wasn't experienced at all, which was all the more embarrassing.

Levi looked at Jazzmine, wondering what was on her mind.

They walked along in silence for a long moment.

Jazzmine had to take a moment to collect her thoughts. Sighing, she began, "Levi, there's something I want to tell you. I would rather you find out from me than someone else." Sighing again, she licked her lips and swallowed hard. "I know that I never told you what happened between Bartu and me. Well, there's a reason for that."

He looked at her with wonder in his eyes. He had been wondering about that. He was beginning to think that she would never tell him. He said nothing, listening attentively.

"Levi, Bartu was my first boyfriend." She listened for a second, expecting him to question her about what she just said. When he said nothing, she went on to say, "Even after he and I got together, I was afraid to let him get close to me. I didn't know how to act around a man. I was afraid that if I let anyone get too close to me that he would break my heart. Bartu and I became close, but," she shook her head, never finishing the sentence. "He pressured me about it a lot, but I couldn't." She shook her head, again.

Levi stared at her with a confused expression.

He had no idea what she was saying to him. He just hoped she wasn't about to tell him that Bartu forced her to do something she didn't want to do. If he did, Bartu was going to be sorry because he was going to be on the first flight home. When he got there, it would be just him and Bartu. Jazzmine wouldn't be able to stop him this time. He still said nothing, waiting for her to finish.

Jazzmine swallowed hard. "He tried to get me into bed on several occasions, but I wouldn't do it. I couldn't. I want my first time to be with the man of my dreams. I want him to be someone I *love*. I didn't love Bartu. I *don't* love Bartu."

Levi arched his eyebrows at her, wondering if she was saying what he thought she was saying. She said *I **want** my first time* and not *I **wanted** my first time*, which was an indication to him that the first time hadn't occurred, yet. "Jazz? Are you telling me that you're still a virgin?"

She inhaled a deep breath with a nod.

Mentally, Levi was doing cartwheels. Jazzmine was pure, which meant that Bartu hadn't slept with her. He was relieved to finally know. She couldn't possibly know how many countless nights he stayed awake in his bed wondering if she was in bed with Bartu. The thought killed him inside. He didn't like the idea of her being in Bartu's arms let alone the thought of her in his bed.

Jazzmine still had the most precious gift that God gave her. He didn't, and he would never be able to get it back. She should be proud of herself. He lost his virginity when he was sixteen. He had been young and stupid then.

With a smile on his face, Levi stopped and

took both of Jazzmine's hands into his own. "Why didn't you tell me?"

When he didn't laugh, Jazzmine looked at him with surprise. Blinking, she had to take a moment to be sure she was actually awake. "I didn't tell you because I thought you would laugh at me."

He frowned, wondering why she thought such a silly thing. He dropped her hands to caress her cheek. "Jazz, I'm not laughing at you. In fact, I'm proud of you. You should wait until you're ready. Your first time should be special. You have a precious gift that you can only give away once. I agree with you. It should be with someone you love, and hopefully he will love you in return. Jazz, I can name several women with whom I've had sex."

At his statement, Jazzmine looked away. She didn't want to know about all the women with whom he slept. She knew he wasn't a virgin.

"But," Levi's voice was soft as he gently turned her face back to him, "I can't name one woman that I've made love to. There is a difference. I've never been in love with any of them," he confessed. *"Because I've always been in love with you,"* he finished mentally. Aloud, he went on to say, "You don't have to tell the world, but you don't have to be ashamed either, Jazz. I wouldn't be if I were you."

Jazzmine gave him a crooked smile, feeling better now that he knew. Now that her secret was off her chest, she was moving on to the next thing on her mind. Placing her hand to his chest, she stepped closer to him.

"Mmm," he thought, *"I like that!"* He wrapped his arms around her waist, pulling her closer.

Gently rubbing his chest with one hand, she smiled up into his eyes. "I got your E-mail today."

"Really? Well, did you know that I meant every word I wrote to you?"

Her smiled widened. She was hoping he did. Teasing him, she opened her mouth, pretending to be surprised. "You did? You mean you actually think about me all the time? You actually enjoy spending time with me?" She arched her eyebrows at him.

He nodded with a slight laugh. "Yes, I do." After a second, he decided that he couldn't hold back any longer. He had to tell her how he felt about her. Yes, he knew that she read his letter, but he wanted to tell her in person. When he wrote the letter, he wasn't able to do that. He was afraid that he would never be able.

Now that the opportunity had arisen, he wanted to gaze into her eyes as he told her. He wasn't afraid of how she would react anymore. He knew that it was either now or never. There was no time like the present. He could not let this opportunity slip away.

Tightening his arms around her, he pulled her even closer.

"Uw," she moaned when she was firm against his hard chest. She laughed seductively. "I like this." It felt so good to be in his arms. She felt all the security she needed in them, and there was no other place she would rather be. She opened her mouth to speak. Then, she closed it again, remembering the night she went to him and climbed into bed with him. At the time she had been there because she needed him for security. Now that she thought about it, she was so glad it wasn't anyone else.

They slept together that night, and it had been the first night she ever slept with a man. A tingly feeling washed over her, causing her to know that Levi Proctor was the man for her, and she would be a fool to let him get away. That night, had he been any other man, she was positive that he would have tried to take advantage of her in her vulnerable state and sleep with her. Levi didn't even try to touch her, which caused her to love him even more.

"Oh, Levi," she moaned, closing her eyes and snuggling up to him.

Levi looked at her with all the love he felt for her in his eyes. "Jazz," he began, his smile widening, "I know you read my message, but I just have to tell you how much you mean to me in person."

Jazzmine smiled broadly, opening her eyes. She wanted to hear every word. She said nothing, listening.

He lowered his eyes. "Girl, every since the day you walked in to the church years ago, I knew you were the woman for me. You just didn't know it, but I begged Sister Fistbourne to introduce us," he confessed with a nod, remembering how he went to one of the mother's of the church and asked her repeatedly to introduce him to Jazzmine because it had been she who invited her to the church the first time she came. "When I became better acquainted with you, your personality was a winner with me. You have always been the same, and I found myself going crazy over you. I dreamed of holding you and kissing you," he gave her a peck on the lips, "forever! I wanted to tell you how I felt, but I just couldn't." He shook his head. "I always thought you thought of me as your big brother, and I didn't want to hear that. That would have crushed me worse than seeing you with other men. Then, you started dating Bartu."

He shook his head a second time, lifting his face to the sky. "I regretted ever introducing him to you. I made up every excuse to him as to why I couldn't do it, but he insisted. I told him you were a very busy woman. He said that he was a patient man. I told him you weren't much of a conversationalist. He said he liked that because that meant you were a good listener, and he liked to talk." He tilted his head, releasing a puff of air. "I'm telling you, he drove me crazy! Then one day, you walked into the studio, and he was right there. I couldn't get around it." He shrugged his shoulders. "I had to do it or else he would have introduced himself. Anyway," he sighed, "I was hoping that things wouldn't work out between the two of you."

Before she could open her mouth, he went on to say, "Yes, I know I should have been happy that you were happy, but I wasn't. I was miserable. The thought of the two of you together in *that* way was too much for me." He smiled broadly. "You don't know how happy it made me by telling me that you never slept with that jerk. I always wondered why he never bragged about it, but after a while, I just assumed it was because he knew I would have stomped a hole in his back if he had."

Flattered, Jazzmine gave a soft laugh. She knew he would have done just what he said he would, but she always thought it would have been because he was just that good of a friend. Now she knew the real reason.

"The night, you came into my hotel suite and

got into bed with me," Levi continued, "you made me the happiest man on earth. Just to hold you all night was a dream come true."

He closed his eyes, remembering how good it felt to have her in his arms all night. Even though she knew he probably wasn't finished with what he was saying.

Jazzmine had to stop him there. She listened to everything he said, and he said a few things she wanted to comment on. "Levi, I have to say something."

He opened his eyes and looked at her. "What?"

"I think that you are sort of a hypocrite on one aspect."

He arched his eyebrows at her, wanting to know what aspect she meant. He couldn't believe she was calling him a *hypocrite*! "What?"

"I think that you should have told me how you felt a long time ago because by not telling me, you were running away from a problem. Aren't you the one who's always telling me not to run from my problems because it will always be there when I get back?" She arched her eyebrows at him. "The same rule should apply for you."

He laughed at himself because she was right. He should have told her a long time ago. He just wished she hadn't used the word *hypocrite*. Letting her slide with the use of the word, he nodded. "Yes, you are right."

"I know!" she teased with a laugh.

He tightened his arms around her. Her hand rode up his chest to wrap around his neck.

They gazed into each other's eyes.

After a moment, she blinked. "Hey! How could

you tell Bartu I wasn't much of a conversationalist? You know that's not true."

Yes, he knew it wasn't true. She could talk about anything. Twisting his mouth with a guilty look on his face, he made the comment, "I don't know that. You talk to *me*. I don't know what you do when you're not around me!"

They laughed together.

She knew he was joking because they were always together, and when they weren't he knew she was going to tell him what happened.

"Oh, Levi," she moaned with a happy laugh and shake of her head. Dropping her eyes after a moment of thought, she sighed. "I am so sorry about that thing that happened with Vanessa," she apologized, regretting that she ever accused him of lying to her.

Remembering, he shook his head. "Oh, Jazz, it's all right. I just want you to promise me one thing."

Jazzmine pulled back to look into his eyes. "What's that?"

"Promise me that you'll always trust me to tell you the truth."

That wasn't hard. His honesty was put to the test, and he passed.

She didn't have to put him through the test again. "I promise!" She kissed him this time, holding him as if to never let go.

He deepened the kiss. "Oh, Jazz, I love you!"

"I love you, too!"

CHAPTER TWELVE

Jazzmine stood next to her father's bed. She was looking at him with sad eyes as she explained that she and Levi were leaving.

James, sitting up in bed, looked at his daughter with the same sad eyes. He wasn't ready for her to go home, yet. She could at least stay another week. He was enjoying having her around, and he was becoming quite spoiled to it. His eyes moved from his daughter to her boyfriend, who was standing behind her embracing her. At least she was happy now that she and Levi were finally together. She deserved to be happy. He couldn't think of a better man for his daughter. Levi was much like him, a good man.

"Levi," his expression softened as he spoke to him, "is there anyway you can talk her into staying a little while longer? I can't do it. I know she'll listen to you."

Jazzmine looked back at Levi. "Oh, Daddy! Don't try to put him on the spot like that!" She turned her eyes back to her father. "If I stay any longer, you'll get too attached, and you won't want me to leave. I think it's best that I just go."

James sighed. "Why are you leaving so soon?"

Jazzmine sighed with a lazy smile. He was acting as if he hadn't heard a word she just said.

As he was asking the question, Vanessa entered the room.

When James looked up, Jazzmine and Levi glanced around to see her entrance.

Seeing her sister, Jazzmine drew a serious expression and looked away. She couldn't stand to be in the same room with her, and she wouldn't be able to enjoy her father's company any longer as long as she was there. She knew that she was going to beg for his attention to steal it away from her. Not wanting to deal with that, she gently stepped out of Levi's embrace to take his hand.

He allowed her to lead him to the door.

At the door as she was passing her sister, she stopped at her side. Giving her a cold stare, she said to her father, "Daddy, if you really want to know why I'm leaving so soon, you'll have to take that up with Vanessa." She looked Vanessa over with disgust as her face drained of all color at being put on the spot.

James frowned at the sick expression on his older daughter's face. He could sense that there was some animosity between his two daughters, and that was new to him. They had always loved each other, and now they seemed to hate each other's guts. "Vanessa, what is Jazzmine talking about?" he insisted as curiosity was pining away at him.

Jazzmine smiled at her father's question, which she expected to hear. She was going to let Vanessa tell her father everything all by herself. When she returned to California, she was going to call her him for assurance that he was told the full truth. If Vanessa lied, she was going to tell him the truth, not leaving a thing uncovered. If she didn't want him to know everything, Vanessa had better tell him enough to satisfy Jazzmine. If she didn't, it would be all over for her.

Vanessa and their father had a loving relationship, and neither one of them wanted to destroy it. She swallowed hard, wondering what to say.

Seeing the sick expression on her sister's face, Jazzmine's smirk grew wider. "You deal with that," she whispered in her ear before she continued her journey out the room.

Levi allowed her to lead him out the room. His expression toward Vanessa was just as cold as his girlfriend's had been. He couldn't smile, however, not even at Jazzmine's comment. He wasn't sure he believed that Vanessa was going to tell her father the truth no matter how much he asked for it. She would somehow put herself in a better light.

PLACE: BEVERLY HILLS, CALIFORNIA
DATE: AUGUST 2016

Jazzmine Proctor sat in the park on top of a picnic table next to her husband of ten years. They were watching Jaylan, their eight year-old son, and Lisa, their five-year-old daughter as they played together on the swings.

Levi turned his attention to his wife, and he reached over to take her hand. She looked at him with a loving smile. "I love you!" he whispered.

"I love you, too," she whispered back.

He sighed and pulled her closer. With a smile, he reached down and rubbed her bulging stomach. In a few months, she would be giving birth to their third child. "So, Mrs. Proctor, what do you think this one will be? Will it be another mama's boy, or will it be another daddy's little girl?" His eyes went to their children.

She laughed. She didn't even care. As long as their child was healthy, it could be a frog. Not answering, she said, "To think, I almost let my sister destroy our relationship all those years ago."

He shook his head, turning his eyes back to her. "It wouldn't have happened anyway. We're together because we're meant to be!"

She concurred. "You're right. Hey, I read in the paper the other day that Vanessa lost her half of the company and her share of the stock. The word is she had to move back in with Daddy until she can get back on her feet because she's flat broke!" She laughed uncontrollably.

Vanessa got exactly what she deserved.

"It serves her right! That only proves that doing evil to someone will catch up with you in the long run!"

"You are so right." Levi raised his eyebrows, and they laughed together.

Printed in the United States
201004BV00001B/1-45/A